P9-DLZ-650

ALSO BY MEGAN MIRANDA

The Girl from Widow Hills

The Last House Guest

The Perfect Stranger

All the Missing Girls

Come Find Me

Fragments of the Lost

The Safest Lies

Soulprint

Vengeance

Hysteria

Fracture

SUCH A QUIET PLACE

A Novel

MEGAN MIRANDA

Outreach - Bookmobile
Fountaindale Public Library District
300 W. Briarcliff Rd.
Bolingbrook, IL 60440

Simon & Schuster

New York   London   Toronto   Sydney   New Delhi

Simon & Schuster
1230 Avenue of the Americas
New York, NY 10020

This book is a work of fiction. Any references to historical events, real people, or real places are used fictitiously. Other names, characters, places, and events are products of the author's imagination, and any resemblance to actual events or places or persons, living or dead, is entirely coincidental.

Copyright © 2021 by Megan Miranda

All rights reserved, including the right to reproduce this book or portions thereof in any form whatsoever. For information, address Simon & Schuster Subsidiary Rights Department, 1230 Avenue of the Americas, New York, NY 10020.

First Simon & Schuster hardcover edition July 2021

SIMON & SCHUSTER and colophon are registered trademarks of Simon & Schuster, Inc.

For information about special discounts for bulk purchases, please contact Simon & Schuster Special Sales at 1-866-506-1949 or business@simonandschuster.com.

The Simon & Schuster Speakers Bureau can bring authors to your live event. For more information or to book an event, contact the Simon & Schuster Speakers Bureau at 1-866-248-3049 or visit our website at www.simonspeakers.com.

Interior design by Erika R. Genova

Manufactured in the United States of America

1   3   5   7   9   10   8   6   4   2

Library of Congress Cataloging-in-Publication Data has been applied for.

ISBN 978-1-9821-4728-0
ISBN 978-1-9821-4730-3 (ebook)

For my parents

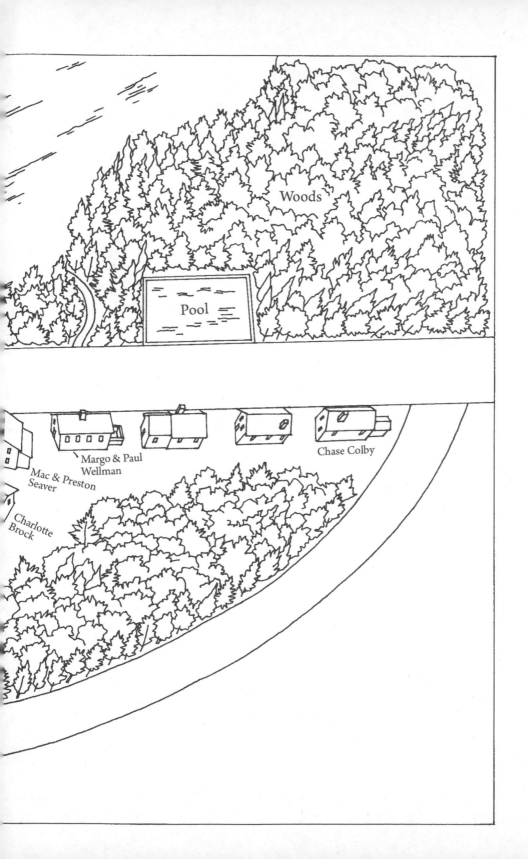

Woods

Pool

Margo & Paul
Wellman

Mac & Preston
Seaver

Charlotte
Brock

Chase Colby

SUCH
A QUIET
PLACE

SATURDAY,
JUNE 29

HOLLOW'S EDGE COMMUNITY PAGE

Subject: SHE'S BACK!

Posted: 11:47 a.m.

Tate Cora: There's a cab outside the house. Did anyone know she was coming back here?

Preston Seaver: What?? Are you sure it's her?

Tate Cora: I'm watching out my window. It's her. It's definitely her.

Charlotte Brock: DELETE THIS NOW.

CHAPTER 1

THERE WAS NO PARTY the day Ruby Fletcher came home. We had no warning, no time to prepare ourselves.

I didn't hear the slam of the car door, or the key in the lock, or the front door swinging open. It was the footsteps— the familiar pop of the floorboard just outside the kitchen—that registered first. That made me pause at the counter, tighten my grip on the knife.

Thinking: *Not the cat.*

I held my breath, held myself very still, listening closer. A shuffling in the hallway, like something was sliding along the wall. I spun from the kitchen counter, knife still in my hand, blade haphazardly pointed outward—

And there she was, in the entrance of my kitchen: Ruby Fletcher.

She was the one who said, "Surprise!" Who laughed as the knife fell from my grip, a glinting thing between us on the tiled floor, who delighted at my stunned expression. As if we didn't all have cause to be on edge. As if we didn't each fear someone sneaking into our home.

As if she didn't know better.

It took three seconds for me to find the appropriate expression. My hand shaking as I brought it to my chest. "Oh my God," I said, which bought me some time. Then I bent to pick up the knife, which bought me some more. "Ruby," I said as I stood.

Her smile stretched wider. "Harper," she answered, all drawn out. The first thing I noticed were the low-heeled shoes dangling from her hand, like she really had been trying to sneak up on me.

The second thing I noticed was that she seemed to be wearing the same clothes she'd had on yesterday during the news conference—black pants and white sleeveless blouse, without a jacket now, and with the top button undone. Her dark blond hair was styled as it had been on TV but appeared flatter today. And it was shorter since I'd last seen her in person—just to her shoulders. Makeup smudges under her eyes, a glow to her cheeks, ears slightly pink from the heat.

It occurred to me she'd been out for twenty-four hours and hadn't yet changed clothes.

There was luggage behind her in the hall—what I must've heard scraping against the beige walls—a brown leather duffel and a messenger-style briefcase that matched. With the suit, it was easy to imagine she was on her way to work.

"Where've you been?" I asked as she set her shoes down. Of all the things I could've said. But trying to account for Ruby's time line was deeply ingrained, a habit that I'd found difficult to break.

She tipped her head back and laughed. "I missed you, too, Harper." Deflecting, as always. It was almost noon, and she looked like she hadn't gone to sleep yet. Maybe she'd been with the lawyer. Maybe she'd gone to see her dad. Maybe she'd tried somewhere else—anywhere else—before coming here. Maybe she'd wrung these last twenty-four hours of freedom for all they were worth.

Then she was crossing the room, coming in for a hug, inescapable. Everything happened on a brief delay, as if choreographed.

Her walk had changed, her steps quiet, more deliberate. Her expression, too—careful, guarded. Something new she'd learned or practiced.

She seemed, suddenly, unlike the Ruby I knew, each proportion just slightly off: thinner, more streamlined; her blue eyes larger and clearer than I recalled; she seemed taller than the last time we were in a room together. Or maybe it was just my memory that had shifted, softening her edges, molding her into something smaller, frailer, incapable of the accusations levied against her.

Maybe it was a trick of the television screen or the pictures in the paper, flattening her into two dimensions, making me forget the true Ruby Fletcher.

Her arms wrapped around me, and all at once, she felt like her again.

She tucked her pointy chin into the space between my neck and shoulder. "I didn't scare you, did I?"

I felt her breath on my neck, the goose bumps rising. I started laughing as I pulled away—a fit of delirium, high and tight, something between elation and fear. *Ruby Fletcher. Here.* As if nothing had changed. As if no time had passed.

She cocked her head to the side as I wiped the tears from under my eyes. "Ruby, if you had called, I would've . . ."

What? Planned a lunch? Gotten her room ready? Told her not to come?

"Next time," she said, grinning. "But that—" She gestured to my face. "That was worth it."

Like this was a game, part of her plan, and my reaction would tell her all she needed to know.

She sat at the kitchen table, and I had no idea where to go from here, where to even begin. She had one foot curled up under the other leg, a single arm hanging over the back of the chair, twisting to face me—not bothering to hide her slow perusal: first my bare feet with the chipping plum polish, then my fraying jean shorts, then the oversize tank top covering the bathing suit underneath. I felt her gaze linger on my hair—now a lighter brown, woven in a haphazard braid over my shoulder.

"You look exactly the same," she said with a wide smile.

But I knew that wasn't true. I'd stopped running in the mornings, lost the lean-muscle definition of my legs; had let my hair grow out from collarbone to mid-back, an inverse of her transformation. I'd spent the last year reassessing everything I'd thought I knew—about others, about myself. Picking apart the trajectory that had brought me here, the conviction I'd always felt in my decisions, and I worried that the uncertainty had somehow manifested itself in my demeanor.

I grew uncomfortable under her gaze, wondering what she might be looking for, what she might be thinking. At the realization that we were alone here.

"Are you hungry?" I asked. I gestured to the food on the counter—the cheese and crackers, the strawberries in a bowl, the watermelon I'd been in the process of cutting—willing my hand not to shake.

She stretched, extending her thin arms over her head, lacing her fingers together: that sickening crack of her knuckles with one final reach. "Not really. Did I interrupt your plans?" she asked, looking over the snacks.

I shifted on my feet. "I saw you yesterday," I said, because I had learned from Ruby that responding to a direct question was always optional. "I watched the news conference." We all had. We'd known it was coming, that she was going to be released, could feel the shared indignation brewing, that after everything—the trial, the testimonies, the evidence—it was all about to be undone.

We'd been waiting for it. Hungry for information, sharing links and refreshing the neighborhood message board. Javier Cora had put the details up, without context, and I'd seen the comments coming through in quick succession:

Channel 3. Now.

Watching . . .

Jesus Christ.

How is this LEGAL?

We knew better by now than to say too much on the message board, but we had all seen it. Ruby Fletcher, wearing the same thing she'd worn the day she was taken in, a banner across the bottom of the screen as she stood in the center of a crowd of microphones: PRESUMED INNOCENT. Simple yet effective, if maybe not entirely true. The trial had been tainted, the investigation deemed unfair, the verdict thrown out. Whether Ruby was innocent was a different matter entirely.

"Yesterday," she said breathlessly, euphorically, face turned up toward the ceiling, "was *wild.*"

She'd seemed so poised, so stoic, on television. A suppressed version of the Ruby I knew. But as she'd spoken, I had leaned toward the television from my spot on the couch. Even from afar, she could bend the gravity of a room her way.

On the broadcast, I'd heard a reporter call out to her: *How are you feeling, Ruby?* And her eyes had crinkled in that charming way she had of holding back a smile, as she looked straight at the camera, straight at me, for a beat before responding: *I'm just looking forward to getting on with my life. To putting this all behind me.*

And yet, twenty-four hours later, she had come straight back here—to the scene of the crime for which she'd been incarcerated—to face it.

THE FIRST THING RUBY wanted was a beer. It wasn't yet noon, but Ruby never worried about such mundane things as public perception or social approval. Didn't try to make an excuse, like the rest of us here might—*summer hours; rounding up*—craving acceptance or someone else to join in our small rebellions.

She stood in front of the fridge, letting the cold air wash over her, and said, "Oh, man, this feels so good," like it was something she had missed. She closed her eyes as she tipped back the bottle of beer, her throat exposed and moving. Then her gaze drifted over to the knife on the counter, to the cubes of watermelon. She picked one up and popped it in her mouth, chewing with exaggerated slowness, savoring it. A faintly sweet scent carried through the room, and I imagined the taste in my own mouth as she licked her lips.

I wondered if this would go on indefinitely: every item, every experience, something unexpected and taken for granted. *Wild.*

My phone buzzed from where I'd left it beside the sink. Neither of us made a move to look at it.

"How long, do you think, before everyone knows?" she asked, one side of her mouth quirked up as she leaned against the counter. As if she could sense the texts coming through.

Not long. Not here. As soon as someone saw her, it would be on the message board—if it wasn't already. When you purchased a home in the Hollow's Edge neighborhood, you automatically became a member of the Hollow's Edge Owners' Association—an official, self-run group with an elected board that decided on our budget, collected our dues, made and enforced the rules.

From there, you were also invited to join a private message board, not officially regulated, initially set up with the best of intentions. It became a different beast after the deaths of Brandon and Fiona Truett.

"Do you want them to know?" I asked. *What are you doing here? How long are you staying?*

"Well, I guess they're bound to notice eventually." She crossed one foot behind the other. "Is everyone still here?"

I cleared my throat. "Plus or minus a few." The renters had all gotten out when they could, but the rest of us couldn't sell without taking a major loss right now. The Truett house was still empty next door, and Ruby Fletcher, longtime resident of Hollow's Edge, had been convicted of the killings. It was a double hit. Maybe we could've recovered from one or the other, but not the combination.

Tate and Javier Cora, my neighbors to the left, were looking to move, but they were two doors down from the crime scene and had been advised by their realtor to wait it out. But there were others who had slowly disappeared. A fiancé who had left. A husband who was rarely seen.

Breaking the case had broken a lot of other things in the process.

Instead, I said: "The Wellmans had their baby. A boy."

Ruby smiled. "Guess he's not such a baby anymore."

I pressed my lips together in an approximation of a smile, unable to figure out the right thing to say, the right tone. "And Tate's pregnant."

Ruby froze, beer bottle halfway to her mouth. "She must be unbearable," she said, one eyebrow raised.

She was, but I wasn't about to tell Ruby that. I was always trying to decrease animosity, smooth over tension—a role I'd long inhabited in my own family. But these were safer conversations than what we could've been discussing, so I ran with it. "And Charlotte's oldest just graduated, so we'll be losing one more by the end of the summer." I was filling the silence, my words coming too fast, practically tripping over one another.

"Can we vote someone else out instead?" she asked, and I laughed, imagining the many names Ruby might propose, wondering which was at the top of her list. Chase Colby, most likely.

It felt like no time had passed. Ruby was always like this:

disarming; unpredictable. *A hypnotic personality,* the prosecutor had declared. As if we were all the victims and therefore blameless in our allegiance.

It was something I repeated to myself often, to absolve myself.

But then I realized why she was asking about everyone, about who was here and who would remain: Ruby was planning to stay.

IN TRUTH, I HADN'T given much thought to where Ruby would go after her release. It hadn't occurred to me that *here* would even be on her mind, with everything that had happened. We hadn't spoken since that day in the courtroom after I testified, and that could barely count—she'd just mouthed the words *Thank you* as I passed.

I'd pretended I hadn't noticed.

If I'd had to make a guess, it might have been that she'd go to see her dad in Florida. Or hole up in some hotel suite funded by the legal team who had gotten her released, working the case angles with her lawyer. I would've thought she'd be more likely to disappear entirely—seizing her chance, reemerging in some far-away place as someone new. A person with no history.

I checked the clock over the fridge, saw it creeping past noon, drummed my fingers on the countertop.

"Expecting company?" she asked. She was looking at the spread on the counter again.

I shook my head. "I was going to bring this to the pool."

"Great idea," she said. "I missed the pool."

My stomach plummeted. How many things had she missed— the cool blast of the refrigerator, the pool, me. Would she keep listing them off, twisting the knife?

"Be right back," she said, heading toward the hall bathroom at the base of the stairs.

I washed the knife as soon as she was out of the room—it was too much, laying out there on the surface, taunting us both, unspoken. Then I picked up my phone quickly, scrolling through the messages piling up.

From Tate: *Why didn't you tell us she was coming back here??*

From Charlotte: *Call me.*

So they already knew.

But I ignored them, instead firing off a quick message to Mac, fingers trembling with leftover adrenaline: *Do not come over.*

I had no idea how long she intended to stay. Ruby's bags were sitting just outside the entrance of the kitchen. Maybe I could get a sense of things without asking directly. I listened for water running in the bathroom, but the house was eerily silent. Just the cat, Koda, hopping off a piece of furniture somewhere upstairs, and the muffled call of a cicada from the trees out back, growing louder.

I slowly unzipped the larger piece of luggage, peering inside. It was empty.

"Harper?"

I yanked my hand back quickly, the side of my finger catching on the zipper. Ruby's voice had come from the top of the staircase, but only her shadow was visible from where I stood. I didn't know what she could see from this angle.

As I backed away from her bags, she came into view, moving slowly down the stairs, hand sliding down the railing. "Is there something you want to tell me?"

Her voice had subtly changed, the way people had pointed out during the investigation—what some called hypnotic but what others called cunning or angry. It was all loaded together on a razor's edge. Either way, it made you pay attention. Made you tune in acutely to whatever Ruby was going to tell you.

"About what?" I asked, feeling my heartbeat inside my chest. There were so many things I could tell her:

Everyone still thinks you're guilty.

I don't know why you're here.

I slept with your ex.

"My things. Where are my *things,* Harper."

"Oh," I said. I hadn't had time to explain. Hadn't thought it would be an issue. Hadn't thought she'd expected any differently. "I talked to your dad. After."

She paused at the bottom step, raised a single exacting eyebrow. "And?"

I cleared my throat. "He told me to donate them." It wasn't that I was unsympathetic, it was just, twenty years was a long time. She acted like she'd been gone a week, not fourteen months.

Ruby closed her eyes briefly, took a slow breath in. I wondered if she had learned this during her time behind bars. It was not at all how Ruby Fletcher used to handle disappointment.

"Did Mac come by for anything?"

God, I didn't know what she was asking. Everything she said was laced with something else.

"I can take you to the store. For anything you need," I said. I could buy her new clothes, new toiletries. I could offer to put her up in a hotel, hand her some cash, wish her well. Wish I'd never see her again.

But she flicked her fingers at the air between us. "Later." She bent and picked up her bag—her empty bag—and returned up the steps.

It occurred to me that I might be witnessing a crime against my property. That she was going to rob me, and I was going to be complicit in it, as it was so easy to grow complicit to the desires of Ruby Fletcher.

WE DIDN'T ALWAYS LIVE together. The situation was unspoken but understood, I thought, to be both brief and temporary.

After Aidan moved out of my place, after Ruby's dad retired and sold their house, it was a momentary necessity—a period of time when we both needed a pause, needed to grasp our bearings, figure things out. Decide what we wanted next.

But she didn't leave, and I didn't ask her to. It seemed that what we both wanted was for her to stay. We had developed an allegiance of convenience, if only for someone to feed the cat.

I'd grown accustomed to the solitude since she'd been gone. I'd grown to value my independence and my privacy, on my own for the first time since college. Knowing that everything here belonged to me.

When she came downstairs wearing my clothes—the maroon tie of a bathing suit top visible under my black tank dress—I didn't have much of a position to argue from, after getting rid of her things. She was taller, and now slimmer, than I, but our clothes were the same general size.

Koda followed her down, weaving between her feet, the traitor. She had been Aidan's cat first, was firmly antisocial, and seemed to spurn attention from all humans except Ruby.

Ruby gathered her hair into a short ponytail, one of my elastics on her wrist. "Do you have an extra pair of sunglasses?" she asked.

I blinked at her. This was like watching a car crash in slow motion. "What are you doing?" I asked.

In answer, she opened the drawer of the entryway table—the same place we'd always kept the keys—the same place Ruby had also kept the Truetts' key, when she walked their dog. For a brief second's pause, I thought she was looking for it, but then she grabbed the electronic pool badge that granted us entrance through the black iron gates. "Going to the pool. Aren't you?"

"Ruby," I said in warning.

Lips pressed together, she waited for me to continue.

"I'm not sure that's such a good idea right now," I said. She had to know it. Of course she knew it.

She turned her face away, but not before I caught what I thought was the glimmer of a smile. "I'm ripping off the Band-Aid," she explained as she opened the front door. But that wasn't quite right. Prison had softened her metaphors. She was flirting with an inferno. She was dousing a gaping wound in vinegar.

She walked out barefoot, front door left ajar—an offering that I had no intention of taking. Not in broad daylight. Not on this street. Not in this neighborhood.

It was bad enough she was *here,* in my *house.*

But I stepped out onto the front porch, watching her walk past the front of the Truett house without a glance toward the empty porch, the darkened windows. No hesitation or change in her stride as she passed the house she'd once allegedly let herself inside in the middle of the night, let the dog out, started the old Honda in the garage, and left the interior door to the house ajar, so that Brandon and Fiona Truett died silently of carbon monoxide poisoning in the night.

My house was situated at the center of the court, six homes around the half-moon edge, a wide-open circle of pavement with a grassy knoll in the middle, with a scattering of trees that blocked the view of the lake in the summer but not the winter.

The pool was on the main neighborhood road, bordered by the woods and overlooking the lake, and from a certain vantage point, with a generous frame of mind, it could pass for an infinity pool.

As Ruby strode by each house, I imagined the security cameras catching her. Watching her. Recording her in jolts of time that could be pieced together later to track her every movement. The Brock house, whose video feed had picked up a noise that night. The house on the corner, belonging to the Seaver brothers, whose doorbell camera had caught the hooded figure striding past, and who had plenty to share about Ruby Fletcher besides.

Ruby was out of sight now, probably passing the Wellman house, whose camera had identified Ruby sprinting into the woods, toward the lake.

I was listening hard to the silence when I sensed movement from the corner of my eye.

Tate was standing at the entrance of her garage next door, half in, half out, arms crossed over her abdomen. Our separate houses were only a few yards from being townhomes with shared walls. We were practically side by side. I felt her staring at the side of my face.

"I didn't know she was coming," I said.

"How long is she staying?" Tate asked.

I thought of the empty bag in my house. "Not sure yet."

Officially, Tate and Javier Cora hadn't seen or heard anything that night—they'd gotten home from a friend's party after midnight, and there was nothing on their camera. Unofficially, they weren't surprised. Now I could sense her teeth grinding together, but I wasn't sure whether it was from anger or fear.

Tate was maybe five feet tall, and small-framed at that. I'd learned it wasn't her true first name only during the investigation. It was her maiden name, but she and Javier had met in college, where she played lacrosse, and everyone had called her Tate then. So did he. She still wore her thick blond hair in a high ponytail with a wraparound athletic headband, like she might be called onto the field at any moment. I could picture it well. She could summon an intensity that compensated for her size.

Everyone knew Tate and Javier as the gregarious couple of the neighborhood. They hosted weekend barbecues and helped plan the neighborhood social events.

"Do something," Tate said, making her eyes wide. Pregnancy

17

had turned her less gregarious, more demanding. But we'd all hardened over the last year and a half. We'd each become, in turn, more skeptical, wary, impenetrable.

I nodded noncommittally.

We both stared in the direction Ruby had gone. "Chase is going to lose his shit when he sees her," she said before retreating inside.

Though Tate was prone to overreaction, this was not one of those times.

If Chase saw her there—

If no one had warned him first—

I grabbed my things in a rush, taking off after Ruby.

CHAPTER 2

I'S FAIR TO SAY that no one here had loved Brandon and Fiona Truett.

On the surface, everything was fine. We smiled, we waved. But we didn't really socialize with them.

Brandon was the head of admissions at the College of Lake Hollow, where many of us worked, and he believed vigorously in a separation between work and relationships. He was standoffish, and judgmental of the rest of us who did not adhere to his personal code of conduct, and kind of an asshole. Fiona was standoffish by proxy, judgmental by proxy, an asshole by proxy.

We liked them more in hindsight. In sympathy.

Their house had been unoccupied since the day they were found. It belonged to the bank now, but no one was offering, and so it sat—empty, haunting. A constant reminder.

In the months after, the yard had run wild and overgrown until we coordinated a schedule to keep up appearances, like we did after Charlotte Brock's accident and knee surgery. We did not have altruistic intentions; we were not such good people. But we cared enough about our own status not to let the property go to hell, bringing us all down with it. We were all dependent on one another here.

19

The neighborhood of Hollow's Edge hugged a finger of Lake Hollow, a semicircle of fifty closely packed homes oriented toward the water, half-moon courts set off from two main roads. The development had been completed about five years earlier, and many of the homes were occupied by their original owners. They were similarly designed and modestly priced; there weren't large industries in the area to commute for. Most of us in Lake Hollow worked for the college, or Lake Hollow Prep, or the public education system.

We were highly educated, though not highly compensated. But we had this: the view, the convenience of a suburb, and the ambience of our own private stretch of nature—you could hear it coming alive at night, down by the water. And the summer: Administrative positions required year-round employment, but the rest had the expanse of mid-June to mid-August for themselves. Two-plus months of unstructured, unaccountable hours. Though I technically had a year-round position at the college, the days turned flexible in the summer, the hours more like a suggestion than a requirement.

There were other, more exclusive subdivisions on the opposite side of the lake, closer to the college: larger homes, more established communities, with lake access and boat docks. Our neighborhood didn't officially have direct access, though there was a cleared path through the wooded area across from the Wellmans' home, a gently sloping path where people dragged kayaks and canoes. A strip of plywood atop the rougher section, to ease anything over the roots without damage.

There weren't many young children here yet, the neighborhood self-selecting based on its facilities. The lack of playground. The pool with no lifeguard. The proximity to the lake. All hidden dangers that parents could see. We were mostly young professionals, upwardly mobile, still establishing ourselves.

Aidan and I had fit right in. We'd been welcomed into the fold as soon as we'd unloaded our things, fresh out of the large academic setting of Boston University, where we'd first met, enamored with the possibilities of the life we would build for ourselves here. We'd both grown up near the water—me, a mile from a stretch of cape where I'd learned to fish and sail and keep time by the tides; him, on the Gulf Coast of Florida, where he'd developed an affinity for biology and boating. We'd felt a pull here, a faint familiarity, like there was something in it that recognized us, too.

Five years later, I could name every family on the street as I walked to the pool, as I followed Ruby.

I thought about stopping at Mac's house on the corner to make sure he'd gotten my message, but it remained dark, the blinds tilted shut. In fact, the stretch of road behind me and in front of me remained still, unnaturally silent, only the cicadas starting up again in the trees, calling out to one another. I was used to hearing my neighbors.

Our backyards collided, high white fences in a grid, granting the illusion of privacy. We couldn't see one another, but we could hear everything, though we pretended we couldn't. Everyone was reduced to a caricature of themselves on the other side of the fence, winnowed down to their most defining features. Sometimes you could see colors moving through the thin slats, the movement of a person, when you thought you were alone.

On a typical weekend morning around this time, most people were up, working on house projects or reading in their backyards. Others would ride their bikes around the lake into downtown, or go for a walk before the heat really kicked in.

But on this particular Saturday, the neighborhood appeared quiet. *Sleepy* is what the news reports once called us, as if we were collectively lazy, oblivious to the danger among us.

21

In truth, summers here were always dangerous. In their luxury. In their sleepiness. With their lack of structure and sudden influx of time. Time to notice the things we were too busy for during the rest of the year. Time to fixate. Time to make a change.

Anything taken to an extreme was dangerous. Here, in the summer, there was nowhere to hide—not from others and not from yourself.

On the surface, Hollow's Edge could still give the illusion of a quiet little neighborhood, but that was a lie. Even if it had been true at one time, the reality was a very different thing now. One thing I could say for sure: We had all awakened.

THE POOL WAS NOT crowded, for which I was grateful. Ruby had already claimed a blue lounge chair, setting herself up by the pool steps. But she had my key, and I couldn't get in without calling her attention.

Chase, thankfully, wasn't here. Neither was Mac.

There was a man in the far corner, a dark hat pulled low over sunglasses, chair angled directly toward the sun, tanned arms resting beside his pale torso. Preston Seaver. Mac's younger brother. I wasn't surprised; he could usually be found at the pool on the weekend, probably on a mission to even out his tan. Preston worked in security at the college during the week and always seemed to know what was happening, in and out of work—and he was usually all too willing to share.

Preston Seaver, who had told the police how one time, when Ruby and Mac were fighting, someone had broken into their home and smashed some dishes, establishing a pattern. Preston, who now held me at arm's length, like I was not to be trusted.

But it was a mutual distrust, and I wasn't sure which of ours was the strongest. The way he'd turned on Ruby so fast. *I warned my brother,* he'd told them. As if he had always sensed some menace lurking in her, threatening to emerge.

Sometimes, when he looked at me, I wondered if he saw in me something untoward. Something worth warning his brother about, too.

Now he remained perfectly still, but I couldn't tell whether he'd noticed Ruby or was sleeping. They had never gotten along, not even before. Preston believed Ruby was full of herself; Ruby believed Preston was irrelevant, an unfortunate extension of Mac's existence. Even before, they could circle each other without interacting. It was a skill, but it worked only by joint agreement, some sort of pact they had entered into together.

Margo Wellman had noticed Ruby, though. She had the baby in the pool, and every few seconds she sneaked a glance—but she didn't change her own plans. She was pulling the baby—a toddler now—in a yellow float, in lazy circles.

I stood at the gated entrance, not wanting to call Ruby's name—not wanting to declare an allegiance, disrupt the balance—when she approached the edge of the pool, crouching down. "Is this your little one?" she asked Margo.

Margo didn't move any closer, but she didn't retreat, either. She was just out of reach of Ruby, and she pulled the float subconsciously closer. "Yes, this is Nicholas." Nicholas had the same curly red hair as his mother, fine and wispy but undeniably hers. Margo had her hair tied up in a bun on top of her head to keep dry, though tendrils had come loose and clung to her neck, waterlogged.

"Hi, Nicholas," Ruby said, waving. She smiled when Nicholas waved back, all chubby arms and baby-faced delight. "Congrats, Margo, he's precious."

"Thank you," Margo answered.

Nothing about Ruby being out or here. No apologies or

condolences or congratulations. Their entire interaction was exquisitely, painfully civil. Nothing about the fact that it was Margo's camera, with its wide-angled view of the lake and the path cutting into the woods, that had caught Ruby running down through the trees that night—making us wonder if she might've been disposing of some evidence in the lake or the surrounding woods, though nothing was ever found.

When she stood back up, Ruby noticed me at the gate and smiled as she let me in. "Look who decided to come after all."

"Hey," I said. I held up my pool bag. "I have towels and sunscreen. And the food." As if her lack of preparedness was my reason for coming. The scorching summer Virginia sun, which she might've forgotten about.

"I can always count on you," she said.

Margo caught my eye as I passed. I wanted to explain. To tell her I was here to diffuse any sort of situation. To keep my eye on Ruby; to deescalate.

With her free hand, Margo hitched the navy blue strap of her swimsuit farther up one shoulder, then the other, her gaze trailing after us. It seemed like Margo's body kept changing by degrees ever since the baby was born, month after month, in subtle re-alignments, so that she was constantly fidgeting with a strap, or cinching a waistband, or holding a neckline in place.

Once I settled in a lounge chair beside Ruby, Margo returned her focus to the baby, gently humming. I handed Ruby the sun-screen, passed her the fruit, watched the gated entrance.

It was easy to fall into old habits—the purple insulated cup, hers; the blue one, mine. The chair closer to the umbrella would be for me, for the shade, because I was more likely to burn than she was, though I never noticed until it was too late.

It was so easy to pretend that everything was normal. We've always been great pretenders here.

24

When I looked over at Preston, he had his phone propped on his stomach, peering down like he was reading something on his screen. But then I thought, from the angle, that maybe he was taking pictures of us. Recording us. It was not the first time I'd thought he was taking photos of people at the pool.

He tilted his phone slightly, and he pressed his lips together, as if trying not to smile. The hair on the back of my neck stood on end, and I sat up straighter, staring straight back at him. His expression didn't change, until I wondered whether I was being paranoid. Whether he was watching a video—he had earbuds in, after all—or reading an article, or texting his brother: *Guess who's sitting on the other side of the pool right now . . .*

He grinned, then placed his phone facedown beside him, resting his head back once more.

No one said anything. Margo kept pulling the baby around the pool; Preston remained almost motionless, only his fingers giving him away, tapping out some beat on the side of the lounge chair.

I wished someone would break. Say what they were thinking. None of us were strangers here. We'd all known Ruby since she was just barely on the cusp of adulthood. And last fall, we'd all testified at her trial.

I'd first met Ruby when I was twenty-five, working in the admissions department, and she was a twenty-year-old student staying with her dad in the summer. That was when Aidan and I moved in, and she was a kid bringing her friends to the pool.

People complained, covertly, passive aggressively, on our message board: *What's the policy on guests at the pool? For example, how many underage college kids can be drinking before someone should say something?*

Flirting, even then, with Mac, who was older than I was and wouldn't give her the time of day, just a nod as he passed with a can of beer in his hand.

I'd always had a soft spot for her. She reminded me of the best parts of my brother. The fun and the joy and the excitement that teetered on recklessness—the parts I imagined must still exist in him, if you stripped all the rest away.

After Ruby graduated, she'd gone on to get her master's, working part-time in our department, giving student tours, and I got to know another side of her. We started having lunches together. She talked about her future.

She got a job teaching English at the prep school right after she'd earned her master's, still staying with her dad, to save. That was the same year Aidan finished his postdoc.

That was also when he left me, in a sudden, jarring blindside— so fast and unexpected that the anger first masked the heartbreak, and even now I wasn't sure whether I was more upset about the loss of the relationship or the way it had happened.

He was leaving *for a better opportunity,* he said, *and maybe it's time we stopped pretending this was working.* This could be an opportunity for both of us. And when I argued, tried to understand where this was coming from, he threw his arms out to the sides and said, *My God, Harper, I just have to get out of here.*

Like some switch had been flipped and he was seeing this place with fresh eyes—the four walls limiting him, the neighborhood roads circling back around, and me, always the thing he was coming back to.

As if I were something that required escaping.

There was nothing secret about our breakup—it was a casualty of the summer, and there was nothing better to do than watch the unraveling. There was a moving truck, because he took half the furniture. I demanded the cat in a moment of insanity. Aidan held a going-away party with the guys in the neighborhood—Javier Cora, Mac and Preston Seaver, Chase Colby—and they all pretended this was a normal thing to do. No one mentioned how I supported him through his education, and then the second he was done, he left me.

Even my dad was unsympathetic when I told him. He'd never been a fan of Aidan, had tallied his shortcomings on both hands when I told him we were moving here together; said it was in my nature to want to see only the potential in people—like it was some great character flaw.

Aidan and I had bought the house together, in theory. But it was only my name on the mortgage because Aidan had terrible credit and an unappealing debt-to-income ratio (one of the many warnings from my dad), so it was easier to qualify without him.

And then Ruby's father sold their house and moved away. When Ruby asked if I could use a roommate, I was still recovering from Aidan's blindside, still caught off guard at the end of each day by the silence here. The unsettling emptiness that seemed to have its own presence.

I gave her Aidan's office, on the second floor, across the loft from the master suite. She piled her things in her car and drove it the two blocks to my place, and I scooped up her clothes from the backseat, laughing. I was twenty-eight, she was twenty-three, and I wasn't sure which of us was doing the other a favor right then.

Now, at thirty and twenty-five, the gap between us felt smaller.

Eventually, Margo made a production of leaving the pool, saying to no one in particular that it sounded like nap time, as if she needed a polite excuse to make her exit. She swooped her gear into the stroller, the yellow floatie spilling over the seat, and hitched the baby onto her hip.

Preston stood next, towel slung over the distinct tan line on his upper arm, and nodded in our general direction as he headed toward the gate. I tipped my chin back, the faintest response, a force of habit. Ruby, committed to the cause, did not acknowledge him.

I checked my phone, but no one else had contacted me. Mac

27

never responded. To be fair, I wouldn't, either—not if I thought she might notice. I would keep my distance. Keep out of it. Hope this was temporary and we could all go back to our lives tomorrow.

No one else came to the pool, though the hours grew hotter, more stifling.

"How lucky for us," Ruby said, reaching into the Tupperware bowl of fruit, "to have the pool all to ourselves."

We passed the time in silence. Sun and drinks and me, always, with my eye toward the entrance.

Ruby dove into the deep end, floated on her back, and I felt myself being drawn into the past. All these things we had done before, as if we could excise the time between. The scent of sunscreen and chlorine and Ruby's steps leaving footprints across the concrete, her hands twisting the ends of her hair, squeezing out the excess water.

She hooked her ankle around the leg of her lounger, pulling it farther away from the encroaching shade, in a sharp kick of nostalgia—so that I could almost taste the extra-sweet sangria Ruby would make, tossing in whatever fruit I happened to have in the fridge at the time, the mixture cloying at the back of my throat. The way my skin would feel on those endless days, absorbing the summer sun, before I showered off back home later, when the sting of the burn slowly revealed itself from the inside out.

And then the neighbors started passing by for a closer look: walking dogs or strolling by, on their phones. One by one, as if it were coordinated. Each one slowing, watching briefly, and then moving on.

These people who, after her arrest, *always had a feeling* about Ruby Fletcher, her perceived crimes expanding in retrospect. Saying, *Money went missing from my wallet at the barbecue; from my living room at that New Year's party; from my pool bag—it was Ruby. I know it.* The paranoia gaining force as people searched for signs, for clues, for how we had missed the danger among us for so long.

Finally, I saw Chase. He wasn't in uniform, but he was walking as if he were. Confident and full of authority, with his large frame and ramrod-straight posture. Stopping and staring from across the street as if he couldn't believe his eyes. Dark hair buzzed short, wide stance, arms hanging stoic at his sides. He stood there for a long time. If Ruby noticed, she didn't let on.

We used to see Chase as *our* cop. We could count on him to fill us in on the cause of the sirens, or the status of the car break-in investigation, and we called on him at neighborhood meetings, plying him for information with beer at the pool. He lent a sense of security. But he became something different after Brandon and Fiona Truett.

The message board had started the same way—as a source of information: *Who has the number for a good plumber?* or *What was that loud noise in the middle of the night?* and *Did you hear about the prowler in the neighborhood up the road?*

Hollow's Edge was a force, as a group, over the last five years. We caught package thieves. We saw a coyote and warned neighbors to keep their small pets inside at night. We caught Charlotte's husband bringing another woman home when Charlotte was out. We solved mysteries. We solved problems. We crowdsourced data and posted the video feed from our security cameras. We extrapolated results.

But the board, too, had subtly morphed with time. After the deaths of Brandon and Fiona Truett were deemed suspicious, eventually, and with Chase's guidance, we believed we had solved the case of who killed them. We pieced together Ruby's movements, her time line, and the police came by for our evidence, our message board comments morphing into official statements.

We were more careful now. In person and on the message board. Posts were deleted as soon as people stopped responding and sometimes sooner.

Ruby picked up her purple insulated cup and raised it toward the iron gates where Chase stood, in a mock salute. Of course she'd known he was there.

He finally turned back up the road, and I breathed slowly, deeply, as he disappeared from sight.

"Okay, you made your point," I said. "I'm baking here. Let's go."

"All right," she said, stretching. "Anyway, I'm famished for some real food."

I SCANNED THE AREA for Chase as we walked back, worried he was somewhere else: waiting in the woods; waiting in front of my house. I kept an eye out for anyone at all. But no one came outside.

They were watching, though. I could feel it in the shadows behind the windows. In the way everyone remained behind the safety of their walls.

All the things that seemed so appealing when we moved to Hollow's Edge: Its insular nature. Its privacy. That close familiarity. The safety of neighbors who would look out for one another.

All of us were held hostage by it now.

The truth was, after the deaths of Brandon and Fiona Truett, we were trapped here. We were trapped with one another and what we had each said and done.

CHAPTER 3

CONVINCED RUBY TO LET me order in, to relax with a pizza in the living room, Koda curled up beside her on the other end of my couch as she sat with my laptop open in front of her.

"You sure you don't mind paying?" she asked as she quickly added an assortment of clothes to the online cart.

"No, of course not." I'd gotten rid of her things, and now she sat beside me, still smelling faintly of chlorine, hair damp and tangled, in more of my summer clothes. She didn't have a credit card, or employment, or a bank account.

She selected one-day rush delivery and passed the laptop my way so I could enter the payment information. "I'm good for it," she said with a wink. I'd never seen her wink before. It was things like this—quirks I didn't recognize—that I found most unnerving.

She scooted closer, the cushions sinking between us, so that I felt her brush against my shoulder as she watched me finish placing the order. "Hey," she said. "Let's see what they're saying."

I froze, my heart in my throat. "You want me to Google your name?" I could only imagine what things might come up—links I'd already clicked, articles I'd read, every one of them already consumed by me in private.

"No," she said, "I mean here. The message board. What they're saying *here*."

My fingers tingled. That wasn't any better. Ruby had never been a member of the Hollow's Edge community page, since she wasn't an owner herself. Charlotte was the president of the board and had established an arbitrary set of rules that dictated who could be permitted access to the message board—*homeowner* being the main criteria. She'd decided back then that Ruby was something between an unregistered tenant and a long-term guest.

But I couldn't deny her now. Not when she was sitting so close, wearing my clothes because she owned nothing of her own. Not when I'd convinced her to stay in—some dark secret I might still be able to contain.

She watched as my fingers flew over the keyboard, typing the URL, my log-in already in place. The page loaded quickly, entries sorted by date. There were no new posts from today. Not a single one.

"It's not the same anymore," I told her. "People don't use it as much." Then I shut the laptop quickly, before she could scroll down, call me on my bluff.

She let out a sigh as she edged back to her side of the couch. "I'm not sure what I expected," she said, reaching for another slice of cheese pizza. "Maybe my picture on every security camera on the street." She smirked, then closed her eyes as she inhaled the scent of greasy pizza. I guessed this was another thing she'd missed. "Did you ever get yours fixed, Harper?"

Once upon a time, I'd had a security camera, too. Angled over the front porch—a deterrent more than anything. But it hadn't recorded that night. Whatever service Aidan set up had long since expired.

"Never got around to it," I said. Though the device still sat there, uselessly pointed at empty space. Those cameras, for our safety, they could just as easily be turned against you. The petty infractions they exposed; the relationships they ruined. I wasn't sure a camera would ever keep me safe when the person convicted had a key.

After we finished eating, I took our plates to the kitchen and tossed the pizza box in the trash can inside the garage, thinking Ruby would be heading to bed soon. Thinking surely she'd be as tired as I was. The sun and the drinks, and who knew how long it had been since she'd last slept.

"Do you need anything before I go to bed?" I asked, turning off the television, hoping she would take the hint.

She shifted positions on the couch, letting Koda settle onto her lap. "I'm good. I'm just—God, it's so quiet. I'm not used to so much silence."

But it was only inside the walls that was quiet. Outside, the sounds of the night came alive, things encroaching from the woods and the lake. The crickets chirping and the tiny frogs bellowing, a sound I once mistook for something larger, until a frog had plastered itself to the front window—letting out a call so sharp and close, I'd thought it was a cry for help.

During the investigation, we had established an official neighborhood watch. A self-imposed curfew. The remnants of our fear carried over long after. We locked our doors and the patio gates, we pulled the curtains tight, we slept with a can of Mace beside our beds—or more. We listened to the silence. We whispered. We reimagined the noises we'd heard drifting from our neighbors' homes. The music at three a.m. The fight. The bang. We stared at the ceilings, slept odd hours, searched through our old camera footage.

Ruby didn't know, she had come back to someplace different.

"Good night, Harper," she said when I hadn't made a move to leave.

"Good night," I said. I hated to leave her there, but I did. Didn't want her to think that I didn't trust her here, that I was afraid.

My room—the master—faced the front, and hers faced the back, a smaller room with a Jack-and-Jill bathroom connecting to the loft, which looked out over the stairway and entrance. Inside my bedroom, I checked my phone one last time. No one else had reached out. I'd expected more calls, more texts, more questions. But the silence said something, too. The nature of my friendships here, too fragile to withstand Ruby's return.

The thing we learned last year, or maybe the thing we had always known, was that there were two versions of Hollow's Edge. There was the one on the surface, where we waved to our neighbor, and passed along recommendations, and held the pool gate, smiling.

And then there was the other, simmering underneath.

I shouldn't have been surprised. I'd witnessed the same from the inside, growing up. With my brother, Kellen, in and out of rehab since he was sixteen, and the strain of my parents' relationship, fracturing under the disagreements and the blame. So different from the facade we presented to the outside, glossing over reality with good posture and white lies.

Eventually, I heard Ruby coming up the stairs. I heard her in the shower. I relaxed, rolling over, eyes fixed on the door. And then I saw her shadow just outside my door. I counted to ten, and it didn't move. I stared at the doorknob, thinking I should've locked it. Then wondering which was worse—Ruby coming in or Ruby realizing I was afraid?

Finally, the shadow retreated. But I heard the sound of her steps on the staircase and then the back door creaking open. I bolted upright in bed, imagining all the places she could be going. All the things she could be doing. Staring at the clock on my bedside table to mark the time—being a good witness.

Maybe there was nothing to worry about here. Maybe I was reading too much into things. Maybe she just wanted fresh air, and who could blame her, really?

But all I could think of was that other night. The one we had to keep revisiting, with the cops, with ourselves—when I'd heard that same creak of the back door and the shower running around two a.m.

It hadn't meant anything to me then. Not even after we'd found them.

No one was afraid at first. Shocked, yes. Upset, of course. But not afraid. Or at least not afraid of anything more than ourselves, what we might've missed. Because when Brandon and Fiona were discovered deceased, we didn't yet know it was a crime—well, nothing further than a domestic crime of murder-suicide (and we could make a case for it going either way). A crime that was self-contained.

But slowly, in the days that followed, the scene shifted.

The carbon monoxide detector—the same model in every home—was no longer in its place, or in the house at all.

The police started coming door-to-door, asking where we were that night, what we'd heard, what we'd noticed. And finally, we understood: Someone else had been in that house with Brandon and Fiona Truett.

Someone who had killed them.

SUNDAY, JUNE 30

HOLLOW'S EDGE COMMUNITY PAGE

Subject: REMINDER! Hollow's Edge Fourth of July Pool Party

Posted: 8:47 a.m.

Javier Cora: Come watch the Fourth of July fireworks with your neighbors on Thursday! We've got a great view of the lake show from our very own pool. All are welcome!

Margo Wellman: Is this such a good idea right now??

Javier Cora: Why wouldn't it be?

/I\   /I\   /I\   /I\   /I\
\I/   \I/   \I/   \I/   \I/

Subject: Neighborhood Watch

Posted: 9:02 a.m.

Margo Wellman: Can we please get this going again?

Preston Seaver: Yeah, we kinda let it drop over the winter. I'd be in to start the rotation again.

Margo Wellman: Chase?? Didn't you help organize this last time?

Charlotte Brock: Chase is no longer a member of this group.

CHAPTER 4

WHEN I CAME DOWN the stairs just after ten a.m., Ruby was cooking breakfast—toast and eggs, and leftover watermelon cubes in an open Tupperware container. I'd been waiting things out in my room, showering in my attached bathroom, checking the neighborhood message board, peering out my front window for any sign of activity—unsure how to approach another day with Ruby in this house.

"Morning!" she called, two mugs of coffee already on the counter, Koda eating from a fresh bowl of food at her feet. From her bright tone and easy smile, I didn't think it was her first cup. She was wearing one of my old T-shirts and gym shorts, bare face and hair pulled back tightly. Her skin had bronzed slightly from the sun, except where it had turned pink high across her cheeks and the bridge of her nose.

"Ouch," she said, reaching out to the base of my neck, two cold fingers pressing into my skin. "You burned."

I'd felt it in the shower, hot and painful under the water pressure. "How long have you been up?" I asked, taking the mug she offered me with an outstretched hand. Old habits. Old roles.

"A while. I think my body is so accustomed to the routine, it doesn't know what to do with itself." Head tilted to the side, as if waiting for me to ask a follow-up question.

The lawn mower started running next door, sparing me, and I peered out the window over the sink. It was Charlotte's turn to cut the grass at the empty house this week, and one of her teenage daughters was out there now. From a distance, I could never tell which. They were only a year apart—seventeen and eighteen—and both had long dark hair and long pale legs and a nervous habit of running their fingers through the ends of their hair as they spoke.

"Do you have work tomorrow?" Ruby asked, jarring me from the window. I wondered if she wanted me out of the house or if she was just making conversation.

"I took off this week with the rest of the department." This wasn't entirely true, but it was believable. We were coming up on the Fourth of July, and the three women I worked with had rented a beach house together for the week with their significant others. They'd invited me to join them, but I'd passed, though the thought of the beach made my shoulders relax, my breathing slow. Instead, I'd joked that someone needed to hold down the fort—even though we worked a flexible summer, and technically, I was the one in charge.

But there was no way I was going in to work tomorrow. There was no way I was leaving Ruby alone here.

"Oh, hey," she said, leaning against the counter, bending one leg, channeling nonchalant, "did you change the bushes out back?" She did not look at me when she said it, instead focusing on some imagined spot through the living room windows, toward the patio.

I tried to keep my voice level, carefree, hands wrapped around the warm mug as I brought it closer to my face. "Oh, in the spring, yeah." No big deal, an afterthought. "Some guys were going around offering to do yard work, and I took them up on it."

Ruby shifted to face me, setting her own mug back on the counter. "What guys?"

The lawn mower passed in front of the kitchen window, the noise grating, and I had to wait a moment before responding. "I don't know, college kids looking to make an extra buck, I guess."

She turned back to the counter, moved her mug to the sink. "Well, looks nice out back. But I think we have rabbits again. Something's been in there."

And suddenly, I thought, *You, Ruby? Have you been in there? Last night, when I heard you go out, were you looking for something you left behind?*

The lawn mower passed again, and this time Charlotte's daughter—Whitney, the older one, finally close enough to tell—cast a glance into the kitchen window. Ruby raised her hand in greeting, and Whitney grinned back. I realized then that she'd been passing by the window over and over, hoping to see Ruby, with that sort of fearless, morbid curiosity best harnessed in the teen years.

Ruby's gaze trailed after Whitney. "There's nothing like a kid you haven't seen in a while to make you come face-to-face with the passage of time."

"She'll be heading to college soon," I said. There'd been a party at the pool last month, and everyone had come, as if we were sending her off into the world and not just to the college on the other side of the lake. But Charlotte was like that, sticking to the milestones, insisting on traditions—she'd even brought both girls in for a tour, waiting in my office with Molly, the younger daughter, while Whitney interviewed down the hall. As if it weren't a done deal.

Ruby watched her move on to the front of the yard. "She used to remind me so much of me at that age," she said. And then, with a smirk, "I think I should warn her." She cupped one hand around her mouth and called, "Watch out!" toward the window—though I was the only one who could hear her.

Ruby had been an English teacher at Lake Hollow Prep, where Charlotte's daughters attended high school. I knew there'd been fallout at the school after Ruby's arrest—parent outrage that a murderer had been in such close proximity to their children.

I wondered what the kids thought. Whether they'd seen Ruby as someone they could relate to at first. Whether they were slower to trust now. Whether they were afraid or intrigued. Back then, when I'd get home from work, I'd sometimes find Whitney doing her homework at our kitchen table while Ruby graded papers, in quiet harmony.

Ruby was just old enough to be their teacher but young enough to tell them they were always welcome here, that they could come to her any time, should they need it—and for them to believe it. Young enough to still call the neighbors Mr. and Mrs. Truett, for people to hire her to feed their pets and bring in their mail when they were away. She'd been the Truetts' dog sitter since she was in college, and if they were being particular assholes, she might give us a tidbit, like: *They sleep in separate rooms, you know.*

Ruby cleared her throat. "I'm sort of scared to ask, but did you donate my kayak, too?" she asked in an abrupt change of topic.

"No, it's in the garage," I said. "But you might need to help me dig it out." I stored a lot of things in there now. After the deaths next door, I'd started keeping my car in the driveway. All the dangers I had not been aware of before. How easy it would be to start a car and forget to turn it off. A slow, creeping death.

The thing that happened after the crime—and I imagined it happened to all of us living nearby, on the same street—was that, at all times, my own mortality felt so close to the surface. It was raw and pervasive and made me feel only precariously alive.

But after Ruby was locked up, that element felt contained, retreating from the surface. Like I had beaten something and endured. Like I had somehow defeated death, sidestepped the danger. The power of watching it come so close and miss.

I felt it again, starting to creep back in. The danger was no longer locked away. Maybe it never had been.

"So you didn't donate *everything,* then," she said.

"Couldn't get it in my car," I said with a grin.

Which made her laugh once, loudly, catching me by surprise. "You always were a terrible liar."

In truth, I kept other things, too. A pair of hoop earrings I'd always loved; her perfect shade of pink nail polish; the handbag she used on special occasions. After her dad came by and told me to get rid of it all, his eyes just barely glancing at the boxes, I took it upon myself to decide. I didn't feel bad about it then. Like I said, twenty years was a long time.

But I couldn't admit that to Ruby—that I'd gone through each item, one by one, deciding what was worth keeping. So yes, the kayak stayed.

In the early afternoon, I helped her carry it down to the lake. In the garage, we pulled out the garbage and recycling cans, the delivery boxes that needed to be broken down, and the bike I had big intentions for but rarely used anymore. We peeled away the tarp and my old camping gear before unearthing the kayak wedged against the wall and covered in dust. The pull cart had broken— one of the wheels turned inward, the metal bent—so we walked down the road single file, Ruby in the lead, the bright pink kayak turned sideways to fit under our arms.

The path through the woods came up before the pool, poorly marked but well trodden, right across from Margo and Paul Wellman's house. I imagined her watching now as I followed Ruby down the sloped dirt, the black iron gates of the pool above us, to our right. I couldn't see anyone watching, didn't hear any voices— just the hum of mosquitoes and the squirrels darting through the brush. Though I was sure people had noticed two women carrying a bright pink kayak through the neighborhood.

Eventually, Ruby's steps echoed over the slabs of plywood, and I could hear the water lapping at the dirt and roots in front of us.

45

On the edge of Lake Hollow, we were accustomed to a breeze, a cool gust off the water. The illusion, at least, as long as the air was moving. Sometimes, in the early morning, I would walk down here, staring out at the expanse of water like I was waiting for something to happen. Something to push back against, like a boat pressing through the current. Remembering that surge of adrenaline out on the ocean, the way you had to shout to be heard, the cold slap of the water, the bitter sting of the wind—feeling the need to move, to act.

But over the summer, the water had started to recede here, a drought that exposed the roots under the shoreline. And the stillness only managed to stir something up in the restlessness. Something quieter.

I saw Ruby scanning the area as we eased the kayak to the ground, like she was struggling to reconcile it with her memories.

"The whole lake has been going down," I said. "It hasn't rained all month."

She kicked off her flip-flops—my flip-flops, half a size too small—and nosed the kayak into the water. "Thanks for helping me lug this thing down here. I can probably get it back up on my own."

"Don't be silly," I said. Not that I believed she couldn't do it. I no longer underestimated all the things Ruby could do. But I didn't want to let her out of my sight. I didn't want to miss what she was doing here. "What else am I gonna do?" I slipped off my shoes and stepped into the lukewarm water, my feet sinking into the mud. "Feels good down here."

"All right," she said, "I won't be too long. I've just spent a long time thinking about getting to do this again."

She set out, heading straight down the center of the narrow inlet, toward the main body of Lake Hollow. If not for the topography of the coastline, the jagged fingers branching out from the main channel, I would've been able to see clear across the lake to the boathouse of the college and, beyond that, the tops of the low brick buildings, stretching into the trees.

As it was, all you could really see was the other side of the inlet—a thicket of trees and overgrown brush, the perfect home for muskrats and snakes. It didn't belong to us. The land was private property, with an area set back from the lake that was cleared but never built upon, and a roughly graded, narrow access road. There was a sign on the closest tree to remind us of our boundaries.

It had taken the investigators a week to search it all for evidence. To hear Chase tell it, all they found were beer bottles, half buried in the dust, and the remnants of a firepit at the center of the clearing from long ago.

The sun reflected off the water like glass, burning my eyes as Ruby cut a path through the still surface. I was watching her, hand shading my eyes, feet sinking deeper into the mud, when I heard a whistle behind me.

I spun around but couldn't see anything. Birds in the trees, calling to each other.

Another whistle, sharper this time, coming from up the slope. I stepped to the side so I could get a better angle through the trees. I could just make out Mac's profile at the concrete edge of the pool in the distance—tall, thin, trademark blue hat, one hand through the iron bars, gesturing me closer.

Mac's light brown hair curled out the bottom of his hat, and he wore sunglasses, so I couldn't tell where he was looking. All I could see was my own reflection as I approached, stepping carefully through the wooded terrain.

He looked over his shoulder once, then circled his hands around the bars, pressing his face closer. "Hey," he said, reaching for me as I came up the slope, fingers circling my wrist to steady me. "Was that her?" Nothing about the text I'd sent him yesterday and the silence that had followed.

"Yeah. She wanted to take the kayak out." With my free hand, I gripped the iron post beside him. But he didn't remove his other hand from my wrist, his thumb resting on my pulse point.

"She wanted to . . ." He shook his head, started over. "I'm sorry, Preston told me he saw the two of you at the pool yesterday, but I'm stuck on the part where she's *here* at your *house*."

"You and me both," I said. He of all people should understand how futile it was to deny Ruby what she wanted.

"I don't know what I'm supposed to say, Harper." *Sorry I didn't text you back. Sorry I didn't call. Sorry you're all alone with this.* I couldn't tell whether his comment was directed at me or at Ruby. His confessions and his questions were often indistinguishable, like this.

"Don't say anything," I said. "Not to her." A pause as his face jerked toward mine, his hand releasing my wrist. "Please."

"I wasn't planning on it." He took off his sunglasses, rested them on top of his hat. There were faint indentations on the bridge of his nose. He leaned closer, lowering his voice even more. "What the fuck does she want?"

"I don't know." In truth, I wasn't sure if she wanted anything in particular.

Mac groaned, ran a hand down his face. "I can't believe she came back here—" He stopped abruptly, turning at a sound in the woods—an animal scurrying. He took a subconscious step backward. "Guess we'll find out more tonight."

"Why tonight?" I asked.

"Charlotte's meeting?"

I shook my head once, confused. "No one told me about any meeting." If it had been on the message board, I'd missed it.

Mac shrugged, glancing behind him, the pool deck empty except for the striped towel designating his seat and the small red cooler on the pavement beside it. "Well, there is one. Charlotte texted. At seven-thirty, I think."

"You're going?" I asked. Mac wasn't much of a joiner. He didn't plan. He stumbled into things, happily surprised by the opportunities that presented themselves.

"Yeah, well, she asked if we could have it at our place instead."

"*Charlotte* did?" We half-jokingly referred to the Seaver brothers' home as the frat house, even though they were the neatest among us. In truth, they were beloved here, our Seaver brothers, with their easygoing appeal, their friendly banter. Like there was something of youth clinging to them instead of the other way around. But I couldn't imagine Charlotte asking Mac or Preston for anything.

"Yeah, she doesn't want to make it a thing so close to where it happened, you know?"

Or so close to me.

He talked like I shouldn't be insulted for being excluded. Like there wasn't a line drawn and me firmly on the other side, with Ruby here.

"Who?" I asked. "Who's going to be there?" Had everyone gotten an invite except me?

"No clue, Harper. I'm just providing the venue."

Sometimes I didn't understand how someone who seemed so bold in personality could be so passive in action. Though I probably shouldn't have been surprised. Mac was solidly in his thirties but had leaned into his lack of ambition long ago. Or maybe his ambition just took another form; he'd found the way to expend the least amount of energy for a relatively comfortable life. But his contentment was contagious. His smile, disarming. The fine lines radiating out from the corners of his hazel eyes—new in the last year or two—only added to his charm.

During the trial, Mac hadn't testified for either side. Hadn't taken a stand one way or another, content even then to let the cards fall however they may. He'd let his brother do the hard part, corroborating the security footage of Ruby from the stand.

Just then the pool gate clicked open, the creak of the hinges crying, as Preston pushed through the gate. His steps faltered briefly when he saw me.

"Hey," Mac called over his shoulder, and Preston raised a hand in greeting before heading to the chair beside Mac's.

When they were close together, Preston looked like a compressed and cleaner-cut version of Mac—a few inches shorter, a few inches broader, the same shade of sandy brown hair kept shorter and neater, held in place with some sort of product. In profile, they had the same ridge to their nose, the same shape to their eyes, but Mac's were hazel to Preston's striking green.

Though five years younger than Mac, Preston was the more successful of the Seaver brothers, the more driven, the more dependable. Even though Mac said he took his brother in after college to help him get on his feet, it was Preston who had secured Mac the job in the grounds department at the College of Lake Hollow. Up until then, Mac had worked at the private dock on the other side of the lake, taking out the boats on the lift, prepping them for their owners.

Mac had developed something of an aesthetic from that job, whether he meant to or not. The bold-patterned board shorts, the worn gray T-shirts over deeply tanned skin, the flip-flops and the way he walked because of them. A slow drag of his heel that managed to stay just this side of appealing.

"Listen," I said, lowering my voice, "just keep your distance. Okay?"

"Okay, yeah. I was going to." Mac looked over my shoulder, toward the water. "I don't know why she doesn't just leave. I would. Wouldn't you?"

"I'll find out what she's doing here. Tell Charlotte. Tell them I'll find out."

"Be careful, kid," he said, tapping the bars once before walking away.

"What was that about?" Preston's words carried across the pool deck as he cracked open a beer, sitting upright with his legs swung to the side of the lounge chair, but I couldn't hear Mac's response.

I sidestepped my way back down the steep slope, half-skidding over the dirt and fallen leaves, listening for the paddle dipping in and out of the water in the distance, growing closer.

It was pointless to show up at that meeting. All of them here with their watching, with their meetings—they were focused on the wrong thing, the wrong part.

No one had budged in their opinion. Not during the investigation and not even now. They believed Ruby Fletcher was guilty.

Back then we believed she had done it because we had to. Because if she hadn't been the one to sneak inside the house next door—to turn that key, to start that car—then it must've been someone else.

It must've been one of us.

CHAPTER 5

THE DELIVERY BOXES WERE stacked on my front porch by the time we arrived back home—all in my name but meant for Ruby. We dropped the kayak in the front yard, and Ruby darted up the porch steps. She scooped up the boxes like a child on Christmas, bringing each upstairs to her room one at a time.

"I'll pay you back," she said as she balanced the final box on her hip. "Promise."

"It's fine," I said.

"I have some cash, but there's not much left."

"You have cash?" This detail, above all, caught me by surprise.

"Yeah, my lawyer gave me some to get me here. To get started." Of course. How else had she taken a cab? Maybe that's why she was here, to retrieve what was left behind. But I'd gotten rid of her things, ruining her plans—and suddenly another path presented itself to me.

"Do you need more?" I asked. The prosecutor had made her out to be a grifter, a thief, a sociopath—take your pick. Maybe I needed to accept that possibility, too. I might be a victim, but I was a willing victim. I held my breath, hoping she would take the offering and move on, move out. Leave Hollow's Edge and never look back.

Ruby paused, one hand on the stair rail. "You've done enough," she said. "But maybe you can get me a job in the meantime?" I stared at her—her expression unreadable, eyes fixed firmly on mine—until finally, she added, "You *are* the director of admissions now, right?"

The air between us felt charged, alive. "Right." A pause. "We're not exactly hiring right now . . ."

Her face split into a smile. "I'm *kidding,* Harper. Oh my God, can you even imagine?" she asked. "Can you imagine if I worked in that department now, after everything? How that would *look*?"

She said it with levity, but I couldn't shake the chill, rooted to my spot. I wasn't sure how she knew that—what sort of information she'd had access to or why she'd been searching: What I had been doing for the last fourteen months. The role I'd acquired. My life, continuing on, while she was locked away—

I needed to get out of this house. Clear my head. But I didn't want to leave her unattended.

When she disappeared upstairs, I stepped outside but stayed close.

I hosed off the kayak, hosed our shoes, muddy water streaming down my driveway. Waiting for one of the neighbors to come out— Tate, demanding to know what Ruby was doing here; Charlotte, filling me in about the meeting—but the street remained empty and quiet.

A dog started barking from somewhere down the street, and— like always—my shoulders tensed, my stomach turned. A sign. A warning. An unshakable reminder that something unspeakably terrible had happened here.

THAT CRISP MORNING LAST March, I'd been outside; I'd gone for a run. When I'd left, I heard the dog barking next door at the Truett house. And I'd thought: *Of all people to neglect their pet. Look who's violating the noise ordinance now.*

When I'd gotten back, thirty minutes later, the dog was still barking out back—louder now, a periodic whimper, and this time I thought: *Maybe Ruby was supposed to walk their dog and forgot.* It was the first day of spring break, and maybe the Truetts were heading out of town. Maybe they'd left the dog out back, assuming Ruby would be over shortly.

But then I'd thought of Ruby getting in at two a.m., the sound of the shower running, and hadn't wanted to wake her if I was wrong.

It was nearly seven a.m., but they were typically early risers. Still, I knocked gently, not wanting to wake anyone on a vacation day. Especially not my boss, who didn't like running into me outside of our work environment.

It was then, as I'd waited on their front porch, that I heard the hum from the garage. The running car, like maybe someone was getting ready to go. I'd waited for the garage door to slide open, but it didn't. I kept waiting until I knew, in my gut, that too much time had passed.

I rang the bell this time, twice in a row, and still no one came to the door.

My hand shook as I reached for the handle. It was unlocked.

I pushed the door open, and I knew. Immediately, I knew.

I did not go in. I stumbled back, looked frantically around, saw another jogger at the corner, and recognized the familiar stride. I screamed for him—*Chase! Chase!*—and there must've been something in my tone that warned him. Because he shifted direction, his stride faster, more erratic. Charlotte must've heard me, too, because she came outside in her pajamas, met me on their porch. *The car has been running,* I said, and her hands rose to her face.

It was Chase who covered his mouth and nose with the crook of his arm as he raced inside to turn off the car engine, yelling at us to open the doors and windows.

It was too late.

Ever since, the sound of a dog barking put me on edge, brought me back to that moment—the moment before I knew, and everything changed.

Thinking about that time was like thinking of another version of this neighborhood, when the perception of our own safety was shattering. When we were realizing that here—with our lazy summers, with our neighbors who were also colleagues and friends, with our cop down the street—we had only convinced ourselves that we would be protected.

This was not the same place anymore, and we were not the same people.

WHEN I WENT BACK inside my house, I heard the shower running upstairs, and I tried calling Charlotte. When she didn't pick up, I texted instead: *Heard about the meeting. Anything I can do?*

I'd long since learned that the best way to get what you needed from Charlotte was to offer to help. As the head of the owners' association, she had enough people stopping her outside or coming by her house at all hours, asking her questions or complaining. Between that and her job as a counselor at the college, she was surrounded by other people's problems.

A door upstairs crashed open, and Ruby came running. She stumbled down the steps in such a rush that a sense of panic spread through the room. The tags were still on her clothes, and her hair was wet and unbrushed, and I looked for the danger, for who was after her. But she stopped in the living room, frantically moving the couch pillows. "It's on, it's *on*."

"What? What's happening?" I stood beside her, trying to help, but had no idea what she needed.

It was then I noticed the phone in her hand. A phone I'd never seen before and didn't know she had. She held it up to me. "My lawyer called. The news. They're doing a program."

"You have a phone?" The wrong comment. The wrong question.

"Yes, my lawyer gave it to me. I don't have anyone's number, though." She was half-paying attention, her gaze roaming around the room until she found the remote.

It was the first time since she'd arrived that I saw behind Ruby's carefully constructed facade. A tremble in her fingers as she turned on the television, eyes wide and mouth slightly open. She was practically breathless, standing in front of the couch, shifting back and forth on her feet.

"That's her," Ruby said, pointing the remote at the screen. "That's my lawyer."

The woman had sleek dark hair, cut blunt to her collarbone, an-gled cheekbones, a sharp suit. Her name was displayed on the bottom left of the screen in bold print: Blair Bowman. And now her words were coming through: "A grave miscarriage of justice. Evidence that could've exonerated her early on had been destroyed by those who should've known better. The crimes against Ruby Fletcher go back further than the trial itself. She never should've been arrested."

Ruby eased onto the couch, perched forward. On the screen, Blair Bowman was sitting at a table with a man and another woman, discussing the facets of the case. How one of the neigh-bors was a cop and never should've been professionally involved; how he'd tainted the investigation from the start, advising others on what to say and what not to say. How the video evidence did nothing but prove Ruby was in the vicinity—and of course she was, she lived there, it wasn't a crime to be outside. How witnesses had lied. "The relationships between all of these neighbors were contentious from the start," the lawyer said, punctuating her point with her hand on the table.

A noise escaped Ruby's throat, and the tension in my shoulders ratcheted up another notch. It hadn't been me. I hadn't lied. I'd been called by the defense—the only neighbor called by their side—to vouch for Ruby, and that was my plan. I thought I'd done the right thing, the good thing.

But in the witness box, in that moment, whatever you were thinking up to that point, it changes. What you say is between you and your god—or your faith in a system. A belief all the same. That the system we built would not wrongly convict or wrongly acquit. That justice can be served only if all play by the rules. And you play by those rules as a belief in something greater than you.

So I told them: Yes, she sometimes walked their dog; yes, I believed she had a key; yes, she was out that night, and I'd heard her come in at two a.m. through the back door, had heard the shower running soon after.

But I also told them she had no reason to do it. I told them we had all known Ruby for years. I told them she was a good roommate and reliable, and there was no animosity between her and the Truetts, no more than the rest of us. I told them the Truetts trusted her.

But I didn't know what the others had said. I didn't know about the footage that was shown. The very tight time line we had created. I did not hear Chase's testimony.

How he'd told them that, on the morning we'd found the Truetts, all the neighbors came running. In the commotion, every one of us came out. Everyone except Ruby. As if she already knew the scene we had uncovered.

I didn't know about the map that was shown of where each of us lived. The evidence attached to each house and the very clear path, established by each witness, of a closed loop—from the scene of the crime to Ruby's return home: Charlotte Brock. Preston Seaver. Margo Wellman. Me.

When I went into the courtroom, I didn't think they had enough. Neither did Ruby, it seemed—who, without bail, had pushed for a fast trial, believing she'd soon be out.

In that moment, on the stand, I did not know I was providing the final missing piece that would convict her.

Ruby leaned forward now, chin in her palm, rapt with attention.

Her lawyer was closing out the discussion. "We are looking into options, but rest assured this is not the last you'll be hearing from us."

Ruby shifted to face me then, practically drunk with some un-named emotion—excitement or power. "We're going to sue," she said.

She smiled then, and I recognized it—her first real smile. The authentic Ruby Fletcher. The one I remembered. And suddenly, I knew why she was here. Knew exactly what she was doing, what she wanted. Even before she said it, I knew: "Someone's going to pay."

MONDAY,
JULY 1

HOLLOW'S EDGE COMMUNITY PAGE

Subject: Sign-up for the party on the Fourth!

Posted: 9:22 a.m.

Tate Cora: BYOB. Preston, will you be working the grill again this year? Everyone, let us know what you're bringing so there's no doubles! I'll bring the lemonade.

Preston Seaver: Of course! I'll also bring the hot dogs.

Mac Seaver: Chips and salsa

Margo Wellman: I'll make my lemonade!

Tate Cora: I already said that.

Charlotte Brock: It's fine. We drink a lot of lemonade. I'll bring the burgers and buns.

⁀⁀⁀ ⁀⁀⁀ ⁀⁀⁀ ⁀⁀⁀ ⁀⁀⁀

Subject: Sign-up for Neighborhood Watch

Posted: 10:47 a.m.

Charlotte Brock: Hey all, a few of us have been talking, and we're going to get this going again, starting ASAP. There will be an orientation meeting at the pool clubhouse today at 7:00. In the meantime, does someone want to volunteer to start tonight?

Mac Seaver: I'll do it.

CHAPTER 6

THERE WAS NO SIGN of Ruby when I woke. When I stepped out of my bedroom, groggy and light-headed, the house was eerily quiet. No scent of coffee or sound of her milling about. How familiar she had become once more, her absence now more jarring than her presence. The door to the Jack-and-Jill bathroom was open from where I stood in the loft, so I could see straight through to her darkened bedroom.

"Ruby?" I called, before taking a step inside the bathroom. The bed was a double pushed up against the far corner, and the turquoise comforter was thrown back haphazardly. The blinds were tilted shut so that streaks of light filtered through the gaps onto the floor.

Last night, after the news program with her lawyer, Ruby had taken a phone call and disappeared upstairs, never to reemerge. I'd heard her through the closed door—the low, periodic sounds of a conversation—but couldn't make out what she was saying. Only her tone: clipped words, rising voice, before the room fell into a prolonged, unnatural silence.

Her room was empty now. I wondered how long it had been this way. Whether she'd gone out last night after I'd fallen asleep.

I backed out of the bathroom quickly, not wanting her to find me snooping, then descended the steps, hoping she was in the kitchen or lounging on the couch.

I didn't see Ruby anywhere, and my heart rate slowly increased. She had no car—there were only so many places she could be. None of them good options.

My eyes scanned the downstairs for anything irregular—the front door was still locked, but the back . . . I walked closer until I could be sure: The back deadbolt was unlocked.

I threw open the door and there she was, on the worn white Adirondack-style chair that she'd moved to the opposite corner of the yard, into the single square of sun, her feet up on the matching wooden ottoman. "There—"

She put her finger to her lips, cutting off my comment. At first I heard only the birds, animals leaping from branch to branch in the trees behind us. But she tipped her head toward the high white fence that separated my yard from the one next door. There were voices, slightly muffled—I could just barely make them out. Not in the yard itself, more like someone had left a window open at their house.

Slowly, as we listened, the voices rose, gaining clarity in steadily rising emotion.

In all the years I'd lived next door to Tate and Javier Cora, I had never heard them fight. Argue, sure, in a gently teasing way—what they must've learned to do in front of others at the local middle school, where they both worked. *If only you had remembered to take out the trash* and *Try not to forget the appointment this time.* But never voices raised, accusations thrown. Not even during the investigation, when tensions were high and relationships were fracturing, fissures exposed everywhere. Tate and Javier had remained a united front.

Oh, but not today.

"You're not *thinking*, Javi." Tate's words sounded like they were forced out through clenched teeth.

"I'm not *thinking*, I'm not *paying attention*—I'm always *not* doing something, according to you. Maybe you should be the one changing. Maybe you should just calm the fuck down for once."

Ruby's mouth fell open in exaggeration, eyes wide with glee. I felt my expression mirroring her own—a shared, delighted shock. I couldn't imagine anyone, let alone Javier, telling Tate to calm down.

A beat passed, and then two—long enough for me to think they'd moved to another room—before Tate's voice, high and tight, cut through the still morning. "Maybe you should get the fuck out of here."

And then the sound of their back door being thrown open, Javier's feet on the steps, and his rapid breathing, so close, on the other side of the fence. A flash of bright blue from his shirt as he passed back and forth.

We were stuck. I was standing at the bottom of the brick steps, trying not to give myself away. Ruby sat on the chair, one hand raised comically in mid-motion. She pressed her lips together. I felt myself holding my breath.

The unmistakable sound of texts being sent and received chimed from his side of the fence; he kept moving, a blur of blue passing through the slats. I wished I could see him, see what he looked like—whether his fists were balled up, whether his face had reddened—but the only way to see into your neighbor's yard was from the second floor, and even then you could see only the back corners of the patio, where the gate gave way to the rise of trees beyond the fence line.

When Aidan and I moved in, Tate and Javier Cora became our closest couple friends. We spent evenings in their yard or ours, drinking beers, grilling, laughing. The guys would go out sometimes in the evenings together, and Tate and I would meet up at the pool, drinks in hand, chairs turned toward the lake, faces angled into the breeze.

After Aidan's departure, it became clear they had known for a while that he'd been considering leaving me; neither of them seemed surprised. When I told Tate—the first person I wanted to see; I showed up on her front porch with righteous anger and a bottle of wine—it was obvious that someone had beaten me to it. And it was then I understood that, at some point along the way, Tate had decided not to tell me that my fiancé wasn't in it for the long haul.

I thought of every opportunity she'd had to tell me. Every time I had mentioned the ideal time for the wedding—*Oh, yes, May is perfect,* she'd agreed, *anything later and you'll melt*—or how we were waiting for Aidan to finish his program first. Afterward, whenever I looked at her, I could only wonder how *long* she must've known. How many times she and Javier had discussed it, how they must've felt such *pity* for me. Something that verged on embarrassment.

It was hard for a friendship to recover from that. Every time I saw them together, I pictured them discussing it, hushed whispers in their kitchen, where they could peer from their window straight into our living room: *It's not our place, Javi. Oh, but poor Harper. I don't think she has a clue.*

Another chime came from the other side of the fence, and Ruby raised one eyebrow, her whole face shifting into a question. I knew what she was implying, letting me fill in the blanks. *Who would Javier be texting after a fight with his wife?*

A window suddenly slammed shut. Their back door swung open, the hinges crying. A pause as some silent communication seemed to be happening: No one was moving; no one was speaking. Like Tate had just realized their mistake—the open window, their voices carrying.

Ruby pushed the wooden ottoman slightly with her bare foot so that it scraped against the brick of the patio, and I didn't think it was an accident. A small smile broke onto her face. I heard Javier take a deep breath, heard his feet on the steps, the door closing, the lock turning with unnecessary force.

Ruby didn't have to make a scene. She could disrupt the balance with the shift of her chair. With the mere possibility of her on the other side of a high fence. Her small smile stretched into a wide grin, and I shook my head, though I was grinning, too. I felt the last fourteen months dissipating—the bond threatening to form once more, the same one that had made our living arrangement so easy.

After Aidan left, Ruby had quickly joined me in my coolness toward Tate, picking up on some undercurrent. There had been a vacancy left behind, a sharp sting of betrayal, and Ruby had filled it.

"Wonder what that was all about," Ruby said, standing from the chair. Then she ambled across the small brick patio, casting a quick glance toward the edge of the mulch bed, where the soil had been disturbed in sections. *Rabbits,* she had said, but it looked too organized. Too deliberate.

"Come on," I said, gesturing for her to follow me inside. "How long were you out there?" I asked once the door was closed behind us. Always, always, tallying her minutes. As if I could control her actions by accounting for her time. Knowing how guilt emerged in the gaps: *The time to unscrew the carbon monoxide detector from its spot on the ceiling; the time to take Fiona's car keys from their spot beside the garage door; the time to start the car and run—down to the lake, down to the woods; the time to dispose of evidence and sneak back home—*

"Not too long," she said. "Hey, can I borrow your car today?"

My train of thought faltered. "I can drive you," I said.

She skirted by me, walking past the kitchen into the foyer. "I have a meeting with my lawyer," she said, her voice echoing as she headed for the stairs. "She's coming through town and asked if I could meet her and the team in private. It's in some business park, and I don't know how long it will take." She paused at the bottom step, one hand on the railing. "Okay?"

It was not. Handing over my car was not the same as an extra bathing suit, a pair of flip-flops. "I was planning to go to the grocery store," I said.

"We can do that tomorrow," she said, and I remembered that, with Ruby, you had to be firm and definitive, had to say what you meant. She would not give you the benefit of nuance or concede a point that had not been earned.

"I'll call you an Uber," I said, and her fingers curled tightly on the railing, the ragged nails bitten down to the quick.

"Harper," she said, "the case is all over the news. I can't have some kid with a license picking me up, driving me around, taking his shot for his fifteen minutes of fame after."

The implied threat: Following her back here. People watching. Media vans camped outside, like they had been the days after her arrest—

Every decision was a balance, and I couldn't see the right option, the right answer. I felt the pieces spinning out of my control.

She didn't even wait for me to say yes.

WHEN SHE CAME BACK downstairs a short time later with that brown leather messenger bag slung across her chest, she went straight for the drawer beside the front door, where I kept my ring of keys. This was another skill of hers, to push you into something, catch you on your heel before you realized what was happening. Asking, half as a joke, *Any chance you could use a roommate,* filling the backseat of her car and taking up residence in your house; saying, with the police on the front porch, *Will you tell them, Harper? Tell them I didn't do it? That*

I don't have their key anymore? That I couldn't have done it? So that the only thing you could possibly say, with her right there, eyes wide and searching, was *Yes, of course, yes.*

"Thanks, Harper, I owe you one," she said, heading for the front door. My whole life, suddenly in her grip.

I followed her outside, watched as she slid into the driver's seat of my car. She started the engine, lowered all four windows as if the inside of my car felt too contained. Hands on the steering wheel, eyes straight ahead—

"Like riding a bike, right?" She gave me an exaggerated grimace, and I wanted to ask, *Do you even have a license? Is it still good?* But more than anything, I wanted her gone—before anyone else noticed her sitting in my car. Ruby in my house. Ruby in my car. Slowly infiltrating my life once more.

"That's what I hear," I said.

She gave no indication that she heard me as the car glided down the slight incline.

I watched from the sidewalk as she drove to the stop sign, turning out of sight at the Seaver house, then I listened as the sound of the engine faded into the distance—not sure what I was waiting for. An accident? A change of mind or heart, my car suddenly returning up that same road? Ruby apologetic, stumbling out of the car, handing me back the keys, all the while saying, *Oh my God, I don't know what I was thinking.*

A flash of movement in the front window of Charlotte Brock's house caught my eye: curtains dropping back into place.

Of course people were watching. Whatever had happened at their meeting the night before, no one was reaching out to fill me in. This would probably make it worse.

I crossed in front of the Truett house and shuddered at the lingering scent of exhaust from my car. A trigger of a memory, my arms rising in goose bumps—Chase yelling at me to open the garage door as he turned off the car, then the mechanical churning so painfully slow as I held my breath—

The smell had taken a while to dissipate. It lingered so long that sometimes I wondered if it was what had brought me to their house that morning to begin with. Some subconscious under-standing of *wrong,* only exacerbated by the barking dog.

Past the Truett house now, I marched up the porch steps to Charlotte's front door, still feeling a chill, like the ghost of a mem-ory following me in the dark.

When I rang the bell, I heard footsteps on the other side of the door—and then silence. As if someone was watching. Deciding.

"Charlotte, come on," I called as I knocked.

The door abruptly swung open. Molly glanced past me.

"Hey, is your mom home?"

She blinked rapidly, long eyelashes and faint freckles on her cheeks, like her mother's. Her gaze finally settled back on me. "No, she had to take Whitney to the dentist."

I noticed her own teeth then, white and sparkly. I'd thought she had braces; she must've just had them removed. She ran her thumb along the top row now, like she was still getting used to the feeling.

As she started closing the door, I caught sight of the duffel bag in the hall, deep blue against the light gray walls, matching the set of landscape photographs hanging in the foyer. As if even this had been coordinated. The layout of their house was much the same as my own, but with a master down along with the two extra bed-rooms upstairs, and decorated with a much better eye for design.

"You going out of town?" I asked.

Molly shifted to block my view, narrowed her eyes, a new distrust—as if the fact that I had harbored Ruby tainted my own character. As if she hadn't known me for years.

"Mom wants us to go stay with our dad. But she didn't check

with him, and he's not home." Hand running through the ends of her dark hair, gathered over her shoulder.

Bob Brock had seemed as generic as his name, tall and thin and nondescript. Blandly handsome in person but nothing to remember. He had the type of face I thought I'd seen before. That had made me ask, *Have we met?* when I'd first moved in. Nothing like Charlotte, who was easy to notice, easy to remember. She had dark hair and freckles and looked much younger than her age. From a distance, walking together, Charlotte and her daughters could all pass for siblings. They were striking on their own, even more so as a group.

Even his job seemed ordinary—he worked in accounting. Which was what made what happened so hard to believe. Bob worked from home, depending on the project, and apparently had a habit of asking his girlfriend to park around the corner, keeping her car out of sight, and walk up our street, entering through their double garage, before she came into frame on their security camera.

But Margo Wellman had noticed the unfamiliar car at the curb, noticed the trend of the timing, and posted a photo to the message board of the blue sedan with a short blond woman exiting, because we had a strict no-solicitation rule. *Anyone know this woman?* she'd written. *She's been parking here every day this week around noon. I've never seen her before.* And then Preston Seaver searched through his security feed and posted a clip of her walking past his house, sunglasses on, head down: *Looks like she was heading up our street.* But she never made it onto Charlotte's camera next door. Charlotte was the one who posted: *She never shows up on my video. Disappears somewhere between your front door and mine. ??*

No one responded, not a word, until the truth sank in, and the drama shifted from the board to reality.

Charlotte was nothing if not detail-oriented and organized. She piled Bob's things neatly into boxes and stacked them out front. We saw the locksmith's van parked along the street before the end of the day.

The girls aligned themselves, as expected, with their mother— remaining here more often than not, even though their parents lived in the same town and shared custody. Bob had stuck it out with the girlfriend. Word was, he'd moved straight in with her on the other side of the lake after Charlotte had kicked him out.

"You shouldn't be here," Molly said to me, pushing the door closed. But she was too old to be wary of strangers—and anyway, I wasn't a stranger. However much the sisters looked alike, their personalities were very different. Even though they were only a year apart, Molly was always the more cautious of the two, the more hesitant, the quieter. Sometimes, if her sister wasn't around, you could forget she was there.

It was the older one, Whitney, who was bold. Who ran the lawn mower close to the window to get a glimpse of Ruby.

"Will you tell your mother I stopped by, please?" I asked.

"Tell her yourself tonight," Molly said. "Isn't there some big meeting at the clubhouse?" Bolder than I remembered, then. Older, anyway.

"By the way, no need to be nervous. She'll be gone for a bit," I said as I stepped back. Molly blinked twice, her face blank of emotion. "Ruby," I continued. "You don't have to hide out inside."

Molly stared at me. "She's guilty, you know," she said, a tinge of disgust in her expression—at me or at Ruby, I wasn't sure. "She shouldn't be allowed to stay here."

"Well," I said, trying to remember myself at seventeen, how I hated being lied to by adults; how all I wanted then was honesty, "they didn't prove it." It was the one honest thing I could think of. I figured it was Charlotte's job to explain the legal system to her children.

"Yes," Molly countered with a roll of her eyes, a spot-on

impression of her mother. "They did." And then she shut the door, effectively ending the conversation.

AS I WALKED DOWN their porch steps, I saw Chase jogging up the street, his familiar broad frame, mechanical stride, quickening pace. I walked faster for home, hoping to avoid him. Knowing that Ruby was currently out in the world, having a discussion with her lawyer. I wondered whom she was referring to when she said *Someone's going to pay,* whether it was only Officer Chase Colby of the Lake Hollow Police Department. Chase had already been placed on leave from the department, pending internal investigation. He had all the time in the world to let things fester. And now the source of all of his troubles, all he had lost, was here—with me.

I strode up my porch steps, head down. Had just shut the door behind me when I heard the steady stomp of his tread passing by. I peered out the front window, watching him retreat. Who needed a neighborhood watch when we knew Chase was watching?

The truth was, I didn't blame him. I didn't blame any of them, walking past the pool to get a closer look, pushing the lawn mower for a peek in our window, jogging by to check up on her—they weren't the only ones who wanted to know what Ruby was doing here.

We're going to sue, she said. On the news, the lawyer had implied that there was contention with the neighbors, with *us,* that Ruby had been wronged by more than the system. I no longer trusted that she would confide the truth to me, not anymore. If she ever had. *Tell them, Harper. Tell them I couldn't have done it—*

It was instinct, at first, to want to believe her. Before her image was found on the cameras. Before the trial and the testimonies. I'd heard the echo of my brother in her plea, appealing to something baser inside of me.

Maybe that's what made me confide in Kellen, in an ill-advised confession on Christmas night, after too much eggnog and not enough sleep. Thinking he would understand, tell me I had done the right thing.

By tradition, we spent Christmas Day with my mother's side of the family, at the cape house we'd grown up in, and where she and sometimes Kellen still lived—occasionally by his choice, more likely by her heavy suggestion.

After dinner, we had made a joint escape from our extended family's probing questions—*Have you met someone new, Harper? How's the job working out, Kellen?*—seeking solace on the covered patio, even in the bitter cold.

We had always looked more similar than either of us would've preferred: large brown eyes and a downturned mouth; high cheekbones and a smile that felt familiar, reflecting back. At times, it made me believe we were closer than we really were.

And so I'd told him, in the dim glow of the yellow light beside the back door, with the voices muffled on the other side. *My roommate was found guilty of killing our neighbors,* I'd said, breaking the silence. *I testified.*

Kellen looked at me with an expression I'd never seen before. Like he wasn't sure who I was, the secrets I kept. *You knew she did it?* he asked.

No, I said. *I wasn't sure.*

His expression shifted again, to something darker, introspective. His breath escaped in a fog of chilled air. *Shouldn't you be sure before you testify?*

But I'd thought that was the purpose of the trial. To present each piece as one, and to know beyond all reasonable doubt. *I only told the truth. I'm not the one who found her guilty.* As if we could each individually absolve ourselves.

The conversation had ended awkwardly, and I'd flown out early the next morning without saying goodbye.

But he'd called me a week later, on New Year's Eve, close to midnight—holidays, the most acceptable times for reaching out—and apologized, as if he'd been thinking about it. Said he was projecting, then tossed in a self-deprecating line about himself— *Like I should talk, right?*—and some comment about how no one could ever be sure what other people were capable of. We'd said *Happy New Year* and hung up the phone and, in another Nash family tradition, hadn't connected again since.

Now I heard the echo of his question: *Shouldn't you be sure?* I wasn't even sure what she was doing here *now*. But suddenly, with Ruby out, I saw the opportunity.

This time I approached her room with purpose.

Since the main door to her bedroom was closed, I entered the bathroom, like I had this morning, so as to disturb as little as possible. I took a closer look. On the counter were the essentials we had purchased online yesterday: fresh toothbrush and toiletries, half of them piled in the far corner, unopened. Humidity lingered in the bathroom, condensation clinging to the mirror, like she'd only just stepped out. I flipped the exhaust fan to circulate the air, and something fluttered overhead.

Above, a tight wad of paper had been wedged between the vent blades. I closed the lid of the toilet and stepped up carefully, balancing with one hand against the wall. Reaching up, my fingers brushed against the edge of a paper—a twenty-dollar bill that had unfurled, flapping with the gust of the fan. I leaned to the side, getting a better look at the roll of cash. If those were all twenties, that was far more money than I would've thought the lawyer would give her to get herself started.

From what I could see from this angle, there was an assortment of small bills—fives, tens, twenties. Like a hand had reached into a bucket of cash and randomly pulled. I couldn't imagine her lawyer opening her wallet, counting out her assorted cash, and handing it over with a shrug, but I couldn't figure out where else Ruby would've gotten it.

I quickly flipped the fan switch off.

My heart raced as I opened the cabinets under the sink, looking for more things she might've hidden, when I spotted a bright yellow pouch tucked behind the plumbing. I knelt on the ceramic tile and pulled it out. A small drybag, like we used when we were kayaking, to keep our phones and keys safe and dry.

It was empty.

She must've found this in the storage compartment of her kayak, buried under fourteen months of junk. Suddenly, I understood. This money hidden in the bathroom; the empty drybag under the sink; her fear that I'd gotten rid of the kayak and her insistence on taking it out—she had hidden her money there before her arrest. Maybe she'd been planning to make a run for it.

And now she was back for it.

A chill ran through me at the realization that maybe the neighbors hadn't been paranoid with the rumors after her arrest. Their claims of money that had gone missing from a wallet, a purse, a house during a party. Maybe I had never known Ruby as well as I'd thought.

But I could feel my pulse slowing again, because I could finally make sense of her actions. She'd sneaked inside that first day, shoes in her hand, empty luggage in the hall. She was here, in my house, for the things she'd left behind. This was a series of steps I could trace forward and back, understand her motivation, see it through to its inevitable end: with her leaving this place.

Koda leaped off the edge of her bed in the connecting room, and I jumped, startled.

Ruby's luggage sat in the far corner of the room. When I checked, it was still empty. I pulled open one of the drawers to the small dresser she'd brought over from her dad's house when she moved, carefully searching through the clothes we had ordered together, tags still on. Some things, like the socks, remained in the plastic bag they'd arrived in.

There was nothing unexpected as I checked the rest of her drawers. I stood at the single window, peering out between the tilted blinds, where her room overlooked the back of our square patio and Tate and Javier Cora's backyard. The branches of the trees outside the fences swayed, though there hadn't been any breeze when I'd been out.

I pressed my face closer to the blinds, my forehead resting on the white slats. If someone was lurking in the line of trees beyond our backyards, I wouldn't be able to tell, with the high fence blocking the view of the ground. Rows of tightly packed evergreens creating the illusion of privacy, so you would forget about the road giving way to another semicircle of houses directly beyond.

A squirrel, probably. We heard them all the time, hopping from the branches and scurrying across the roof. A quick pitter-patter of feet that set my heart racing every time.

I checked the closet last. Inside, the few wire hangers on the metal rod remained empty. A heap of dirty clothes was stacked in the dark corner, like she wasn't sure what to do with them just yet. I dug my foot into the pile of fabric just to check. Nothing.

There wasn't much else in the room to go through. A beige towel hung from the edge of the bed where the cat had been sleeping, and I resisted the urge to pick it up and hang it in the bathroom before it mildewed.

Before Ruby's arrest, I had let the police in here myself, given them permission to search, when they were looking for the missing carbon monoxide detector. I was so sure they wouldn't find it here—and they didn't. The police ultimately believed that was why Ruby was spotted on Margo and Paul Wellman's video feed, running toward the lake: to dispose of the evidence, though nothing was ever found.

I'd watched as they searched her room back then, methodically and carefully. I remembered all the places they'd checked. So I flipped the pillow over. Ran my hands along the comforter, then along the seams where the bed was pushed against the wall.

Finally, I reached between the mattress and box spring, sliding my arms up and down the length of the bed. My pinkie caught on something sharp near the head of the bed, and I jerked back. A dot of blood, the beginning of a wound; I brought it to my mouth to stop the sting. Then I reached my other hand carefully under the mattress again, and my fist closed on something small and metallic.

I recognized the item right away. It was a small paring knife. A familiar black handle with a sloping shape. Part of the set from my kitchen. Taken by Ruby from downstairs and stored, within reach, under her bed.

Like she was afraid of something.

I stood for a long time in that spot, listening to the sounds of my empty house. Wondering if I needed to be afraid of something, too.

CHAPTER 7

GREW RESTLESS AND UNSETTLED, pacing the house. Watching the clock. Eating dinner while standing over the kitchen counter, in case I needed to shift tasks at any moment.

My mind kept drifting to that knife. Why she felt the need to take it. What—or who—she was afraid of, when half the neighborhood was making plans to deal with their fear of her.

I'd replaced the knife under her mattress carefully, in the same spot I'd found it, not wanting her to know I'd been through her things. Imagining what she might already be telling her lawyer: *Harper got rid of everything I owned, can you believe it?*

It was nearly seven p.m. and Ruby wasn't back.

Had she told me when I could expect her return or where she was going? *Some business park,* she'd said. She implied it was close, that her lawyer was coming through town. But she'd left no room for follow-up, no chance to shake out the specifics.

The mantel clock over the fireplace ticked loudly in the silence. I could feel my jaw clenching.

I heard people talking out front, and the noise drew me to the dining room window—the irritational hope that I might see Ruby stepping out of my car, chatting with one of the neighbors like nothing was amiss.

But it was Tate on the sidewalk, calling for Javier, "Come on already, we're going to be late," as he locked up behind them. Her expression turned light and friendly as Tina Monahan approached from her house next door. Tina strode toward them with her usual air of efficiency, brown hair pulled back in a low ponytail, short bangs she appeared to cut herself, and an assortment of colored scrubs she rotated with regularity.

"Hey, there," Tate called with a hand on one hip, "can you believe this?"

Tina shook her head once. Though I couldn't see her expression, I couldn't imagine Tina saying anything negative. Tina—*What would I need a security camera for, Officer?*—was a saint, perpetually optimistic. She seemed to be the only person in the neighborhood the Truetts had liked, someone less frivolous than the rest of us.

Tina was a registered nurse and worked at the college. She had brought both of her parents to live with her the year after Aidan and I moved in, was the type who said, *It's a blessing to get to spend this time with them.* Her father was in a wheelchair. Her mother wasn't able to care for him alone. Tina's model home had a master downstairs, so, she said, *Truly, it was an easy decision.*

I had never heard her complain, never heard a negative comment. I believed that her demeanor was authentic after the murders. She never had to look at the people who lived with her and wonder what they were capable of. She never had to account for their time line. When the police came to investigate, she said there was no need for surveillance because someone was always home.

I waited until they were out of earshot and then locked up behind me, following the rest of my neighbors to the clubhouse.

THE MEETING COULDN'T BE held in the clubhouse, which was just a series of three doors set in a low building directly off the pool deck, accessible only from inside the pool gates. It amounted to nothing more than two bathrooms and a meeting room, the last of which doubled as the lost and found. That was where the neighborhood board met, but the space wouldn't hold more than fifteen people or so. Our neighborhood meetings always spilled outside, onto the pool deck, where we sat on loungers and vinyl-strapped pool chairs, their metal legs scraping against the concrete as we settled in.

But the people in charge always filed out of that meeting room like they had come from some pregame briefing, deciding what to share with the masses. Whenever the door swung open, we could briefly see into the room: the edge of a table and a large gray bin filled with an assortment of floats and goggles, unclaimed items that had accumulated over the years, now available for residents to borrow when needed.

Charlotte Brock was the president, Tina Monahan was the secretary, and Margo Wellman's husband, Paul, was the treasurer. They'd held their positions for years. No one was interested in the extra work or the grief.

Even though this gathering wasn't board-sanctioned, Tina was standing beside Charlotte outside the meeting room door when I arrived. I looked around for Paul Wellman—the business-casual attire he always wore, regardless of the fact that we were outside, at a pool, while the rest of us were in cover-ups and athletic apparel; the prematurely salt-and-pepper hair that gave him an air of responsibility—but he was nowhere to be seen. Margo was here, though, sitting at one of the round pool tables, moving the stroller back and forth with her foot as Nicholas fidgeted. I took the chair beside her, though she didn't seem to notice. "Hey," I said, scooting the chair a little closer.

Her eyes widened as she looked at me, and she peered over my shoulder like she might see Ruby. Just like Molly had done earlier in the day.

"It's just me," I said, and she nodded. Up close, her nose was burned and starting to peel, and her lips were chapped. In her thirties, Margo had a round face with soft features and large blue eyes; between her wide eyes and her hair, which was never fully contained, she always looked caught slightly off guard. She and Paul were a contrast in demeanor, but they seemed to balance each other.

"About yesterday," I said. "I didn't know Ruby was coming. I followed her to the pool just to make sure nothing happened—" I checked the crowd behind me, lowered my voice. "Between her and Chase."

Her shoulders relaxed, and she leaned closer. "I had no idea she was back," she said. "She talked to me, and I froze."

"Well, she walked in my house, and I froze."

That got half a laugh, at least. I needed to work my way back like this. Make sure they knew I was on their side.

When I was called to testify in Ruby's defense, I had put myself on a definitive side of the line. The neighborhood had grown tense in the lead-up to the trial, when we knew who was testifying and who was not. But after Ruby was convicted, it didn't seem to matter anymore. We had all just presented a piece of the truth, and no one could fault me for that.

Afterward, everything was surface-level fine and polite smiles and waves from the car. But look deeper, and you could find the divide. The texts I didn't receive; the invitations that weren't extended. I wasn't always in on the secrets anymore.

"Is she gone now?" she asked.

I closed my eyes briefly. "She's out with that lawyer. But she's not gone."

From the stroller, Nicholas started to cry, and Margo lifted him to her lap, smoothing down his red baby-fine curls. "Well, then," she said absently, and I wasn't sure if she was talking to me or the baby.

"Where's Paul?" I asked. Come to think of it, I hadn't seen him in weeks. If something had happened with them, no one had mentioned his absence; his was a silent retreat.

"Stuck at work," she said, patting the baby's back, then shushing him, not giving me room for a follow-up question. "I told Charlotte a seven o'clock meeting wouldn't be doable for everyone. But you know how she is."

As if on cue, Charlotte's voice boomed over the space. "Can everyone hear me?" she called, hands held out from her sides, as if summoning something.

The chatter fell to murmurs. I looked around the pool deck at the rest of the neighbors pulling closer, and I felt claustrophobic. The families from the street behind ours, scraping the chairs against the pool deck. Eyes darting away when my gaze met theirs.

Mac was just walking in through the open gate, side by side with his brother, Preston. They maneuvered through the sea of chairs, heading toward an open spot near the back, nodding to neighbors as they passed. At least half of the households were represented here tonight. Word had spread quickly.

"Thank you all for coming out tonight." Charlotte's voice always rose above the crowd, though she wasn't loud; it was more that the others quieted to compensate. "I know we've been over this before, but I thought it would help to revisit protocol. Please, please, remember we are all volunteers, so let's not demand more of people than they're offering. Okay?"

A shuffling of fabric. A cough near the back.

Charlotte nodded to herself, then continued. "We are asking for as many people as possible to sign up for one full evening, so the requirement will remain low on each person. I know it's difficult to give up a consistent time slot, week after week. So we found that this works a little better. You give a full night if you can, and then you can be done with it for the month. We ask for periodic walk-throughs from dusk to dawn. Obviously, if you want to split the responsibility with someone else, be my guest. I'll leave a sign-up sheet here, and we can go over any logistics together. We just want to know who to contact, who to be on the lookout for each night. I remember last year, my girls were nervous because they didn't know Javier had a new car." A wink in his direction, a light chuckle through the crowd.

"As a reminder, or to those of you new to this . . ." She scanned the crowd. None of us was new to this. "Here's a quick recap of what you are and are not permitted to do."

We had heard all of this last time from Chase, who had stood up in that very spot in his police uniform and walked us through exactly where the legal line lay. As if he himself weren't crossing it at that moment.

"You do have the right to tell someone that this is a private neighborhood," Charlotte continued. "You do have the right to ask who they are visiting. But you do not have the right to detain them. Most crimes will be deterred by the presence of someone in authority. Regardless, you should call the police promptly after a suspicious encounter to have it on record. We recommend keeping a log of anything you see, anyone you speak with who isn't from the neighborhood."

"Who counts as from the neighborhood?" A voice boomed behind me, and I turned to see Preston Seaver, hand raised even as he was already speaking. "For instance, what if the issue is with someone already staying *in* the neighborhood?" Beside him, Mac remained perfectly still, eyes forward. As if he had no opinion in the matter.

Charlotte gave him a tight smile. "If there's an issue, same rules apply. Call the police."

"I mean, we're allowed to walk at night, though, right?" another man asked, sitting at a table to my right. He lived in the court behind us, alone. He'd been engaged, but his fiancée had left sometime last year. He shifted forward on his chair, and I briefly caught sight of Chase, leaning against the side of the entrance.

"Of course," Charlotte said. "We all know one another here. Use your discretion, Pete."

We knew what these questions were implying and what Charlotte's responses were acknowledging. We were all here to keep track of Ruby Fletcher. To watch out for her. To watch her.

Ruby had been at this meeting the last time, when it was Chase up there laying out the ground rules. Before a woman who looked an awful lot like Ruby was identified on the Seavers' security camera—and the investigation, and Chase, turned their focus on her.

Back then Ruby was still one of us, getting in line, signing her name. *Split with me, Harper? We can go out together.*

"If that's everything," Charlotte said, placing the paper on the white rectangular folding table in front of her, "let's let everyone get back to their evening."

We formed a line, just like last time, the very picture of civilized community. I slid into place, inching forward, wedged near the front between Charlotte and the Seaver brothers.

Mac, sensing me, stepped back slightly. "How'd you manage to sneak out?" he asked, speaking from the side of his mouth, like this was all a game.

"She's gone," I said.

Preston, facing forward, let out a noise—something between

disgust and amusement. Mac raised an eyebrow but was next in line and never had a chance to respond.

"I think we should all take the first week, that okay with you guys?" Charlotte was saying to them now.

We were our street. Our group. Our clique. *We* were the people who overlapped at work and at home, conversations and jokes spilling over, with no defined boundaries. *We* were the row of homes, from our court to the pool, who had caught Ruby on camera. We were the people who had testified.

We were the people who might pay.

"Good idea," Preston said, and I lost the rest of their conversation under the sound of Margo Wellman attempting to calm a squirming Nicholas.

When it was my turn next, Charlotte's expression did not falter. "Harper, thanks for coming out. What evening works for you?" She held the pen over the sign-up.

"Put me down wherever there's a gap, Charlotte. Also, I've been meaning to talk to you. I stopped by the house today."

Her finger slid down the list of dates, eyes focused on the page. "Molly told me. Sorry, it's been chaos, I scheduled a bunch of appointments for this week. Is there something urgent?"

I leaned in closer to get her attention. Pressed my fingers into the plastic table until she met my gaze. "I think I know why she's here."

Charlotte blinked twice, then brought her long hair over one shoulder, like I'd seen Molly do earlier in the day. Her gaze flicked to the gate and back, her lips pressed together. I followed her line of sight, worried I'd see Ruby, that she had caught me here. But it was Chase, leaning against the black iron bars.

"We haven't done coffee in a while," she said. "Can you make it to my house early tomorrow? Say nine?"

I nodded. She scratched my name down in an empty slot, then

smiled at Margo behind me. "Margo, truly, you don't need to do this."

"He's up every few hours teething. I'm awake anyway."

"I remember that stage," Charlotte said with a sympathetic expression as I walked out of earshot.

I looked for Chase on the way out, but he'd disappeared in the last few minutes. He wasn't in the line or on the pool deck. I started to think I'd manifested him from nothing. Déjà vu from the last time we did this, a cycle repeating itself. While we grasped for the illusion of safety with structure and routine.

Chase's house was in the other direction when exiting the pool, toward the left, at the opposite corner from Margo and Paul Wellman's home. Before the Truetts' deaths, Chase had a career and good standing in the community. Authority and reputation. Power. I wondered if people here ultimately blamed him for Ruby's release.

The evening had turned overcast, like it might rain, even as dusk was settling in. The streetlight on the corner flicked on automatically, illuminating me.

I walked faster than I needed to. Imagining Ruby waiting at home, with free reign over the place. Waiting for me.

I SHOULDN'T HAVE WORRIED. My car wasn't back. Even if she could've fit the car inside the garage, the lights were off inside, as I'd left them. Even the porch light was off; I fumbled the key into the lock in the shadows. As I pushed the door open, a paper skittered across the entrance floor.

I flipped the foyer light, then bent for the paper. It was simple printer paper, folded in half, black ink visible through the other side. Something slid onto the floor as I unfolded the page, a message in bold ink staring back:

YOU MADE A MISTAKE.

One line, that was it. No name. No indication whether this was meant for me or for Ruby.

But on the hardwood floor, staring up at me, was a photo. I crouched closer until I was kneeling on the floor, photo in hand. It was an image, blown up and slightly blurry, only part of the scene fitting on the standard-size glossy photo paper. But I could tell that it was a picture of a hand clutched around an item. A still frame from a camera.

From the angle, only one thing was clearly visible—something small and shiny, protruding from the bottom of the closed fist. A key chain in the shape of a dog bone. Metallic, I knew. Something that got hot in the sun, cold in the winter.

A gift from the Truetts when Ruby was a teenager starting a dog-walking business. It had once been kept in our entryway drawer but had long since disappeared.

The police had been looking for this. The front door of the Truett home had been unlocked that morning. As if someone had snuck inside with a key. They never found it.

But someone else had seen this. Had captured it on camera and kept the proof for themselves.

Until now.

CHAPTER 8

FOOTSTEPS TRAIPSED UP THE front porch stairs—too heavy to be Ruby's—and the image of the key chain trembled in my hand. I scrambled from my spot on the floor and flipped on the porch light in a rush before throwing the front door open. Mac stood there, mouth agape, hands held up in surprise.

"What are you doing here?" I asked, even as I was sliding the photo and note into the back pocket of my shorts.

"You said she was gone," he said with half a smile. "We haven't gotten a chance to talk." He slipped inside, stepping around me and scanning the open front area.

I closed the door behind him, realizing he was planning to stay. "Well, she's not here *right this second*. But she'll be back. Anyway, aren't you supposed to be on watch?"

He paused to look at me from the corner of his eye. "She's not here, Harper. What the hell do you think I'm watching for? Nothing's gonna happen right now, you know that."

It wasn't Ruby I was worried about now. It was the knife she kept under her mattress for protection. And the note and photo of missing evidence that had been wedged into my door while I was at the pool meeting with everyone else.

My mind went straight to Chase. I tried to remember who had left before I had. Who had arrived after. Who would've had the chance to leave this here without me noticing.

But then Mac's arm was at my waist, and he was guiding me toward my own kitchen. "Come on, you look like you could use a drink," he said. All of us in Hollow's Edge moved around each other's homes with ease, each model so familiar that you felt at home even when you weren't.

I felt my shoulders relaxing. I'd been running on high alert since Ruby's return, feeling like I was two steps behind, trying to keep everything under control. I needed to relax. Make sound decisions. Think things through.

There was something contagious in Mac's demeanor— something I lacked on my own—an ability to live in the moment, never looking too far ahead or too far back.

Once we were in the kitchen, Mac stepped to the side of the fridge, deferring to me, which I had come to appreciate as part of his allure. I opened the fridge and pulled out two beers, held one to the back of my neck for a moment while handing him the other.

"You all right there, kid?" he asked, twisting the top off his beer, tossing the cap on the kitchen table.

"Yeah, fine," I said. "You scared me."

"Everyone's so jumpy right now. She's just a person. One person. I asked Charlotte, you really think she'd do anything now that she's out?" He shook his head, leaned against the counter beside me, waiting for me to take a drink. He held his bottle out until I clanked mine against his.

I knew exactly how this would go, and there was a comfort in the simplicity, in seeing the steps laid out before me, predictable and dependable. It had been much the same the first time.

He'd come over after Ruby's trial, looking lost, like he couldn't believe what had happened and didn't know what had brought him to my door, except that maybe I was someone who might understand. I was someone who had seen the other side of Ruby, who was willing to speak in her defense. That day, like now, Mac kept staring deep into the heart of the house, like it was all some trick and Ruby would arrive from around the corner of the living room at any moment. I'd offered him a beer then. *She called me,* he'd said, his voice cracking with emotion. *It was an automated message, a call from . . .* He'd let the thought trail.

Did you take it? I'd asked, picturing Ruby standing against a cinder-block wall, one hand over her other ear.

He shook his head and looked up at me. *Did I do the right thing?* he'd asked. And I got it suddenly. Him. The way Ruby had chased after this feeling, on and off, for years. The way he looked up from the seat at my kitchen table, the puppy-dog gleam in his eye. The way his words felt raw and honest, like he was confessing something deeper. The gently lilting drawl that pulled you in. The way he deferred to my judgment, to my opinion—it was its own brand of power.

I swallowed the lump in my throat. *You did the right thing,* I had told him.

Well, I feel like an asshole. Head in his hand, twisting the bottle of beer back and forth on the tabletop.

Twenty years is a long time, I told him, as if absolving us both of what was still to come.

There's also the double homicide to consider, he'd said, one side of his mouth raised in that private smile I'd come to know better. It was the first time anyone could, or would, make a joke. I had laughed, loud and unrestrained, more than was warranted. An emotion that had been bottled up. I hadn't laughed since before we'd found the Truetts' bodies. As if everything since then had been tamped down with a heavy weight. And now that it had been released, I assigned it disproportionate significance.

But everything back then was raw emotion. The fear, the loyalty, the shame. Everything felt so raw and exposed that it was easy to think: *So what? What's a little more?*

So when he said, *We weren't that serious. I mean, you know that. We never were,* I could answer: *I know.*

I knew roughly how it would go after that, had watched the same routine with Ruby. The way he called her *kiddo,* the way he skirted around her, stayed in her orbit, always making sure she was turned to him, following.

He'd stood and placed the empty beer behind me on the sink, leaning close. *I needed that,* he said. I was no longer sure what he was referring to, and I no longer cared.

BEFORE MAC, BEFORE THE trial, before the sound of the engine humming too long in the garage next door, I had often felt like I was standing on the edge of something, looking down, always careful not to get too close. Growing up with my brother, I had always felt the pull toward the other extreme. Like I was fighting to maintain a delicate balance; like any slip would send the rest of our family into a spiral. I'd believed strongly in the necessity of control—for myself and for others. I'd spent my entire life staying within the confines I'd established for myself or the boundaries others had set for me.

What would happen, I'd suddenly thought, if I breached those confines? If I did not pull back but leaned forward instead, giving in to the impulse and recklessness of the moment?

The answer, it turned out, was both relieving and terrifying: nothing. There was no repercussion, no slide I'd set in motion, and there was something alluring about that realization.

But now, as Mac stood beside me, it felt more dangerous, more deliberate. Back then, what was the harm? There was no fear in being found out, no consequence we would have to face—other than the side-eye from Tate, the knowing look from Preston. It had felt justified, even. Two people who could understand each other. Whose lives had been shaken by proximity to Ruby Fletcher.

Things had been easy and simple with Mac. We weren't serious, either. We were a convenience. I couldn't imagine Mac ever being serious about anything. Whatever we had then had dissipated by winter vacation, only to start up again early last month—some Pavlovian response to the changing seasons.

Mac placed the beer bottle on the counter, standing closer. The room felt charged, like he was testing me, but in some game— something elicit, something exciting. A rush. Like he was waiting for Ruby to catch us.

"Wait," I said. Because the decisions weren't as easy to make when there wasn't a twenty-year buffer and cinder-block walls between us. Then I thought, *So what if she found me? What would she do? Leave? Would that really be the worst thing?*

I didn't put up much of a fight when Mac leaned in, his mouth on my neck. But he must've felt my resistance. "Don't let her get to you, Harper," he said, breath next to my ear, body pressing mine into the counter. "Are you afraid?"

"No," I said, even though I was listening for a car, watching the front entrance. But the thing I'd learned about fear was that it heightened everything, even this. It solidified whom you trusted and whom you didn't. It clarified things—about others, about ourselves.

A noise coming from the patio made me jump. Even Mac jerked back, knocking the beer bottle over in the process, so that it rolled against the countertop, too loud in the silence.

"What was that?" he asked, peering at the darkness through the living room windows. It had sounded like something had fallen on the patio.

Mac stayed put while I crossed the living room toward the back entrance. I pulled open the door, heard nothing but the sound of crickets and a creaking hinge. The back patio was empty, but the high back gate of the fence had come unlatched and kept swaying back and forth.

That gate should've been locked from within. There was a bolt to turn from the patio, and it was unreachable from the outside. I'd started locking it after the Truetts. I never forgot. Without the lock, the gate could be unlatched by someone from the outside, occasionally from the wind or neighbors jostling the fence line.

I walked down the back steps, crossed the patio, and peered outside the fence into the row of trees. The sound of the crickets grew louder, but there was nothing visible between the shadows of the evergreens, overlapping. I couldn't even see the streetlight on the other side of the road beyond, where the next half-moon court sat, a little more elevated than ours.

I pulled the gate until the latch clicked, then turned the lock. Maybe Ruby had left the gate unlocked when she was out here earlier today. When we were listening to Javier and Tate. Maybe she'd gone out for a walk and had forgotten to secure the fence after. But she'd been barefoot this morning; I didn't think she'd been outside the fence.

"I think someone's been watching the house," I said, retreating to the safety of inside, locking the back door behind me. I turned to face Mac and felt once more the image of the key chain hidden in my back pocket. I wondered if whoever had placed it there had been trying to sneak closer to watch my reaction.

Mac was still staring out the window, and I didn't know whether he believed me.

"Maybe you should get back out there," I said, irrationally angry. Like he was the one at fault.

"Harper," he said, "it was probably just the wind. Don't let her get to you."

My irritation only grew. As if Ruby's presence was shifting the fabric of my reality. As if I was seeing danger in the places it didn't exist.

As if Mac had come for any other reason than because he was drawn to the danger of the moment himself.

AFTER MAC LEFT, I flipped all the outside lights on, made sure the blinds and curtains were closed. And then I spent the next hour reconnecting that old camera over the front porch, the one Ruby had mentioned. It was basically an old webcam, something Aidan originally placed over the door when word first went around about packages going missing before the holiday. Once I got it working, I could access the feed and watch the livestream, but I didn't have a service set up to record.

Ruby still wasn't home—if not for the cash left behind in the bathroom, I would've thought she'd taken off with my car and this was my punishment.

Upstairs, I stuffed the image and the note in the bottom of my pajama drawer. Close by yet hidden.

As midnight approached, I left my laptop open in my bedroom, screen beside my bed, so I could see who might come by. Who might've left this photo. Who might still be watching. Listening to the noises of the night behind the safety of closed walls and locked doors. The sounds of the lake in the distance—a steady buzzing, a rising hum—drowned out anything softer, closer. I would hear no careful footsteps, no quiet struggle.

I watched until I fell asleep, my dreams fitful and dark. I kept jerking awake, wondering what had woken me. Pressing a button on the laptop until the screen came into focus again, watching the shadows of the grainy footage. Wondering whether it had been Mac walking by. Ruby coming home.

Or someone else.

TUESDAY, JULY 2

HOLLOW'S EDGE COMMUNITY PAGE

Subject: Neighborhood Watch Schedule

Posted: 8:24 a.m.

Charlotte Brock: Just posting the final schedule for the upcoming week from the meeting last night. If you can't make your shift, please find a replacement and update it here so we know who to expect. P.S. Thanks to Mac Seaver for taking the first shift last night.

> JULY 2—*Tate & Javier Cora*
> JULY 3—*Harper Nash*
> JULY 4—*Margo & Paul Wellman*
> JULY 5—*Tina Monahan*
> JULY 6—*Charlotte Brock*
> JULY 7—*Preston Seaver*

CHAPTER 9

I **WOKE CURLED UP ON** my side, facing the laptop, with the faint tinge of a hangover, though I'd had only the single beer. My head could get like this sometimes, regardless of the liquor—the stress or adrenaline causing a dull ache, a persistent nausea. It was barely morning, the soft glow of dawn just starting to seep through the cracks in the blinds.

It took me a second to remember what I was doing, why I was so disoriented—waiting for Ruby; watching for whomever had been lurking.

I pushed myself out of bed, steadied myself in the open doorway. "Ruby?" I called, walking toward her room—dark and stale and empty—before heading down the stairs. Still in my pajamas, I opened the front door, even though I knew what I would see: an empty street, the vacant driveway. My car and Ruby still gone.

But the street wasn't dead, despite the hour. Preston Seaver was heading in the opposite direction, head down, hands in the pockets of his gym shorts, striding toward home. He didn't notice me on the front porch, didn't change pace, just continued toward his house on the corner. Probably covering the last part of Mac's shift from the night before.

Despite the adjusted summer schedule, Mac worked early mornings—earlier than the rest of us, getting a head start on the outdoor work. Last I'd heard, he was overseeing the brickwork being redone across the quad in center campus.

I eased the door shut, running through my options: report the car missing; find that lawyer's information and contact her about Ruby's whereabouts; wait.

Maybe Ruby just did not think of others as I thought of her. Maybe she got lost in the freedom of it—fourteen months with no one dictating her schedule, accounting for her every move. Or maybe she was telling me something.

I got rid of her things, and she took my car. Everything a push and pull.

Like she said, someone was going to pay.

I LOOKED AT THE clock; I was due at Charlotte's for coffee in fifteen minutes. When I first moved in, I loved the standing coffee dates she would organize at her place. The promise of close friendships and secrets kept. There was something about Charlotte that made you want to open up—it was probably what made her so good at her job as a counselor at the college. Or maybe it was a trick she'd learned in her training. Either way, it was common to be welcomed into Charlotte's home for coffee only to leave with half your issues addressed, feeling lighter.

All of us were different now. Held tighter to our secrets and our trust.

I left my hair to air-dry—Charlotte would probably be put together, but there was no point in me pretending. When I stepped outside, Javier was sitting on his front porch in a worn gray T-shirt and blue pajama pants. He had a coffee beside him and a cigarette in his hand. I knew he'd supposedly quit years ago and that Tate wouldn't put up with smoking in the house. I also knew the scent carried through the slats of the back fence some nights, long after she must've gone to sleep.

"Morning," I said, heading down my porch steps. He tipped his cigarette toward me in faint acknowledgment, not speaking. I wondered if Tate was still inside, sleeping.

Javier Cora leaned into summers with conviction, so different from the persona he adopted on school days, with his quirky bow tie and loafers and dark hair tucked behind his ear, as if shrugging on the costume of Favorite Teacher. He would probably be unrecognizable to them with his summer hair, longer and unstyled; a beard he shaved only once a week, if that; the cigarette, a scandal to middle school parents everywhere.

Here, to our neighbors, we revealed a side of ourselves that we kept hidden from our colleagues and acquaintances. The person we were at five a.m. on garbage day; the hours we kept; the lives we led. We were closer to being a family than not, knowing each other's schedules, and visitors, and insecurities.

We knew who didn't make it in to work (and whether they lied about the cause); we noticed whose cars didn't make it home at night; we saw whose recycling bins were overflowing at the edge of the driveways (though we were rarely surprised); we listened to the arguments carrying from open windows and backyards, feeling more like confidants than voyeurs.

I rang Charlotte's doorbell precisely at nine. She answered the door barefoot, in leggings and a flowing tank over a sports bra, like she had been working out. Though there wasn't any evidence other than the clothing. Her hair was shiny and blow-dried straight, and her house smelled of coffee and freshly cut flowers. There was no evidence of the luggage from yesterday in the hall, or her daughters.

"Hi," she said in a faux-quiet voice. Then she gestured to the staircase behind her. "The girls are still sleeping." A quick roll of her eyes. "Teenagers in the summer. Come on in. They won't hear us in the kitchen."

I followed her past the stairway, down the hall, into the kitchen, where three barstools were tucked under the counter dividing the kitchen from the living room, the lack of a table opening up the space.

Charlotte still had a faint limp, if you knew what you were looking for. An accident in the midst of her divorce that had landed her in a ditch with her leg pinned the wrong way. A resulting knee surgery. It was more pronounced when she was barefoot, like she was still being careful. A residual fear of the damage. I rarely saw her in shorts, so the limp sometimes caught me by surprise. But I found it reassuring that there were things outside all of our control. That even she couldn't anticipate a deer darting out from the woods. That even her instincts—cutting the wheel in the wrong direction, toward the lake, where the road sloped into a ditch—could be wrong.

"Are the girls going to Bob's?" I asked her.

She faltered, looked over her shoulder at me, and said, "No, they're spending the holiday here."

"Oh, yesterday Molly mentioned—"

"Yes," she said, waving away the comment, "there was a mix-up on his end over who had them for the long weekend." She poured us two mugs of coffee and sat on one of the counter stools, leaned her chin in one hand, and waited for me—for what I'd come to say.

I always felt insecure when I was alone with Charlotte. As if our contrast was too great not to acknowledge. Ever since Bob left, it seemed like she'd doubled down on herself. Calm and unflappable before and after. The fact that her marriage had fallen apart in such a public way, that she was aware we all *knew*—it must've killed her. I knew what it was like to have the whole neighborhood watching as the life you'd built abruptly fell apart. But instead of humanizing her, it had done the opposite. She'd fortified herself, daring you to find a weakness.

"First," I said, hands held out in the universal proclamation of innocence, "I had no idea she would turn up at my house. Scared me to death, to be honest."

"Mm." A noise that could've meant any number of things. Her face remained porcelain. "I can imagine." She spooned some sugar into her mug, the metal clanging against the side.

"She just . . ." I leaned forward conspiratorially. "She just walked right in like nothing had changed."

"And?" she asked, raising the mug to her lips, steam rising.

"I think she came back for her things." I didn't specify the money she'd left behind, hidden in her old kayak. I cleared my throat. "And . . . did you see her lawyer on TV the other night?"

Charlotte shook her head, mug frozen. But the lack of movement gave her away—she was holding her breath. Intrigued despite herself. I wanted to shake her, break through the surface, share a secret. But it was like she thought any show of emotion lost her the upper hand. Like she had to be the person you wanted something from, needing nothing in return.

"Ruby said they're going to sue," I finally said.

Charlotte lowered the mug back to the counter. "Sue *who*, exactly?"

I tipped one shoulder, then added cream and sugar to my mug. I really did need the caffeine, my head fuzzy from the sporadic night's sleep. "She didn't say. But she went to meet with the lawyer yesterday."

She raised her eyebrows again. "And?"

"And she hasn't come back yet."

Charlotte let out a deep breath. "Maybe she's *not* coming back. Maybe this has nothing to do with"—she waved one manicured hand over her head—"any of us." The same thing I had hoped.

"Well," I said, after taking my first sip of perfectly brewed coffee, "she has my car. So I do, in fact, hope she returns in this case."

Charlotte closed her eyes and laughed softly despite herself. "Oh, Harper," she said, and I knew I was forgiven. That I was back in the role she expected me to inhabit. Too trusting, too naive. Too blinded by my desire to see the good in everyone. The last to know when Aidan was going to leave. The last to accept the truth about Ruby but forgivable for the pattern of my own nature.

"I know, I was caught off guard. I didn't exactly tell her she could use my car," I said. "But in her defense, I didn't tell her she couldn't."

Charlotte gave the tiniest shake of her head and a look that bordered on patronizing. Like she was getting ready to impart some sage advice; she'd gazed deep into my soul and found the flaw, and now she would expose it, to fix it. "Well, I think you're going to need to tell her to leave. Once you get your car back," she said.

"How, exactly, can I do that?" I asked. Half sarcastic, but also, I wanted to know. She was the mother of two teen girls, elbow-deep in the issues of an entire school community, and you knew she could put things into context. I wanted to imagine what Charlotte would've done had Ruby walked in her front door unannounced.

"It's not her house, Harper. It never was."

"She paid rent," I countered. She was up front with the checks, paying me in installments of three months at a time, the ideal tenant. Said money always made things awkward, and she didn't want me to have to ask her for it. She made sure she was always ahead of the curve.

Charlotte put a hand over mine. "You're a good person, but you don't owe her, Harper. She is a *criminal*." I pulled my hand back abruptly, and her eyebrows pushed together, the single line between them deepening. The only sign of her age. "You don't think she's innocent, do you?" she asked. Leaning forward finally, like we would share that secret after all. Her face scrunched up in disgust for a fleeting moment. "It was a technicality, Harper. An injustice."

Except it wasn't a single technicality. The entire investigation and trial had been tainted from the start. Chase wasn't a misfiled piece of paperwork. He was a very real person involved in a very real investigation, with a hand in every corner of it. The message board had been the proof. According to Ruby's lawyer, there was more that we didn't even know. Evidence that had been withheld. People who should've known better.

"We don't know that," I said. "The whole thing, the investigation, it was so fast, don't you remember?"

Once the focus settled on Ruby, the dominoes fell quickly and succinctly, improbably sinking her. Her half-smile on all of the news pieces. The time line, forced between camera still shots.

Charlotte folded her hands on the counter, the very vision of a mother advising her children. "Look, let's pretend. Let's go ahead and pretend. Ruby was out there that night. She was seen by various cameras. At the very least, she knew something, and she said nothing. She was seen running down to the lake. She lied. You heard her sneaking in the back door at two in the morning. Does that strike you as an innocent person?"

It didn't. But Ruby didn't strike me as guilty before her arrest, either. "There was no motive," I said, looking out the kitchen window, where you could see straight into the Truett house next door—the curtains gone, the entire house stripped and empty. That was what had irked me the most. Apparently, you didn't need a motive to convict, but it kept me up at night. Kept me on her side longer than most. There was no reason for Ruby to do it, so I could therefore believe she hadn't done it.

"She stole from them, you know. From Brandon and Fiona."

My gaze jerked back to Charlotte. "What? Did you tell the

police this?" After Ruby was arrested, there were so many rumors. I'd just never heard any related to this.

She sat back on the stool, mug in hand again. "Of course. But they couldn't bring it up in trial. There was no one to vouch for it. But Chase knew. They all knew. Fiona said money had gone missing."

"She thought it was Ruby?" Fiona still let Ruby walk their dog, still let her have a key. It didn't track.

Charlotte shrugged. "Never said. You know how Fiona was, though, a little . . ." She let the thought trail as if we could not discuss the limitations of the dead. But I knew what she meant. *Removed. Condescending. Uninterested in the rest of us.* Charlotte continued, "I only remember because she opened her wallet once to pay me for when we all got the group rate to aerate the yards, remember? She opened her wallet and frowned, and I could tell something was wrong. She was clearly flustered, called Brandon asking if he'd taken the money in her wallet. And when he said he hadn't, she was shaken, I could tell. She looked straight at Ruby, who was out washing her car." Charlotte pressed her lips together, and I knew what she was remembering: Ruby in a bikini top, cut-off shorts, everyone looking despite themselves.

"It could've been anyone," I said. "Or maybe Fiona was wrong. Ruby didn't need the money." They called her a grifter, but that wasn't true—she'd paid me to stay after Aidan left me with the mortgage; she'd helped me out of a bad situation. They called her a charmer, a fake. A person who got what she wanted. But she was locked up for the last fourteen months, and no one believed her, so that wasn't true, either.

Even as I said it, I pictured that money again, stashed in the bathroom, damp in my hand—

Charlotte shrugged. "Who said she needed it? Like some spoiled, bored child. It's not the first rumor I heard about Ruby, though I assumed she'd grown up since then. Always seeing what she could get away with." As if everything could be traced back to boredom. "My guess, the Truetts knew it was her. Maybe they confronted her. Maybe they asked her for the key back, and she knew she had to do something."

"You can't think she would kill over that? Come on."

"Is there a good reason to kill them, Harper?" She took a slow breath, started again. "Look, something like that gets out . . . we're all so connected here. The college. The school. Our jobs. Even small things have big repercussions here."

I couldn't stop my mind from drifting, then, to every time I thought I'd misplaced something. Of the times I'd been surprised to be short on cash or I'd found a piece of jewelry in a different place than I thought I'd left it. Things I'd attributed to being busy, not fully focused on the simple actions of the day. Now I was seeing something else: Ruby, hand in my jewelry box, thumbing through my wallet, seeing what she could get away with. Watching my reaction for her own entertainment.

"Ruby never liked Fiona," Charlotte said, voice lowered.

Like she was any different, any better. I didn't say what I was thinking: that none of us did. On a good day, we rolled our eyes at them, emboldened by our shared sentiments, bonding the rest of us together. It made us feel more righteous, more right. On a bad day, Brandon and Fiona represented something bigger, something that preyed on our insecurity—that there was something unworthy about the life we were living.

A creak in the ceiling directly overhead cut through the silence: someone walking in the loft, if their upstairs layout was the same as mine. We both looked up.

Charlotte checked her watch. "About time," she said. Then, to me, "I think you should go before the girls come down. I don't want them to hear us. I don't want to upset them."

111

Though, judging from my conversation with Molly the other day, Charlotte had already managed to do that herself.

I nodded, heading down the hall. "Thanks for the coffee, Charlotte."

"Of course," she said. "And, Harper?" I looked back, hand on the doorknob. "Tell her to go."

"I will," I said.

IT WAS BROAD DAYLIGHT, midmorning, but no one was outside. There was something off about the entire street, like an abandoned set.

The Truett house, blending in with the still surroundings. Nothing, except for the lack of curtains, to set it apart. Nothing to declare: *This is the murder house*. In the months after the trial, people would drive by, slow down, watch. Try to see something inside now that the danger had passed.

I'd never peered inside those open windows myself—I'd already seen inside once, and that was enough. The reality burned on the inside of my eyelids. The bedroom upstairs; Chase's expression. The scream rising in the back of my throat.

Something caught my eye now as I passed. A flash of movement in the dark windows. A trick of the light. My memory and imagination overlapping.

But I found myself walking up those porch steps again, listening closely.

I pressed my ear to the door—*the rumble of the car engine, a dog barking from the backyard*—but there was nothing. This time, when I reached out to check the handle, it didn't move. It was locked. My imagination, then.

I released the handle, backed away, could see the gleam of my thumbprint left behind on the brass knob. During the investigation, Ruby's fingerprints had been found on this handle, along with mine, Brandon's, Fiona's, and more. I thought about that now—about how much of ourselves we leave behind in every interaction. How every place we've been, everything we say, can be used to craft a story.

But Ruby's fingerprints had also been found on the back door, where the dog was left. On the bedroom handle upstairs, like she had peered in on Brandon and Fiona sleeping before steeling her nerve. Her cold gaze, her cold heart. And on the car door in the garage, the most damning place of all.

Ruby's defense was just that—of course she'd been in their house. She had walked their dog when needed. She couldn't tell what she might've touched or when. If she might've brushed against the car when it was out in the driveway.

She was just *out* that night. For a walk, she said. And why not? Was that such a crime? She'd left her phone behind because who was she planning to call in the middle of the night? What did she have to fear here? This was a safe place. Lake Hollow Prep was on spring break. She was twenty-five years old. There had been other people out there, she told anyone who would listen, she'd heard people down at the lake and gone to check it out.

This was the point she kept maintaining: There were other people out. She wasn't alone that night. But the cameras did not back up her claim.

And neither did anyone else.

The neighbors testified with their videos that had been posted on the message board. They testified to the time stamps, the locations of the cameras, and described what they saw: A woman walking from the Truett house; a woman racing toward the woods. A woman who did not reappear on any cameras on her way home—who must've cut through the woods to the other side of the inlet, ignoring the sign marked PRIVATE PROPERTY.

Sneaking back by an unseen route—the dirt access road, the dense woods—creeping around behind our street, hoping no one saw her. Maybe she'd left her phone at home, they decided, because she didn't want any evidence of where she had been.

Most of the devices recorded only when motion triggered. There was no more activity on our street.

The jury was satisfied: Nothing else had happened that night.

But. The image of that key chain left inside my house.

There were things people here knew. Things people had seen.

I wondered, not for the first time, what else they might've seen—and what they'd decided to keep hidden.

CHAPTER 10

WAS STANDING IN THE hallway outside the kitchen with my cell phone in my hand, debating, when I heard the mechanical hum of my garage door. Nearly thirty hours after Ruby had left to go meet with her lawyer. Enough time for me to research local business parks and pull up Blair Bowman's information, debating whether to make that call—or whether to call the police, report my car missing.

I opened the front door and stood in the entryway, staring at Ruby in my driveway, watching as she rifled through the trunk. She didn't even look my way until she was halfway up the steps, in a different outfit than when she left. She pushed through the doorway, two tote bags full of groceries on one arm.

"Hi!" she said, bags extended in my direction. "Hold on, there are more." Nothing about being gone, being missing. The new clothes, the lack of contact.

She turned down the steps, gathering the last of the bags, closing the trunk with a resounding thud. Half the street probably heard, heading for their front windows.

Ruby strode past me in the entrance with the three remaining bags. She waltzed into the kitchen, humming as she emptied the groceries. The tote bags were my own, stored in my trunk, now brimming with the staples of my kitchen.

"Ruby," I said, unmoving at the entrance.

She paused, turned around, lips pressed together when she took in my face. "You're mad," she said, her posture deflating.

"Of course I'm mad," I said, not bothering to worry about the level of my voice, whether anyone could hear. "You were gone for two days with my car! I was"—*furious, worried*— "I was *this close* to calling the police."

I heard the echo of my mother in my head, following Kellen into the house after one of the many times he'd disappeared for a night, a weekend, or more. The nights my parents had spent arguing over whether to call the police or his friends. Whether to lock him out or lock him in. Over who had abandoned him and who had enabled him. The relief evident on her face at his return, even as her voice rose in anger—

Ruby blinked rapidly. "Oh, God, I'm sorry. I know, I wasn't thinking. I just . . ." She lifted her arms, closed her eyes, feigning contrite. "I got carried away. I wanted to call, but I didn't know your number. Not by heart. It used to be in my phone, you know." She fished around in her messenger bag, pulled out her cell. "Here," she said. "Tell me your number."

I recited the numbers by rote, and my phone began ringing in my back pocket. She pressed "end." "Now we're connected," she said. "It won't happen again." As if the fault had been out of her hands until now.

"Where have you *been*?" I asked, because it was my car, my house, and Charlotte was right. I didn't owe Ruby unfettered access to my life.

She let out a sigh. "It was late by the time we finished up, and we'd been drinking over dinner, and I just thought . . . I should stay. Last thing I need is to get pulled over now, right?" Eyes wide, like she was sharing a secret. "I would've called you if I had your number, I swear! And then I wanted to make it up to you by getting the groceries, since you mentioned needing to go shopping. I found these bags in the trunk. Very resourceful. Very conscientious." A grin. "And I'm making you dinner," she said, a tentative smile. "To make it up to you. And to thank you. For everything." She blinked once, slowly. "Forgive me?"

I nodded, started emptying boxes from the closest tote bag. Because what could one say when she was in your house, with your keys, and she'd been locked up for the last fourteen months?

"I really am sorry, Harper," she said, voice lower, more confessional.

"You scared me," I said, our eyes locking over the span of counter between us.

She held my gaze, unmoving, until I looked back to the tote bags. There was something almost eerie about the groceries she'd purchased. She knew exactly what I'd been needing. A new carton of eggs, the type of orange juice I drank, everything that was running low—she'd gotten it all and then some. I thought of the money in the bathroom. How much more of it did she have? She'd come back in new clothes with new food. I assumed she'd stayed at a hotel near her meeting, but maybe I was wrong.

"Go," she said, and I was shocked by the word—the one I'd been thinking to say to her instead. "Go relax. I've got this. Please, let me do this."

When I didn't move—because it was my house, my kitchen, my cabinets she was currently opening—she pulled out the wine from the last bag. "Here," she said, "still your favorite?" And something softened inside me, because it was. Because, fourteen months later, a lifetime later, she still knew this. And I remembered the other side of her, before the investigation: how thoughtful she'd always been. When I'd had a bad workday, when Aidan had left, she'd somehow known exactly what to say or do.

She'd brought me flowers—lilies, my favorite, in an assortment of colors that brightened the room. She'd stood on my front porch with the vase in her hands and said, *He's an asshole, and I'm sorry.* I'd invited her in, and she looked around my half-empty house, and it was then, seeing the empty spaces that needed to be filled, that she asked if I could use a roommate. When all I could feel were the people who had been our friends, who were no longer reaching out, as if my heartbreak might be contagious.

It wasn't a roommate I needed in particular, but Ruby filled up the space with her things, her laughter, her thoughtfulness.

Ruby checked the right drawer on the first try, held up the corkscrew, and opened the bottle, pouring me a healthy portion. I took it from her hand, our fingers brushing.

"Now," she said, with a crooked grin, "let's see if I remember how to use a stove."

This time I smiled, too. I went along with it, leaning into the awkwardness, the way she just embraced it, made it a part of her, didn't try to fight it or pretend it didn't exist—the opposite of Charlotte, in so many ways.

I took the glass of wine out back, sat in the Adirondack chair with the chipping white paint, watching the shade creep across the brick patio. Thinking about how the trial had painted her, the way they wanted to make her into a manipulative villain instead of someone fully formed. Who could be both generous and careless, fearful and feared.

Next door, I could hear the daily monotony of Tate and Javier's dinner routine—banging cabinets, the rattle of a pan on the stovetop, Javier's muffled voice. Whatever had happened yesterday, they seemed back on track today.

I curled my toes on the wooden stool, watching the bees darting from flower to flower in the mulched garden against the house. The far-right corner of the mulch bed was disturbed—Ruby was right, though it wasn't obvious unless you sat at a distance. An abrupt gap between the flowers and the edge of the brick, the mulch between them dark and overturned.

When Ruby swung open the door a while later, her face was shiny, and the scent of garlic and oregano trailed after her. "Dinner is served," she said with a flourish of her arm, beckoning me inside. She was brimming with nervous energy, watching for my expression as she led me past the kitchen.

She'd set the dining room table off the front foyer, which we never used. It ended up functioning as a holding area for mail or packages, usually. We typically ate at the kitchen table, or standing at the counters, or on the couch with plates balanced on our laps, wineglasses on the coffee table.

Now the chandelier looked like a candelabra, dimmed and atmospheric. Half the lights had burned out over time, and I'd never found the replacements, which gave the room a certain ambiance, shadowed and quiet.

"That's you," she said, pointing to the place setting against the far wall, without the wineglass. Her glass was poured fresh, next to her dish in the place beside mine, facing the front window. She had made shrimp and pasta, a salad, garlic bread. With intense formality, she gestured for me to sit first. She was watching me closely, every movement, waiting for my reaction.

"This looks really good, Ruby," I said, and I meant it. It had been a long time since someone had cooked for me.

"I hope you're hungry?" She said it as a question, and wasn't it? Wasn't this a test of some sort? Whether I believed she was a killer. Whether I believed she could become one. The ultimate question: Did I trust her?

Would I move the food around, looking closely? Would I chew

119

tentatively, wondering at each bite what she would be capable of? Would I eat it?

Of course I would. I didn't even wait for her to take a bite first, twisting the pasta around my fork, closing my eyes as I chewed. With Ruby, I knew, you were all in or you were nothing at all. "Oh, God," I said around the bite, "it really is good, Ruby. Like, really fucking good."

She smiled, her entire demeanor relaxing as she speared some lettuce on her fork. "You know what I missed the most inside? Being able to break from routine. Not just the big freedom—that's not the worst. It was the little ones. They were harder to deal with than the bigger concept, honestly." I saw her throat move, her eyes drift somewhere over my head. "Just the idea that I could cook dinner for someone . . ."

It took me a second to realize what she meant by *inside.* That she didn't mean *within her.* She meant a place. A place where she had existed for fourteen months. And this, even cooped up with me, with the neighbors watching—this was *out.* She could finally do anything she pleased. Whether that was staying out a night without checking in, on a whim; buying a new outfit because she could. And could I fault her for that, really? Every day, a steady notch. An accumulation of weeks that became routine. Adding up to an unforgiveable passage of time.

Time to grow a child. For a child to grow teeth, learn to speak, turn from baby to toddler. To graduate and become an adult. And for us, time to decide on something. Come to terms with the truth—let it seep into your bones, gather weight, and become part of your understanding: *Ruby was guilty. A jury agreed. We were right.* All changes that were impossible to undo, in reverse.

I cleared my throat. "How did the meeting with the lawyer go?"

A pause. "Good," she said. "And you? How was the meeting?"

I froze, then reached for my glass of wine, trying not to show

how she shook me. How did she know about the meeting here? Had I mentioned it? Had she seen it on the message board somehow, logging in to my computer when I wasn't looking? Had she spoken to someone else here?

But I felt my allegiance shifting in her presence. The wine, the food, the honesty. The words at the bottom of the television screen the day of her release: *presumed innocent.*

"As expected," I said. "They're starting a neighborhood watch."

"Is that why I just saw Javier Cora walk by?"

I hadn't noticed. But Ruby was facing the window, and I wondered if that was on purpose. Whether she'd grown accustomed to keeping an eye on her surroundings. Whether she was watching for something now.

Her gaze trailed after something out the window; for the first time, I could see the signs of fatigue on her: the thin skin under her eyes, dulled and discolored; the slightly sunken cheeks, like she was ravenous for something to drink.

"Probably," I said. It was dusk.

"Or maybe not," she said with a wry grin. And for a second I thought her look was for me—that she'd caught me watching her too closely.

I didn't respond; didn't know whether Ruby's throwaway lines meant anything at all or if I was reading too much into every word, every gesture.

"Well, anyway. What about you? What have *you* been up to?" she asked.

I thought of Mac last night, Charlotte this morning. "Hmm?"

"Fourteen months," she said. "What did I miss?"

"Oh, nothing much." Nothing I could tell her, the mundane things I'd taken for granted with the freedom she'd lacked. She already seemed to know about my new job somehow. But now I was really thinking about it—how maybe I, too, had been in a holding pattern for the last fourteen months. That I'd somehow understood—or believed, or feared—that someday she'd be back, and I had lost trajectory of my own life in the process. That I was only waiting for her return.

Fourteen months, and what did I have to show for it?

"I know one thing," she said, fork resting in her hand. She stared at me, and I held my breath, and then she smiled, teeth first, before it reached her eyes. "You turned thirty, and I missed it. I hope you celebrated."

Though I was stuffed, I made myself eat the last bite just to have something to do with my body. "We did a work thing," I said. It was February, solidly winter, and Mac and I had cooled with the season. I'd gone out to dinner with my group of friends from the office; it had been nice and fun, but I had also become their boss, which altered the dynamic.

My friendships in the neighborhood had drifted since the trial. Maybe even before that. What I'd lost after Aidan—the couple friendships, the joint activities that were no longer possible—what I'd gained with Ruby. The easy way she could say, *Your ex is a moron* or *You're really pretty* in the way girls used to in college, the type of simple compliment that we no longer gave or received outside that close confinement.

"Well, let's do it now," she said. "There's no *rule* against that." She left for the kitchen and returned with a second bottle of wine—I couldn't remember when we finished the first, didn't notice how much she'd kept pouring. How close some things were to the surface.

"How do you want to celebrate?" she asked. "We can do anything, really."

The way she said it then, like I hadn't looked far enough or close enough—like I'd taken my options for granted and had no perspective on the things that were possible, because they had never been taken from me.

I wondered then what I really wanted—maybe, for the first time in a long time, I really considered it. I'd gone to my father's alma mater, and moved to a new part of the country with Aidan, and taken over Brandon's job on an interim basis because I was the one with the most seniority left behind—then I'd worked so hard that no one could find a reason to take it from me. I'd learned to hold tight to the things I had earned. But sitting with Ruby, every path I'd taken seemed so narrow, so preordained.

Maybe it was the wine, or maybe it was her, but I couldn't help thinking of all the things that were suddenly possible beyond the walls of this house; beyond the borders of this town.

But I thought of Javier on shift, patrolling, keeping watch and reporting back to a community who believed they were keeping themselves safe. The note I'd found last night. The picture left inside. The dangers out there.

"This," I said. "This is how I want to celebrate."

She raised her glass to mine, nearly empty. Insisted on doing the dishes after, even though she'd cooked, while I found an old movie we both liked.

I gave over to it, to this, to her. Drunk on the wine and the freedom she'd just unveiled. With her face close to mine as she bent over laughing on the couch, her legs hanging over the end, everyone else seemed so far away. Another life, another world.

That morning with Charlotte, I'd lied, of course.

Of course I wouldn't tell Ruby to go.

WEDNESDAY, JULY 3

HOLLOW'S EDGE COMMUNITY PAGE

Subject: Watch last night

Posted: 5:35 a.m.

Javier Cora: Just finished up my shift, and yeah, there were definitely some kids hanging out down by the lake. Heard them in the woods but couldn't get a good look. Didn't call the police because they left fast. Think they had a boat on the other side of the inlet.

Margo Wellman: Didn't some local kid drown out there a few years ago at night??

/ı\   /ı\   /ı\   /ı\   /ı\
\ı/   \ı/   \ı/   \ı/   \ı/

Subject: July Fourth party rules

Posted: 10:52 a.m.

Charlotte Brock: Due to the fact that this is being partially sanctioned by our HOA fees, we are unable to accommodate any nonresidents.

Preston Seaver: That's some bullshit. We're bringing the food.

Javier Cora: Yeah, you can't actually prevent us from bringing a guest to the pool. The rules already say we can bring up to two.

Tina Monahan: I don't think this was directed at you guys.

Preston Seaver: Well maybe she should be more direct next time.

Charlotte Brock: Ok sorry for the confusion, after talking things over with the board, you are correct on the rules. Just an FYI though we may not have enough food for everyone. And just a reminder, you are responsible for your guests.

Preston Seaver: Don't worry. I'll tell my guest not to eat.

CHAPTER 11

I ALWAYS WOKE EARLY AFTER a night of drinking. Jolting awake in a panic while my mind raced to catch up, trying to remember what I might've said or done.

I was in my bed, the bedroom door wide open, the sun shining through the gap in the curtains. I couldn't remember all the steps that had gotten me here. There was Ruby's dinner, the movie, our conversation—and though I couldn't pull every specific topic to mind, I remembered mostly laughter. Fits of it, doubled over, clutching our stomachs, the armrests of the couch, each other.

And then: more wine out on the back patio—I couldn't remember how we'd gotten there—and then Ruby coming in from the dark, the warm gust of air following her as she tripped through the doorway. More laughter. Her saying, as if she'd merely stumbled onto a thought, *We should call Mac. He was always good for a party.* And me at least having the presence of mind to say, *No, no, thank you, it's my party, anyway.*

Playing the game even way past sober. Something that had been deeply ingrained.

And then: Ruby perched on the edge of my dresser, singing a really terrible rendition of "Happy Birthday" while I fell into bed.

In a panic, I lurched from my bed to that dresser and pulled open the top drawer, reaching my hand into the bottom. I let out a breath at the feel of the paper folded up under my pajamas: the image inside, safe and secret and secure.

My head spun from standing upright too quickly, and I gave serious thought to getting back into bed and remaining there indefinitely. But the other part of me needed to see Ruby, to know where she was, and maybe discover where she had been. How quickly I'd fallen back under her spell last night. All for the price of one home-cooked meal and my favorite wine.

I tiptoed out to the loft, approaching her room. The bathroom door was closed, but the door to her bedroom was cracked open. Peering in, I saw her facedown on the turquoise comforter, dressed in yesterday's clothes, with one arm over the edge. Her face was turned toward the wall, so all I could see was her dark blond hair, the slight but steady rise and fall of her back. The cat glared back at me from the edge of the bed.

I got ready for the day quickly—a fast shower, hair in a wet braid, no breakfast, so as not to wake her—and let myself out the front door, my key ring safely back in my possession. I would probably be back before she woke.

In the car, I adjusted the mirror she'd moved last, a fingerprint smudge on the edge. Then I backed out of the driveway, eyes on the front door of my house as if I expected her to come outside and beckon me back. As if I were her prisoner, oblivious to the boundaries that held me.

But she didn't emerge, and I drove down the street, passing in front of the pool, where I stopped for a moment.

I wanted to look for clues of where Ruby might've been for those thirty hours. Where she'd met the lawyer with the blunt haircut and sharp cheekbones and catchy name; where she'd stayed after, where she had shopped—picking up the new clothes, the fresh groceries—before returning to me. Her words a chill on the back of my neck: *Someone's going to pay.*

I checked the odometer, but I couldn't be sure of what my mileage count had been when she left. Inside the glove box, I looked for anything out of the ordinary, rifling through my own assortment of old receipts stuffed around the car handbook. I dipped my fingers into the cupholders, the pocket on the door, finding nothing but loose change and a hair tie. All that remained was a scent, like an air freshener. Like something else had needed to be covered up.

Maybe Ruby had smoked. Maybe she'd driven with the window down, wind in her hair, arm held out the window with a cigarette between her fingers. Maybe she'd dreamed of driving forever and gotten carried away by the feel and the scent and the freedom.

Maybe it was nothing: hours at a business park, like she said; drinks over dinner; the lawyer pointing out a hotel across the street, a big box store across a highway where she'd picked up a change of clothes and groceries on the way home; the scent of the hotel soap lingering.

All these little mysteries. Did they even really matter? Or was I letting my mind get carried away, like this entire neighborhood had done, working themselves into a frenzy, piecing together their story?

Look where it had gotten us.

We had been raised on true crime and the promise of viral fame. We'd consumed unsolved mysteries and developed our deeply held theories. Believed that neither law experience nor a criminal justice background was necessary to see into people's true hearts, to root out the truth. That all you needed was a clear perspective and a sharp mind.

Other than Chase, I was the only one here who had any real experience with the law. My brother, Kellen, was first arrested at sixteen; my dad had called it in himself. Thought it would shake him up, wake him up. But that was before we understood that once you were in the system, it was nearly impossible to get out. That you had to be careful, had to be sure. Neither Kellen nor my mother ever forgave him.

I started driving again and turned on the radio, but the sound made me jump, jab my finger at the power button—the noise was too loud, harsh and instrumental, tuned to a different station from my usual.

Suddenly, I felt that I was the intruder instead.

MY DRIVE TO AND from work was so different from the typical highway work commute. Here, the road meandered around the lake, trees stretching outward in either direction, toward the water or deeper into the woods. The only traffic I ever encountered was in the drive-through of Bakery by the Lake, a small but busy local shop that had carved a spot out of the woods, halfway between my home and the college.

I stopped there now for a bagel and a coffee. Then I sat in the parking lot, eating in my car, head tilted back, windows down, headache slowly dissipating. The irony of finally feeling free while being contained in my own vehicle. When I was done, I continued along the curving, tree-lined road, tracing the border of Lake Hollow.

I wasn't sure how long Ruby intended to stay and when I'd feel comfortable leaving her for the full day, so I wanted to grab the week's work, should I need it.

The College of Lake Hollow was located on the opposite side of the lake from our community. Whenever I used to borrow Ruby's kayak, paddling out to the main channel, I'd just be able to make out the college's boathouse on the other shore, the students practicing for crew, sleekly moving across the surface of the water. And then the lush green of the trees and the brick buildings and the glass windows reflecting the sun, depending on the angle. Some of the young professors who lived in communities with docks and lake access would take a Jet Ski across in good weather, their materials kept safe in a waterproof backpack.

Of course, the flip side to this idyllic scene were the tragedies. The accidents that we anticipated and accepted over the years, something we chalked up to part of life on the water. The Jet Ski that collided with the kayak a few years ago, killing the kayaker, a man in his sixties who hadn't worn a life vest; the visitors in the summer who couldn't swim but thought that a lake meant placid and calm, not that it could have a current, an endless depth—things that could snag you under the water when you jumped from a rented boat, trap you and disorient you. The high school kids who anchored and tied up boats together at night, at the edge of an inlet, not realizing until too late that someone had gone missing.

There were also the stories told on campus—stories that were based loosely on fact. The kids who dared to swim across the lake one night, thinking the shore was far closer than it was—four going out, only two returning. (The other two were found by lake patrol, clinging to a buoy, after their friends had called it in.) The yearly middle-of-the-night plunge taken by the incoming freshmen during orientation in August, in the dark, half-dressed and semi-sober. Supposedly as an offering to the lake so it would not come for you later.

All tradition was steeped in legend. All risk was heightened by stories.

In truth, it was a safe campus, a safe college, a relatively safe location. Up until the crime, the most dangerous aspect of living in Lake Hollow was the deer. The road was sinuous, snaking around the coastline, and if you weren't careful, you'd turn a corner to see the glow of eyes staring back. If you were unlucky, you wouldn't have time to see it darting from the woods, straight in front of your car—like Charlotte.

The lake accidents mostly happened in the summer, with no college students to witness the tragedy. But the biggest tragedy to date was the truest: the murder of Brandon Truett, head of admissions, and Fiona Truett, who managed a string of tutoring centers. Locked away for the crime was a former student of the college and neighbor of the victims.

Ruby Fletcher was a legend in the flesh, and now she had returned.

When the students moved back in the fall, if Ruby was still here, I imagined they would start coming by our neighborhood to get a closer look. A new dare. I wondered if the local kids had already started.

The campus on Fourth of July week was mostly empty, especially given the early hour. Even if people were working, they probably wouldn't come in until closer to ten, other than the grounds department.

I pulled into the lot behind the admissions building, a low brick building with glass inset into the triangular top of the roof, making it look like there might be a second story. Each administrative building in this section was small and quaint and separate.

There was another car back here in the small lot. Most visitors ended up parking in the main visitor lot and walking across the picturesque green at the center of campus, following the snaking brick paths to other brick buildings. This lot was unlabeled and set back, accessible via the narrow faculty roads, requiring a permit on the windshield.

I didn't recognize the white SUV in the back-left spot, under the shade of an oak tree. The rest of the staff was supposed to be on vacation. I parked on the other side of the lot, closest to the building's back door.

We didn't schedule any prospective campus tours or meetings from our office for the holiday week. But sometimes people came on their own during family road trips, taking in the colleges along the way, giving themselves self-guided tours. Others parked in our lots on the weekend to ride bikes through campus or have an afternoon picnic on the green.

I used my key to let myself in. The lights turned on automatically as I stepped inside. "Hello?" I called, just in case it was someone from tech, updating our systems. But the lights were motion-operated, and since it had been dark until my arrival, I couldn't imagine someone else in here. The three offices beyond the front lobby stretched into darkness, though each was glass-walled—a modern renovation inside a classic, traditional structure.

I locked the entrance door behind me, which I always did when I was alone in here. It was a policy first implemented by Brandon Truett. He'd told us about a student who showed up after being rejected, demanding to know why. There'd been implications of a weapon. Campus security was called by the receptionist when she heard what was happening. Brandon said that was why we were to keep doors locked after hours, when campus security wasn't the press of a button away. Especially if we were alone.

Back then, I'd thought he was overreacting, as I always did. Suspected his story, even, chalking it up to another legend that grew out of the old brick buildings. His story seemed less unlikely after his death. And any time I wanted to believe in Ruby's innocence, I was reminded of this: someone who could've been angry enough to harm him. I told the police that there were thousands of people with motives. That his job made him the figurehead of rejection. Which, one way or the other, was a common motive for killing. Something that struck you to your core, sharp and fast.

"Anyone here?" I called, just so I wouldn't spook someone. No one responded.

I had a different key for my personal office—a lock I'd had changed after taking over Brandon's space, in the days when paranoia crept in. Those first few months, I couldn't look at my office without seeing the version that had existed before: the large desk in the center of the room, the worn chair, the single frame on the clean surface. College of Lake Hollow paraphernalia decorating the walls, a framed portrait of the lake and surrounding campus taken from above.

This office had never truly seemed like my own. Maybe it was the memory of a moving truck, of the empty places in my house—the fear that everything was temporary; that anything could be taken from me.

I'd replaced the chair first, the imprint of his body something that had sent a chill through me the first time I'd sat there, and I'd added my own decorations to the office, including a quirky blue bookshelf I'd put together myself, and a potted plant in the corner that was currently in need of water. But I'd left the College of Lake Hollow decor and the framed photo of campus. Put anything else left behind in the storage closet.

I used my black mug from the bookshelf—HELLO THERE! it declared in cutesy white text to whomever might be sitting across from me—to bring water from our shared bathroom in the hall back to my office, taking three trips in my continual attempt to keep the plant alive.

Then I grabbed the stack of blue files off my desk, where they'd been waiting. Brandon had kept most of his work organized in a system hidden from sight: in his desk drawers or in file boxes in the corner closet of the room. But I preferred everything where I could see it so I wouldn't forget—a visual to-do list.

I used that same closet now to store all the things Brandon had left behind—the things not taken by the police during the investigation. I knew it was odd, all this time later, that his things still sat in a closet, gathering dust. But I was not the person who should've been responsible for deciding what to do with it all. And so these items remained, waiting for someone else to make that call.

His laptop had been at home, so I imagined the police had kept that; and his appointment calendar was kept electronically, with secondary access by Anna, at reception. There was nothing unusual on either.

What remained: a personal framed photo of him and Fiona, both of them dressed in khaki and white, standing on a beach, sunburned and carefree—so unlike the version of them I remembered; memos that had been sent his way but not received before his death; his most recent birthday card signed by the staff, along with a Visa gift card because we didn't know what else to get him, stored in the bottom drawer; a fishing magazine that he'd accidentally routed to the school instead of home, which had kept coming month after month until it hadn't been renewed; and a small package that had been sent to the school instead of his home. It had arrived when I was already working here, and Anna had left it on my desk, washing her hands of it. Staring at his name, I'd felt a chill and stored it in the closet with the rest of his things.

I had never gathered the nerve to throw it all out. The only next of kin was Brandon's brother, and he'd had no use for anything but the dog. He'd never even set foot in this office, and I couldn't bring myself to ask him: *Do you want the vacation photo that was on his desk? A half-used Visa gift card?* I'd grown accustomed to the contents of the closet, the same way I could walk by the Truetts' front door without flinching. But now I stared at the closed door, a chill rising. Ruby's return had shaken up everything, every memory. Nothing was spared.

As I stood there with the files tucked under my arm, I heard something from the other side of my office door, but I couldn't tell whether it was coming from inside or outside the building. Whether it was the pipes resettling after my trip to the bathroom, an older system tucked behind the remodeled walls. Or whether it was someone trying the front door.

The hair on the back of my neck stood on end, and I turned to face the glass walls, the empty space. Here, with the historic brick buildings, we didn't have cameras. We believed in the honor code—for our students and for ourselves. We believed we were an isolated community and that the community was ours—the town an extension of the college or the college an extension of our town. Either way, we had been conditioned to believe in our shared safety.

I stood listening to the silence. I counted to ten, then to twenty. Hearing nothing else, I decided it must've been the old building, the hidden pipes and air-conditioning that had not been updated during the renovations.

I locked my office behind me and walked faster than necessary for the exit. Outside, that white car still sat at the other end of the lot.

And that was when I heard it clearly: a heavy step at the side of the building, boot on gravel. I spun in time to see Preston Seaver walking into the lot.

"Hey there, Harper," he said. I couldn't tell if he'd been waiting or had just arrived. Whether he'd been here all along.

He was in his security uniform but on foot, not in his car or on one of the electric golf carts the security team often used to get around.

I stepped back, on instinct. "You gave me a heart attack," I said, looking around the lot. "You're working this week?" I'd seen him early yesterday morning, finishing Mac's watch, and assumed he had off this week.

"Just the morning shift, making sure all the buildings are secure for the holiday. Anyone in there with you?" His green eyes skimmed over me quickly.

"No," I said, holding up the files that had been wedged between my purse and my body. "Just bringing some work home. It's empty in there otherwise."

He nodded, then tipped his head to the white SUV in the lot. "You know whose car this is?"

"No, haven't seen it before. I assumed it was someone giving themselves a tour."

"It was here yesterday, too. There aren't any plates."

I looked again—the tinted windows, a contrast to the mud-caked tires. "Was it in the same spot?"

He chewed the side of his cheek. "Don't remember."

It reminded me then of what had happened after Brandon's death. How the media had come to his home, our neighborhood, and then to his place of work, reporting from our lot, while we watched from behind the windows, our doors locked. How Anna had to call security to get them to leave. Murder wasn't good press for the college, either.

"You could get it towed," I said. "If there's no permit."

"You don't want to tow the wrong person's car, here, by accident." He walked closer, peering in the windows, completing a slow circle.

I unlocked my car and dropped my purse and the files on the passenger seat, preparing to leave before he could question me about something else.

"Guess I'll see you tomorrow?" he asked.

"Yeah, see you at the party," I said, easing myself inside.

When I drove out of the lot, I checked the rearview mirror. Preston was standing beside the white SUV, hands in his pockets, watching me go.

CHAPTER 12

AS I TURNED IN to Hollow's Edge, past the stone sign and the fresh flowers and the mock lanterns at the entrance, I caught a glimmer of the lake before the road curved, and my breathing stilled, like always. On the drive in, it sometimes felt like you were sliding toward the water, especially in the dark, with only the porch lights to guide you down. I knew the graded roads and elevated plots were to give the impression that each house could have a view, but sometimes it created the illusion of the entire neighborhood sloping toward the lake, like we were all fighting some gravity.

But for all our differences, this was it—what we were here for, what drew us in. We were a group who appreciated a certain aesthetic, a certain lifestyle. We gravitated here, and to one another, from this commonality alone. We assumed things about one another because of it. We assumed we were alike.

We had kayaks and paddleboards and fishing lines. We spent summer weekends in our bathing suits underneath cover-ups, coolers ready to go, an assortment of insulated mugs to keep our drinks cold. We had midday happy hours and late-night barbecues, hair tangled from the wind or the water.

Maybe Brandon and Fiona hadn't known what they were getting into when they moved here. To be fair, neither did I. I'd toured the area with Aidan before we moved, thought it looked calm and peaceful and quiet, that it was the type of place that would settle into me—that it would settle me. Turn me into someone still driven but more carefree, like Aidan. But that was before we were both ultimately surprised by the people we turned out to be. Seeing each other for the first time out of context when we moved here. Maybe Aidan seemed so academically driven only because he preferred it to the finality of what came next. Something he was actively avoiding.

And maybe I seemed outdoorsy and adventurous only because I'd been pushed outside all my life, sent to camps, enrolled in activities—anything to avoid the pitfalls my brother had fallen prey to. Maybe I became this way only because my parents were terrified of what could happen to me when I remained stationary. Like there was something sinuous that targeted stillness, always waiting to sneak up on me, sneak into me. This fear that I was at the whim of something greater, outside my control.

It was easy to forget now that the Truetts were one of the first families in. And maybe that tainted their perspective, too—that someone was always moving in, changing the rules, changing things on them.

A large subset of us at Hollow's Edge overlapped at work. It wasn't just Brandon and me, in the admissions department, and Ruby, who had been a student. It was Tina in the health center and the Seaver brothers in grounds and security. Paul Wellman in alumni giving; Charlotte, as a counselor; and Tate, who helped coach lacrosse as a second job.

It was the reason, I believed, that our neighborhood sometimes took on the approximation of dormitory living. Like we were an extension of the college in both location and age. Conforming ourselves to the unique structure of a private post-secondary education.

Except for the Truetts.

Every time they lodged a complaint (the backyard parties on summer weeknights; the fireworks on New Year's Eve; the garbage can left out too long), the animosity grew around them. No one knew why they wanted to live here. They were never seen down at the pool on weekends. They had never shown up at a neighborhood party. Had never walked barefoot from the edge of the road, through the woods, straight into the water.

The shore wasn't technically for swimming, though we all did it. The finger of water kept us sheltered from the current in the main channel. It was private and belonged to us alone, just one more secret of the community.

In the drought over the last few months, though, something had gotten lost. The hidden edges of the shore had slowly been revealed, the roots and mud and dirt and debris. The trash brought out on boats and left behind, washing up, catching on the decaying logs. Secrets rising from underneath.

Sometimes, at night, you could hear rats scurrying out from the edge.

Sometimes I thought all of this was because of Brandon and Fiona Truett. That nothing beautiful could ever last here again. That the story we told ourselves about this place was rotten, and now this, too, must rot.

RUBY WAS OUTSIDE.

She stood on the corner of my street, in front of the Seaver house. Currently no less than six feet from Mac, who was halfway down his walkway, rocking back on his heels, hands on his hips.

Five feet now, as he stepped even closer.

I tapped my brakes as I approached, then eased to the curb. Ruby was turned away from me, but Mac was smiling at something she'd said. His expression didn't change as he saw me pull up beside them.

I lowered the window. "What's up?" I called.

Ruby turned quickly, ponytail whipping behind her. "What's up with you?" she asked. "I woke up and you were gone."

"Had to grab some things from work for later," I said, and Ruby frowned, quick and fleeting. I said to Mac, "I ran into Preston on campus. Thought maybe you'd be working this morning, too."

His hands were in his pockets as he shook his head. "Not me. The project is off this week. Half the crew was on vacation anyways."

I shifted my gaze to Ruby, who made a show of stretching, leaning to the side, hands on hips. "Well, I'm running," she said. "Preparing to run. Thinking about running." She laughed to herself, and I heard Mac's laugh in echo.

"If you wait a minute, I'll catch up with you," I said. Even though it was too hot and I was nursing a hangover. Ruby, on the other hand, seemed fully recovered.

"Oh, no," she said, "I'd better embarrass myself on my own. Enjoy the peace and quiet, Harper!" And then she took off, slowly but confidently. I watched her in the rearview mirror until she disappeared down the road. Mac was watching, too.

"What did she want?" I asked.

"To say hey, I guess." He scratched at the side of his face, in need of a shave. "I thought it would be worse if I ignored her. You know how she is. Persistent."

Didn't we both. "*Hey?*" I said, arm hanging out the window, practically searing against the hot metal in the sun. "That's all?"

"Harper, come on," he said, glancing to the side quickly before approaching my window. He bent down, tan arm resting beside mine on the window frame, his free hand tucking the hair behind my ear. "*You're* the one who kicked me out the other night."

I brushed his hand away. "Mac, seriously, what did she say to you?" I said. With Mac, I had learned to ask things directly, knowing he would be direct in response.

"I think she said, *Hey, Mac, long time. How's it been?*" He smiled, the corners of his eyes crinkling. I rolled my eyes, and he squeezed my arm. "Be fair, Harper. I'd think by now you'd do me the favor of at least acting like you trust me."

And that right there was the reason I had stayed in this casual limbo, even though neither of us seemed interested in taking it any further. I *did* trust him, in a simple, straightforward way, and there was something to appreciate in that. He didn't hide who he was or what he was interested in. I wouldn't wake one day to find him halfway out the door with half my furniture in tow. It was the easy path. The simple path. The one that required no commitment and no promises.

He tapped the car door once as he stood. "Although," he said, "she also wanted to know where you were. She asked if I'd seen you. Maybe she knows. Maybe it's fine." He lifted one shoulder in a slow shrug, half his mouth in a careless grin.

My eyes widened. Ruby had my number. She could've called if she'd really wanted to know. I hardened my gaze. Made sure he knew I was serious. That this was serious. "Mac, it never happened," I said.

His expression shifted—confusion and something else. Resignation. Acceptance. He nodded once. "If you say so," he said, stepping back, erasing all that had come before. Like we could rewrite history, undo our missteps, go back and take a different path. And it was like we both understood, right then, that it was over.

Our end, as easy as our beginning.

He looked toward the woods. "Better get out of here, then," he said. "Before she makes it back around and wonders what you're still doing here."

THE NEIGHBORS HAD STARTED emerging again. Whitney, sitting cross-legged on the top porch step, smiling at the phone in her lap; Tina, pushing her dad in his wheelchair with her mother beside her, waving to someone out of my sight. There had been a shift; a return to normal.

People could get used to any change. All we needed was time.

THERE WAS A PHONE ringing somewhere in the house. Muffled, but with a high-pitched generic ringtone, coming from upstairs.

Ruby's phone.

I carried my files from work upstairs but went straight to her room first. Her phone sat on the edge of her bed, facedown. I flipped it over before I could talk my way out of it, wondering who might be calling her.

An ID flashed on the screen—*BB,* a name she had added to her contacts. It took me only a second to work it out: Blair Bowman. It had to be. The lawyer whose name I'd seen on the television screen. The phone stopped ringing, now showing the message *5 Missed Calls.*

The phone chimed once in my hand as I was staring at the display. A text this time, from the same caller: *We need to talk. Pls call me back ASAP.*

Definitely the lawyer, who couldn't be bothered with the extra milliseconds needed to type out the word *please.*

A door opened downstairs, footsteps heading across the foyer. I dropped the phone back on her bed, hoped I got the positioning right, and rushed out of her room. I was just passing the top of the stairs, files still in hand, when Ruby started up in her new jogging shoes.

"That was quick," I said.

Her steps slowed as she approached, a sheen of sweat over her exposed arms, the top of her chest. "What are you doing?" she asked, looking at the files.

"Work," I said. "Grabbing my laptop." Like I needed to account for any movement in my own house. And then, like I could beat her to it, save myself with a piece of the truth: "Hey, I heard a phone ringing. You just missed it."

She stepped to the side, pacing through the loft. I could see the muscles in her calves, in her upper arms. The tendons in the back of her neck. "Probably spam," she said. "I think I was given a phone number that must've recently belonged to someone else."

I wanted to tell her, *No, it was the lawyer.* I wanted to hear what she had to say. But there was no way to do that without giving myself away.

She pulled one leg back into a stretch. "I barely made it around the block. It's too hot to run," she said. She started to laugh. "But Mac, my God. He acted like . . ."

I waited, hanging on her every word. Desperate to know what she saw, what she knew.

She wiped her face with the bottom of her green tank top. "You know," she said, "he came to see me once."

I shook my head slowly before finding my voice. "No, I didn't know that." I wondered if it was before or after the day he'd shown up in my kitchen, telling me about Ruby's call.

More than that, I didn't like where the conversation was going—the guilt that had lodged deep inside and was being dragged to the surface. I hadn't gone to see Ruby. Not once. Cutting her out after the trial as someone who had existed and then no longer did. How easy it had been for the rest of us.

"I guess he wanted to make clear that we were over. Just in case I wasn't sure," she said.

I tried to picture it, Mac sitting on the other side of some plastic shield or maybe across a table—I didn't know how it had gone. Ruby crying. Or not crying. Narrowing her eyes at him. Laughing at the situation, at his cowardice.

But no, I was the coward. Mac had been brave, had gone to see her where I had not. I had read him all wrong, pegged him as someone who avoided adult responsibility, when really, he'd been the only one to do what the situation called for.

"Now I look at him and I don't remember what I saw in him," Ruby continued. She smiled to herself. "Well, I do remember." A single high-pitched laugh. "I remember, anyway, when I was too young for him. God, I loved the chase. Loved it because I knew he was always looking at me, even when he wasn't supposed to."

I flinched. Ruby hadn't been a kid when they'd met. She'd been nineteen or twenty. Too young for him, yes, but not *that* young. From my perspective, he'd barely tolerated her back then. I wasn't sure which of us was misremembering.

"Something about those Seaver boys, huh?" she asked. She gave me a look halfway between a grin and a wince. I didn't know what she was implying. "They love them around here, those boys who never seem to fully grow up. Not the girls, though. Not people like me."

She was right. Hitting on exactly how the neighbors here viewed her. Maybe it was because Ruby had been in college when we met her. She'd walked dogs and brought in our mail, come home late or not at all, owned roller skates and laughed loudly, spoken more from impulse than from tact. Maybe it was because her father never seemed to have a handle on her himself, always asking if we'd seen her.

"How's your dad?" I asked her. As if she needed a reminder

that she had somewhere else to go. Somewhere else to be now that she'd gotten what she'd come for. One of those missed calls, of course, could've come from him.

Her expression darkened, her eyes narrowing on the edge of mean before her gaze flicked away. "He died," she said. "I thought you knew that."

"Oh. Oh, no." I shook my head, a sudden wave of grief washing through me, though I hadn't had much contact with Mr. Fletcher other than when he'd neglected to accept Ruby's things. He'd seemed too mellow for his daughter, too lost, like he'd given up attempting to control her long ago. The path my own father had taken with my brother, whereas my mother had gone to the other extreme.

When Mr. Fletcher retired, he moved to Florida. Perhaps figuring Ruby was old enough to figure things out on her own, like the rest of us. And she'd shuttled herself the two blocks over, to me.

"I didn't know," I said. I closed the distance between us, placed my hand awkwardly on her upper arm. "I'm sorry."

"Well," she said, stepping away, "I'm gross right now, sorry. I really need a cold shower." And that was that.

Maybe the calls from the lawyer were about her inheritance. Maybe her staying with me was a waypoint on her journey, then she would ultimately collect her father's estate and start fresh.

Ruby retreated to her room, but I settled on the love seat in the loft, listening for the call I knew she'd be returning. About her case, or her dad's estate, or whatever she planned to do with the rest of us—the people who were going to pay.

But she remained silent. There was nothing, nothing, from the other side of the wall, until the sound of the water in the pipes. And then, moments later, the faint hum of her off-key tune in the shower.

CHAPTER 13

RUBY DID HER LAUNDRY.

Ruby made French toast for lunch, the scent of syrup permeating the downstairs.

Ruby went for a walk down by the lake—for some fresh air, to clear her head—and had to clean the mud from the bottom of her new white sneakers after.

In the late afternoon, Ruby ran her fingers over the books on the built-in shelves on either side of the television, pulling out titles she'd never read. Flipping to the back cover, opening to a seemingly random page, skimming the words.

My gaze trailed her through the house from my spot at the kitchen table. I had set myself up with my laptop open, files stacked on the table beside me, pretending to work, distracted by her every move.

She did not mention her phone or any calls. She did not talk at all unless responding to a direct question. The silence had grown into something solid, something that took on too much meaning, too much possibility. All the things I was keeping hidden. All the things I thought she might know. A tension building throughout the house until it had to break.

"I'm on watch tonight," I said, clearing my throat.

She turned from the bookshelf, crossed the room, long strides and silent steps. "Whose idea was that?"

"I told Charlotte to put me down whenever they needed me. I guess they needed me tonight."

She laughed once. "Of course it was Charlotte's idea." She sat in the chair across from me, fingers splayed on the stack of blue file folders between us. "What are you watching for, Harper?"

I shook my head. "Suspicious activity, obviously," I said. I tried to get my smile to mirror hers, like we were in on the same joke.

"Let's make a bet," she said, slouching back in the wooden chair. "Let's keep it fun. I'll write down what I think you'll see out there tonight, and you can tell me how close I was after."

At least this was better than her offering to come with me, which had been my first fear.

"What do you get if you win?" I asked. Because there had to be a trade. Every game had a winner.

"The knowledge that I was correct," she said, eyes boring into mine. "That I can still guess every little thing happening around here." She punctuated each word carefully, deliberately. "Write it down, Harper. You'll see."

A chill ran through me, but I forced a grin. "There won't be anything to report," I said, trying to match her nonchalant posture. "Everyone's going to be staying in tonight." That was the whole point of a watch in the first place. We knew people were out there, and we all stayed put, a self-imposed deterrent.

She tilted her head, almost smiled. "Oh, I am willing to bet anything that you won't be the only one out there tonight."

I flinched, remembering the noise from the patio when Mac was here; the still-frame image left behind while I was at the clubhouse meeting; the knife I'd found under Ruby's mattress.

She was probably right. Hadn't we learned that before? In Hollow's Edge, someone else was always watching.

I PREPARED TO LEAVE for my first pass at dusk.

Ruby was lying on the couch, head resting on a folded arm, watching the evening news. I kept thinking she was waiting for something. Blair Bowman with a new announcement, maybe; or an update on the case, a shift in a new direction. But the main topic of discussion was the drought, the current level of the lake, the fact that we might have to implement water restrictions, our squares of lawn turning brown and brittle.

I pulled the front door quietly shut behind me without saying goodbye. In the settling darkness, I saw an unfamiliar car at the curb, a figure walking up the porch steps at the Brock house. "Hey, Charlotte," I called as I headed her way, but the figure didn't pause. The car drove off in the other direction, and it took me a second to realize it wasn't Charlotte on the porch but Whitney, arriving home. Long hair covered the side of her face as she threw open the front door, just as Charlotte's disappointed tone carried out into the yard. "You missed dinner."

The rest of the neighborhood appeared to be winding down. Lights had started turning on in the houses down the street, illuminating my path.

A figure approached from the corner, slowly moving up the road. Tina, pushing her father in a wheelchair, his hands folded in his lap.

"How you doing, Harper?" she asked as they approached. She brushed her dark bangs to the side of her forehead.

"Okay," I said. Her friendliness and sincerity were a welcome relief. "I'm on watch tonight, just getting started."

"That girl back?" her dad asked, suddenly alert. Mr. Monahan had a stout frame, his head sunken almost directly into his broad shoulders. He looked like someone who had once been strong. Tina had that same frame, short and broad, her loose clothes camouflaging her strength—I'd seen her load the wheelchair into the back of her vehicle like it was weightless. Her mother, on the other hand, was petite and frail-looking and probably would've had difficulty caring for her husband even in her youth.

"Dad," Tina said in warning.

"She is," I said. No point lying when we all knew the truth.

Mr. Monahan raised a hand to his thinning white hair, his fingers trembling as he smoothed a few flyaway strands to the side.

Tina sighed. "I better get him home soon or my mom will worry," she said.

"You don't have to talk about me like I'm not here," Mr. Monahan said with a childish roll of his eyes. Tina squeezed his shoulder, then gave me a small smile as they continued toward home.

"Good night," I called after them.

"Be careful," her father called back.

As I continued my walk around the perimeter, I took stock of the routines of our community: Paul Wellman turning his silver sedan into his driveway, pulling straight through to the garage, the mechanical door lowering before he'd even exited the car. A couple leaving the pool at closing time, barefoot and wrapped in towels, their laughter trailing behind them.

Porch lights turning on, fragmented scenes visible through the open curtains. Flashes of television screens, the scent of burgers cooking on a grill, as I walked the road that backed to the high white fences of our patios.

When I arrived home, I debated how many more passes I really needed to do.

"All safe on the home front?" Ruby called. She seemed to be in exactly the same position on the couch.

"All clear."

The television was tuned to the same news station, though the volume had been lowered, more for background noise than active listening. She had a book in one hand—a paperback, cover folded over so I couldn't read the title.

I returned to my spot at the kitchen table, opening my laptop again, deciding I'd go out once more before bed. Split the night at a reasonable hour. Surely no one would complain when the person they really wanted to keep an eye on was currently inside my house. The more I was home, the more I could keep an eye on her.

At eleven, Ruby stood and stretched, turning off the television now that the main news broadcast had finished. "Well," she said, book in hand, "good night and good luck. Wake me if you want company?" Like we had done last time, sharing our shift for extra security.

But I had become someone different, too, in the time she'd been gone. "I'm good," I said.

She paused in front of the kitchen table, standing there until I looked up from the screen of the laptop. "Let me know who you see out there," she said. Her eyes flicking away, like she didn't want me to read any more into her bet. Like it mattered what I saw. That it wasn't just a game.

I WAS LATER THAN I intended. I left again just after eleven-thirty, taking a flashlight from the kitchen drawer this time. Flicking it on as soon as I closed the door behind me. At night, the stillness seemed rife with possibilities. The stifling humidity, the crickets and the frogs, the faraway sound of an animal darting into the woods, a door slamming shut inside one of the homes.

Ruby's words echoed as I passed the Seaver house: that I wouldn't be the only one out here. My eyes trailed to the upstairs right window—Mac's bedroom—where I could see the warm glow of a lamp beside the closed curtains.

I was standing there, staring up, when I heard it: the sound of metal on metal. A gate opening or closing. From the direction of the pool.

I kept the flashlight trained ahead of me—maybe the couple I saw leaving on my last walkthrough, neglecting to secure the gate behind them.

But the gate was closed now. I pulled at the bars just to check, but the latch was secure, the clang of metal against metal echoing through the night. I paused with my hand on the iron rungs, listening closely. I arced the beam of my flashlight across the surface of the pool—still and quiet—and then the pool deck.

A trail of water. Footprints leading from the pool, across the white concrete, to the gate where I stood on the sidewalk, then disappearing into the black pavement of the road.

At the pool, so close to the lake, the sounds of the night became almost deafening: the lapping of the water at the roots and rocks, the wind through the leaves of the trees, the frogs no longer in the distance but here—surrounding me in the trees around the pool deck. I slapped at my leg but felt the welt of the mosquito bite already rising.

It was probably a resident at the pool, anyway. Someone with a key, even though it was technically off hours. A midnight dip. A violation of our owners' association rules but nothing worth reporting.

Still, I shuddered, imagining all the things that could happen at night with the rest of us oblivious, behind locked doors and closed walls. I started walking faster, planning the route, keeping to the sidewalk, with the flashlight guiding the way. I wanted to be home, to be done with this. Of course there were other people out at night. It wasn't a crime. That had been Ruby's defense, after all.

"Hey." A soft voice up ahead stopped me in my tracks before

I could see anyone. At first I wasn't sure if I'd imagined it under the sounds of the night. I scanned my flashlight to the side and stopped at the figure sitting on the top porch step. Chase stood up. "I was hoping to catch you," he said.

But his porch light was off, and he was wearing sneakers and gym shorts and a dark T-shirt stretched tight across his shoulders. I wondered if he'd been watching me. Following me. From here, in the daylight, the pool was just barely in sight. He could've been out here all along.

"You're sitting in the dark," I said, as close to an accusation that I could get, even as I started moving again, passing his front door.

"I didn't want you to avoid me," he said, hand extended in my direction, palm up, case in point.

I stopped walking but didn't get any closer.

"You need to be careful, Harper," he said, walking down the steps.

I made myself stand my ground, not showing my discomfort. He wasn't a cop anymore; I didn't have to follow his instructions. "Or what?" I said. "People will talk?"

He frowned, suddenly another step closer. "She tried to get in my house yesterday morning. When I was out for a run. I know it."

I shook my head, but I understood. The paranoia had taken hold of him, taken him over. "She was gone all day yesterday," I said. "Until dinner."

"Says who. Her?" When I didn't respond, he continued, "Look, I left the garage open, and someone tried to jimmy the inside lock—who else could it be? She's dangerous, Harper, and you don't even see it. You always wanted to protect her, and sometimes I wonder why."

The space between us had disappeared, and I was aware of his size, his anger. "You need to keep out of this," I said, my voice low. "She could get a restraining order." Reminding him who was at fault here. Who was really the danger.

He took a step back. "No, she can't. I've never threatened her. I've never laid a hand on her. I'm going to be cleared. Everyone knows it. I did everything by the book. Where was the lie, Harper?"

There hadn't been a lie. It had been the way it was handled. The lines we all knew we were walking. All in the name of self-righteousness and good intentions.

"I heard you," I said, so he would know. "My house is right next to Tate and Javier Cora's. You hear everything." Through the fences and open windows, voices carrying in the night. I'd heard him talking to Javier during the investigation.

Chase looked at me closely, the only sound his breathing. "What are you talking about?" Head tilted to the side.

"You were discussing the strategy. That everyone needed to keep it simple. *Don't complicate things*." That was the one specific that stuck in my memory. Like he was telling them what pieces of evidence would help and which would not. "So tell me again, Chase, how you're going to be cleared?"

"That's not . . ." He scratched the back of his head. "I don't know what you *think* you heard, but you're wrong. She was a suspect, and we worked the case. A jury found her guilty." His gaze flicked to the side. "When we found them, she didn't come out. You know it." His voice had lowered, as if he were seeing that same unspeakable scene.

I squeezed my eyes shut, chasing away the image. "Ruby was sleeping. She sleeps like the dead," I said. She'd been out, after all, until two a.m. "She said someone else was out there."

"You're seeing what you want to see," he said.

"Or you are," I countered. "We all knew there were cameras everywhere on the street." This had always bothered me; it must've bothered him, too. What I should've said on the stand if given the chance. What I should've explained to the police in the first place. Our cameras had caught Charlotte's husband cheating.

158

They'd trapped package thieves. Why would Ruby waltz right by them, knowing she would be recorded, if she was committing a crime? If she had killed the Truetts?

Chase flicked his hand at the air as if swatting at a bug. "Don't put this on me. You were the one who testified that she came home at two in the morning through the back door, that you heard her in the shower. She moved fast, and she tried to hide what she had done, washing away the evidence. She knew it was a mistake. Killers, Harper, they aren't always thinking clearly. They're not always methodical or logical. A crime is chaotic. Sometimes it's just the heat of the moment, but they're still a killer. They may not be master criminals, but they're still guilty."

"The lawyer said . . ." I began, because hadn't he watched the same program? Heard the same implied threat of her statement? "She said there was evidence that would've exonerated her." *Someone else was out there,* Ruby had insisted, and maybe there was proof—

He spread his hands in front of him as if unveiling the end of a magic trick. "Do you see this mysterious evidence?" he asked. "You think, if it really existed, they would have waited until now to show it?" He shook his head. "They're playing a game for money. They want to sue the police department, to get everyone doubting. Before they decide to retry her. Look, she's been out less than a week, and they've already got you."

"They don't *have me*. She's innocent until proven otherwise."

His head jerked to the side, like he thought someone was listening. Then his focus turned back to me. "Don't you think it's weird that she came back here? That she came back to *you*?"

I did. I'd thought she'd take the money and go. But she was still here. Still waiting for something. "She trusts me," I said. "I was the only one who spoke in her defense."

His expression twisted up in confusion. "You can't possibly think she trusts you."

"She thanked me. After I gave my testimony." I shrugged, remembering that final communication as I stepped down from the witness box. The last time I'd seen her.

"She . . ." He trailed off, shook his head. "That's not at all what she said."

"You weren't there," I said. He had testified earlier in the trial, so he couldn't watch the rest.

"I know, but plenty of my friends in the department were there. They sat through the whole trial, and it's all they could talk about after. What she said when her roommate stepped down." His eyes widened, the whites glowing in the moonlight. "They were legitimately worried for you, Harper. If she hadn't been found guilty."

I blinked rapidly. "What—"

"How she turned to you, clear as day, with everyone watching, and mouthed: *Fuck you*. Like she didn't even care if the jury saw."

My mind was scrambling, trying to make sense of the scene. I shook my head, stepped back. "No, she didn't," I said. I was there, and he was not. But I couldn't stop my mind from returning to that day, the way my head was light and dizzy as I stepped down from the witness box—all those eyes on me, and the questions, and Ruby sitting right *there*. I'd felt ungrounded and removed, everything distorted through a filter. And this time, in my memory, as I passed Ruby, I saw her teeth catching on her lip at the start, her message becoming something else—

"Seriously, Harper," he said while I was still caught on my heels. "Be careful." I closed my eyes, trying to see. The memory morphing each time: *Thank you. Fuck you.* "Hey," he said, hand on my shoulder. "You have my number, right?"

But I shrugged him off. Ruby had known this would happen—that there would be someone else out here. Someone else watching. Chase had ruined his own career, his entire future, and now he was desperate to get it back.

"Stop watching us," I said. Because he was obsessed. Had been back then and was still now. Jogging by my house, standing outside the pool, waiting for me, even now.

He raised his hands in proclaimed innocence, heading back inside.

I couldn't get away from him fast enough, and I wasn't paying attention as I rounded the corner, up the next road, behind our street. My mind was stuck on that scene in the courtroom—Ruby's face, turning my way; Ruby's eyes, meeting mine—so I didn't tune in to the noise at first.

A car driving off. Brake lights disappearing around the curve ahead.

There were plenty of possibilities: someone lost; someone curious; someone who knew that Ruby was here and was watching.

As I stood there, staring at the space where the car had disappeared, I sensed something off in our backyards.

Something moving. Not behind the patio gates but closer—in the trees.

I ran my light through the pine trees, looking for any sign of someone else. I was worried that this was the person whom Chase might've mistaken for Ruby, testing the boundaries of his house. Who had been in my backyard when Mac was over.

I stood perfectly still, then heard that same familiar noise—of a gate creaking.

I paced the line of fences until I came to the unlatched gate: at the house beside mine.

The Truett house.

I pushed open the gate, shining the flashlight into the corners. But there was nothing inside the patio fence. A rusted spot on the brick where a grill had once stood. Dark, uncovered windows giving way to the empty house.

I pulled the gate shut, unable to lock it from the outside,

wondering how it had gotten unlocked in the first place. Whether someone had found a way in and was snooping around.

And then I stopped.

Maybe it was Chase's words, or thinking back to my testimony, but I stood frozen in place. Contemplating once more what I'd heard that night. The story it created.

Ruby, leaving through the front, taking the keys to the Truett house. Bringing the dog outside. Peering into the Truetts' bedroom, watching them, making sure they were asleep. Taking Fiona's car keys, starting the car, leaving the door ajar—

Planning it so carefully. So methodically. So ruthlessly. From the moment she took those keys.

In which case, what was she doing, waltzing in front of the cameras after?

If she'd been planning to return by sneaking in the back gate, she wouldn't have let herself be spotted in the front by half the cameras on the street.

Either she planned it carefully and was not careful at all, or it was a crime of chaos. Both of these things could not be true.

Chase had to be wrong. About her, about what she'd said.

I hugged the edge of the fence line on the way around the block, passing each enclosed patio, until I could circle to the front of our street again, at Tina Monahan's house. Without the porch light, the corner was pitch dark. As I passed in front of Tina's house, a bright light suddenly shone across the driveway. They must've had a motion detector.

It illuminated my path until I approached my front steps, where I'd left the porch light on for my return. I tried to unlock the front door, but the key didn't turn—it was already unlocked. Had I forgotten to lock up after myself when I'd left? With the late hour and all that had happened, I couldn't be sure.

Stepping through the front door, I almost slipped. Under my

sneaker, a paper had been left in the center of the entryway, folded on the hardwood floor of the foyer.

The room buzzed, and I remained perfectly still, listening to the silence of the house. Someone had been inside.

Maybe someone still was.

My shoulders tensed and I held my breath, trying to hear the sound of an intruder, but all I could hear was my own heartbeat, the pounding inside my own skull steadily increasing. I felt the adrenaline coursing through me—fight or flight; stay or run.

I flipped the lights on, thinking this would set someone fleeing, but nothing happened. A clatter as the ice maker dropped newly formed ice in the freezer, and I jumped, hand to heart.

I stepped silently around the paper on the floor and continued deeper into the house, flicking on each downstairs light as I passed. A rustling upstairs, and I paused at the base of the steps. I could feel my pulse in my fingers, gripped to the banister, as I listened. Ruby, probably, turning over in bed.

I took the steps slowly, cautiously, my senses on high alert, until I stood in the entrance of Ruby's darkened room. The light from the hall stretched across the carpeting, and I saw her facedown on the bed, her legs moving in some restless dream.

Feeling more secure, I checked every corner of this house, assuring myself that we were alone. Checking each lock, closing the curtains.

All the while, thinking of Ruby sleeping upstairs with the knife under her bed. The blasé way I'd walked outside, unsure whether I'd left this house unsafe, unguarded, when everyone knew I was on watch tonight.

How sure I had been when I'd told Ruby that no one would be out there tonight.

How wrong I had been. How unquiet our street truly was.

Heart still racing, I picked up the paper left behind in the foyer, and a photo slipped out once more.

It was a printout of the same image, of that dog-bone key chain. But the frame had been pulled farther out, everything else gaining context: a person running down the sloped wooded path toward the lake—the water nothing more than a darkness stretching into the distance.

A black line obstructed the left side of the frame, and it took me a moment to make it out.

A black iron bar, surrounding the pool.

The photo had been taken from a distance. But not from the security camera of someone's house. It had been snapped from the corner of the pool, from inside the fence. Where Mac had stood the other day, beckoning me closer.

The image was black and white, taken in the dark, but I could make out different details this time. Jean shorts and pale legs and sneakers, the Nike swoosh reflecting in the moonlight.

Details that could be identifiable.

A scene that someone had silently watched, standing at the edge of the pool deck.

I unfolded the paper it had arrived inside. Two words typed in black ink. A simple, stark message: WE KNOW.

THURSDAY, JULY 4

HOLLOW'S EDGE COMMUNITY PAGE

Subject: Are we really doing this??

Posted: 9:20 a.m.

Margo Wellman: I'm sorry, but this party just seems like a really bad idea right now.

Javier Cora: We're all going to be together. What's the problem?

Margo Wellman: Yeah, drinking.

Preston Seaver: I will not let my life be ruled be fear.

Charlotte Brock: Look, come or don't. No one's telling you what to do. But you can't stop people from going to the pool they all pay for with their dues just because you don't think it's a good idea.

/|\   /|\   /|\   /|\   /|\
\|/   \|/   \|/   \|/   \|/

Subject: Heard something . . .

Posted: 10:13 a.m.

Tate Cora: . . . outside last night. Woke me up around 2:45. Just went through my security footage, but there's nothing on the camera. Harper, did you see anything??

Harper Nash: Nothing out of the ordinary last night.

CHAPTER 14

I HADN'T GONE OUT AGAIN. Not since arriving home to realize someone had been inside. I'd remained in my room, behind a secondary locked door, knowing that neither could truly keep me safe.

I stared at Tate's note on the message board again, then slammed the laptop shut as Ruby appeared, coming down the staircase. Her steps slowed when she saw me, sitting at the kitchen table. "You okay? You look like you've seen a ghost."

"Just tired," I said, the image from the photo that had been left in the foyer last night seared into the back of my mind. Someone had gotten into my house while I was out, and I hadn't slept, and now there was this: a collision between a party that no one would cancel and the sudden return of Ruby Fletcher, fear and paranoia commingling at critical levels.

"Well?" she asked, pouring herself a coffee from the pot on the counter. "Was I right?"

I shook my head, not processing.

"About last night," she continued, taking the seat across from me. "Run into anyone else out there? We can compare your notes to my guesses."

She felt so close. My eyes drifted to her lips on the edge of the coffee mug as she took her first sip. Trying to remember that day in the courtroom. *Thank you. Fuck you.*

"No," I said. "There was nothing to write down. It was quiet."

She raised an eyebrow, reached a hand for my wrist, and flipped it over, exposing the fragile skin there. I could feel the blood pulsing. "What's the matter?" she asked, leaning closer.

I felt boneless, my arm limp in her grip, not sure what I could trust—my memories, even; my perception of events. The words she might've spoken in the courtroom. The knife she kept under her mattress and the threatening pictures left inside. Whether she was afraid or someone to fear.

The way she'd sneaked in here the first day, barefoot, with no warning. The fact that Chase believed she'd tried to break into his house, the missed calls from her lawyer, and this sudden thought that maybe she had taken my car and gone absolutely nowhere. That she'd been here all along, watching. That she'd had fourteen months to let things fester, and now she was back for a reason.

"Ruby," I said quietly. "Ruby, you can't go to that party today."

You can't be here at all.

Her eyes narrowed, and her face became impenetrable, nothing but hard angles and flat expression. "You know what no one does around here? Talk to each other face-to-face. Ask questions or demand answers. It's contagious, the way people act to save face." The corner of her mouth twitched. "Smile on the surface, and whisper something else to the police. Cut someone out of their lives and pretend she never existed."

I held my breath, held my expression still, refusing to look away. Not knowing whether she was speaking with generality or specificity.

"I've been ignored for a long time, Harper."

I thought of Charlotte and what she would say. Chase and what he would do. What I was truly afraid of. "You can't go," I said. Direct and to the point. "Don't go." A plea instead.

She pushed back her chair slightly so the wooden legs cried against the tile floor. "Is this coming from you or them?" she asked.

I swallowed around the dryness in my throat. "It's coming from me," I said.

Her eyebrows shot up, like I'd surprised her. But she stood abruptly, turning away. "Don't worry," she said as she opened the fridge, pulling out the containers of fruit, placing them beside the bottles of red wine lining the back of the counter. "I won't show up empty-handed. Wouldn't want to be a bad guest, would I?"

I WAS GOING TO be sick. The last time I'd felt this ceaseless nausea, this unstoppable force heading my way, was in the days leading up to the trial. When I knew I'd have to face her and everyone else. I was barely able to eat the entire week.

Margo was right—a party was a bad idea. I couldn't tell whether their insistence on the party was fueled by stubbornness, or animosity, or naïveté, but as the day progressed, the setup began, undaunted.

I had no control over Ruby Fletcher. I was naive to think I ever had.

From my bedroom window in the early afternoon, I saw Javier and Chase carrying the white folding tables from Javier's garage. I heard the sharp pop of bang snaps being tossed in the street, and someone yelping with delight.

I needed to stop this.

Downstairs, Ruby had the music on too loud, so the entire

house seemed to vibrate with the beat. She was mixing a second pitcher of sangria and didn't seem to notice when I left.

I stepped outside to the sound of laughter, could smell the lingering smoke drifting from Charlotte's driveway, where her daughters stood barefoot on the edge of the dry grass, tossing bang snaps onto the pavement.

Molly darted across the hot asphalt, and Whitney tossed one at her feet, both of them laughing as she leaped out of the way, smoke rising in her wake.

Music was already carrying from around the corner, probably the pool.

"Hey," I called, walking across the Truetts' lawn. "Where's your mom?" I asked Whitney, who was the closest, standing on the Truett side of the driveway.

"Setting up," Whitney said, thumb jutting over her shoulder. I could see the outline of her American-flag bikini under her white tank. Behind her, across the driveway, Molly wore a red-and-white-striped cover-up and jean shorts, not coming any closer. I wondered what would happen if she saw Ruby out here. Molly tossed a bang snap close to the spot where Whitney stood, still turned away. Whitney yelped, leaping into the air.

"Nice moves," Molly deadpanned as Whitney returned fire.

I kept moving, passed the Seaver brothers' house. The pool came into view. The gates were propped ajar, neighbors filing in and out, setting up. Their movements were rapid, almost frenetic, like they knew what they were doing—taunting fate; taunting *her.*

Like if they moved as one, they became a force and would be protected.

Chase wheeled a grill to a spot near the front fence where Charlotte stood in a flowing pale blue cover-up, partially sheer and hitting just below her knees.

"Charlotte," I called, and she turned her head quickly my way.

"Right here, Chase." She gestured to her spot on the concrete. "Be right back. What's up?" she called, meeting me at the entrance.

"She's going to come," I said, sounding breathless even to myself. "Doesn't matter what I tell her."

Molly and Whitney came in right behind me, like they'd been following me, but Charlotte held up a hand as they passed through the gate. "Did either of you remember the sparklers?"

"We can go back when it's dark," Whitney said.

Charlotte shook her head once. "Now, please."

Molly rolled her eyes, but they both turned back for the house, obeying their mother. When they were out of earshot, Charlotte turned to me. "I think it's best to ignore Ruby, don't you agree? Seems what she wants is a reaction."

How calm she seemed, how measured. As if Ruby were a stubborn toddler who would change course when she failed to elicit the desired response.

"Look," Charlotte continued, gesturing somewhere behind me, "even Margo decided to come."

Margo was crossing the street, wheeling a large cooler behind her. I stepped to the side as she leveraged it through the gate and under the white tables. She pulled out two large containers of lemonade and placed them on the counter, then used a Sharpie to label the cooler with a piece of tape that declared: ICE.

Charlotte had returned to her to-do list, currently unspooling the wire from a box fan. Tina poured a bag of chips into a purple bowl, then helped Charlotte set up the fan at the edge of the table to keep the bugs away.

I felt caught between worlds. Just like in the days before the trial—on the outskirts, looking in.

Tate and Javier arrived next, and Tate set out her dueling

pitcher of lemonade, wrinkling her nose at Margo's on the other side.

I watched, dumbstruck, as Tina set up at one of the pool tables in the corner with her parents, angling the umbrella for shade. Whitney and Molly returned with the sparklers, dragging lounge chairs out into the sun, stripping down to their swimsuits. Charlotte called, "Don't forget sunscreen!" I couldn't decide whether people were being deliberately obtuse or wielding their own sense of power, going on with their lives like nothing was amiss, like nothing could touch them.

Preston barreled through the gates with the shoulder strap of his own cooler slung over his arm, heading straight for the grill. He started pulling apart frozen burgers that Charlotte had stacked on the stand beside him, then scanned the crowd. "Hey, anyone seen Mac? I asked him to bring the gas for the grill. Can't start without him." When no one responded, he called my name. "Do you know when Mac is coming?" He said it so loudly, it carried over the crowd, and everyone stopped talking.

I whipped my head toward the entrance, terrified I'd see Ruby there, thankful that she hadn't arrived. "No," I said, walking closer so our voices wouldn't carry. "Why would I?" Like I'd know any better than he did.

Preston cocked his head to the side. Lowered his voice as he closed the distance between us. "Does she not know?" He shook his head, then grinned at my wide-eyed reaction. "She's got no right to be mad at you. Really, it's only fair."

I stared at him, at the twitch of his lip, at his smug expression. Daring me to ask. Needing me to do so. And me, with that pit in the center of my stomach, hating how much I needed to know what he meant. "Fair, how?" I said.

"Well," he said, "you know." A wave of his hand, dragging it out, making me wait. His captive audience. Seeing if anyone else would join to listen. Scanning the crowd to check that they were. "After Aidan."

My head whipped to the closest person listening, to Javier, and I could tell by how fast his eyes darted away that it was true. That the guys, at least, all knew. Tate was staring at her husband with the same intensity—with her own version of surprise.

I closed my eyes and saw it again, the day Aidan told me he was leaving. How he'd stood in the center of the living room, eyes to the windows, pleading with me, like I should understand. *My God, Harper. I have to get out of here.* His arms stretched wide, and I'd thought he meant this house, this life, with me. But maybe it was something more. A mistake that was following him. A mistake that wouldn't let him go. And I was the person worth sacrificing for his own fresh start.

Preston was looking at me with an exaggerated grimace. "You really didn't know?"

The anger seared at the pit of my stomach. At Aidan, at her, at everyone who knew. At fucking Preston Seaver, shit stirrer, who would drag your baggage out in public, just to broadcast your reaction.

"Well, I mean, anyway. Like I said, she can't really complain." And then Preston turned toward the entrance. "Hey there," he called to the young woman walking from a car parked along the street. His date, I guessed by her beaming smile. She looked like an athlete, tall and lean-muscled, with long, sleek hair, blond at the roots, dark at the ends. I thought I recognized her—a student on campus.

Preston beckoned her over, grinning like he had not just up-ended my entire life thirty seconds earlier. Then he craned his neck, calling out to the entrance, "Look who finally decided to come," as Mac walked in with the container of propane for the grill.

"Hey," Mac said, frowning at the state of us, quiet and tense. "I thought this was a party?"

But everyone was looking behind him. At the figure waltzing down the middle of the street, head high, a smile I could see from the distance.

My heart leaped and then hardened.

Ruby was here.

CHAPTER 15

IF NOT FOR THE music, the silence would've cut through the moment. All eyes on Ruby Fletcher, sauntering through the pool gate.

It was then that some of the neighbors started to leave. Pete, from the court behind, and the couple who'd arrived with him.

But not us. Not the ones who knew her best.

Ruby pretended not to notice the eyes on her, leaving the sangria in an open spot on the table, pulling our insulated mugs out of my pool bag. "You forgot yours, Harper," she said, arm extended my way. She pretended not to notice my coolness, the fact that I had asked her, *told* her to her face, not to come.

"Hey, Charlotte," she said as Charlotte moved the fan on the table for a better angle. Ruby waved her fingers at Whitney and Molly on the lounge chairs. Only Whitney waved back. "The girls are looking more and more like you each day."

Charlotte pressed her lips together, nodding once, before carrying the sunscreen over to her daughters. *Ignore her.* That was Charlotte's policy, but I didn't see how it could possibly work when Ruby was standing in the middle of the pool deck, greeting each person one by one.

"Tate, wow, look at you." A pause. A grin. "Javier." His name drawn out, like she knew a secret. "Is that Chase? Chase!" she called, arm raised over the crowd. "I didn't get to say hi the other day!"

Stop. I wanted to shake her. Send her back. Send her away.

People were whispering. Preston to Mac. Javier to Chase. And I couldn't help thinking it was about me. About what I didn't *know*. How naive and clueless I had been. How wrong I had been about Ruby Fletcher all along.

I pivoted to Margo, who was busying herself at the white table, organizing the food, moving things around absently. I didn't know why she hadn't stayed home if she really thought this was such a bad idea. "Where's the baby?" I asked, trying to tune it all out. Keep the tension from brewing over, stifle everything down inside me.

"Napping. Finally. Paul is watching him so I could get out by myself for a little while. It's so rare these days—"

"Hi there, Preston." Ruby's voice carried over the group, my ear tuning in to hers above anyone else's. She had worked her way into the circle of people standing around the food, and I was trapped between the table and the crowd. I couldn't look away. Her confident smile. Her fearlessness.

Mac stood off to the side, appearing awkward for maybe the first time in his life, with a bag of chips in one hand and a bottle of beer in the other.

Preston's date smiled and stepped forward, like she was excited to be in proximity of such celebrity. Shook Ruby's hand, even, something performative about it, like it was for Preston's benefit. "Hi," she said, "I'm Madalyn. It's *so* nice to meet you."

I wanted to shake this girl, too. Tell her he wasn't worth trying to impress. Tell her how Preston had told the cops that Ruby was crazy, that she didn't take rejection well, and he'd do the same again. I wanted to tell her that Ruby Fletcher wasn't worthy of her attention, either. That she craved it, fed off it, was here because of it. I was seeing her clearly, finally. Like Chase did. Like the prosecutor claimed. A grifter, a thief, a sociopath, take your pick—

Then Madalyn pivoted to me, and Preston introduced us. "Right," she said. "You're the one who works in admissions?"

I looked to Preston, confused. "We saw your car," he said.

"Yesterday? I didn't see you there," I said to Madalyn. Just Preston, creeping around the edge of the parking lot.

"No, the day before?" she said. "I was keeping him company before we went to lunch. And he saw the cars in the lot, said he knew you. That you were his neighbor."

But I was shaking my head. "I wasn't there." The day before yesterday, Ruby had my car.

But before I could ask him about it, ask Ruby where she'd really been—*with my car, with my entire set of keys*—Ruby raised her purple mug toward the sky. "The gang's all here!" she called, spinning away.

Someone turned the music up, as if we could celebrate by blunt-force approach, and Preston guided Madalyn away.

Ruby stopped to talk to Molly, then Whitney, Charlotte watching from afar. I was surprised she didn't physically intervene, pulling her daughters closer, putting her body between them. But Charlotte stuck to her decision. She was ignoring her as best she could.

Ruby was reveling in our discomfort. How long had she waited? Had she imagined this each night, each week, each passing month? What she would do if she could?

Of course, we should've realized when we saw her at the press conference that she would not move away and start fresh. That she was not interested, ever, in getting on with her life or putting everything behind her. That had never been Ruby's nature. This had always been the difference between us: She had a good life, a solid

179

life, and felt a compulsion to shake the foundation. To destroy the gift of relative stability. An addict of a different sort.

Ruby had always acted like she had nothing to lose—until, suddenly, she did. She lost her freedom. Fourteen months of her life. The trajectory her life would take forever after.

Oh, but she had taken it back. She had emerged.

Now she seemed more or less invincible.

She pushed Mac into the pool, fully clothed. Laughed at his good-natured grin after as he shook his hair out of his eyes.

"Jesus," Javier said, suddenly beside me. "This is going to be a shit show."

THE FIREWORKS WOULD HAPPEN just after dusk, and then people would scatter, breaking off into smaller groups, retreating to their patios, or front stoops, or living rooms. Into smaller, exclusive subsections.

And then I would have to deal with Ruby on my own again.

When I exited the bathroom beside the clubhouse, Charlotte was gathering up a stack of used plates and napkins at the long white folding table, while Ruby was pouring herself a drink. The sangria had run out, and she was moving on to the lemonade. As she reached for it, Charlotte jerked back, and Ruby laughed. "Seriously, Charlotte?" she asked.

Charlotte didn't respond, didn't give her the benefit of any reaction. "Girls," she called over her shoulder, "it's time to go home."

Molly looked her way, but Whitney had her earbuds in, lying on a lounger, sunglasses on even though it was nearly dusk. Neither moved from her seat.

"Ruby," Charlotte said, in case she would listen to Charlotte instead, "I think it's time for you to go." Loud and firm, for all to hear. What she would've said the second Ruby walked into her house. Strong, where I was weak.

And that was when Ruby turned. Like all she was waiting for was a switch. This moment. Something she could weaponize.

"Why are you all acting so afraid?" she asked, arms extended to the expanse of us. And then she laughed. "I know why you're all scared. It's not because of *me*. It's because of your little lives, with your little problems, and your little worlds. You're afraid that no one will even *notice* if you're gone. Honestly, if it wasn't for the dog, would any of you have realized something had happened to the Truetts?"

We had always avoided them. Happier not to run into them out front, to hear their complaints or see their condescending looks. The barking dog had been the only thing I noticed.

"Fucking cowards," she said, and even Preston's date flinched. "I know what you did." Her gaze moved so fast, over all of us, I couldn't be sure who she was talking about.

"All right." Mac broke the silence, stepping forward. "Come on. Let's go talk." Hand on her arm.

She jerked her arm back. Brought it forward again into an accusing point. "And what about you, Mac? Aw, shucks, I don't know," she mimicked. "I mean, maybe my girlfriend is a killer. I can't say for sure." She gave him a slow drawl, a lazy affect. "My life can remain exactly the same, either way." A step closer, and I got a chill. "I can still go three doors down. Get laid without leaving the street."

"Ruby, come on. Come walk it off," Mac said.

"Walk what off, Mac? Walk the last fourteen months off? Walk off my anger that all of you, every single one of you, conspired to have me convicted of a crime I did not commit?"

Silence as we all stared back. The thing she had finally given voice to, unavoidable now. An open accusation that the Truetts' murder was not at her hand but at one of ours. But I wasn't on her side anymore, and the drinks had steeled my nerve. I saw what they all saw now. The things Ruby was capable of. A liar. A dangerous liar.

"Preston told me," I said, because it was the only thing I could do to alter the course, redirect the train wreck of this conversation. "He told me about you and Aidan." Ruby turned my way slowly, blinking once. "God, Ruby, you had me fooled. But you really are a terrible fucking person."

Her lip twitched. "He was an asshole," she said. "And nothing even happened, Harper, I swear. Though not for his lack of trying. I told him I'd tell you, and what did he do? Ran, to save face. Your fiancé? Please, he was making a fool out of you. I did you a favor. Not like anyone else did for you here."

She stepped closer, one eyebrow raised. Like she was giving me one last shot to change course, rethink my side. And then she shook her head. "And this one, I mean, seriously?" She gestured around the group. "Is it the big brown eyes that have everyone fooled?" She widened her own eyes in a play at faux innocence. "Has no one thought this was odd? That she takes the job of the guy killed next door *and* my boyfriend?"

I shook my head as if I could deny it. People looked down, looked away.

"I see you," Ruby said, softer now. "I see everything about you, Harper." She was up in my face. I was tired of being pushed around by her. I was so, so angry. Not just about her actions; anything could be forgiven if you chose to forgive. And the past, with Aidan, was so long ago. But because of the way I found out, from Preston. That sharp, hot humiliation—the thing that made me ache with the need to push back. To do something.

I pressed my hand to her shoulder and shoved. Hard enough that she stumbled. "I took you in," I said as she regained her footing, eyes wide from surprise.

"Oh, like hell you took me in. You're just too scared to tell me to go. And why, Harper? Why is that?"

"What are you saying?" I asked. Because if she said it, I could defend it. If she said it, I could accuse her. An equal and opposite reaction. "You think I hurt them?"

"No, I don't think you have it in you." She said it not as a compliment but to imply a lack of backbone, a lack of agency. "I think you're an opportunist, Harper. That you only know what you don't want. I don't think you can ever be happy as yourself."

My eyes burned under her unflinching gaze. Something stirring in the wake of her words. Something too close to the truth. The way I had crafted myself in reaction to something else: in contrast to Kellen; to Aidan; to her.

"Get the fuck out of here," I said, the words barely audible. Out of this party, out of my home, out of my life.

"Come on, Ruby," Mac said once more, arm out like he was the one who could calm her. His hand made contact with her arm, and she flinched. "Don't," she said, and I wondered suddenly how much he had hurt her. How much she had the capacity to let herself be hurt. I'd thought she didn't have it in her anymore. That she had hardened herself, by necessity, for her survival.

"Please," he said, and this time she followed him. Out the pool gate, down the trail, to the water's edge. I couldn't see them clearly through the trees. Couldn't tell whether she was taking a few deep breaths or whether he was talking her down. What she was saying in response. Until I saw her head lower, her shoulders contract, and her body retreat into Mac's chest, where his arms wrapped around her back.

In the silence, Tate refilled the container of lemonade from her cooler under the table. "I see she hasn't changed," she mumbled, and someone laughed, the tension dissipating.

My hands still shook from the adrenaline, and I felt lost,

ungrounded. Ruby's words returning again so I could see myself only as she might. Seeing only what I didn't want to be. What I couldn't be. A career helping others begin the next stage of life but neglecting my own in the process. Staying on the same path, letting the momentum carry me, so I wouldn't have to look too closely.

"Harper?" Javier had taken over at the grill, flipping the burgers. "Cheese on your burger?" He tipped his head, his dark eyes friendly, like nothing had happened. Like we were all expected to resume our roles now; we'd settled something, dealt with it, and could continue on.

My stomach rolled. "No, thanks," I said.

I looked around for my blue mug, which I'd left on the white folding table, but I couldn't find it. I only saw the purple one, left on the concrete, behind a chair; Ruby must've misplaced hers and taken mine. I rinsed hers out in the water fountain, where Charlotte was refilling two plastic cups for the girls. She gave me a sympathetic smile as I scooped up the water, letting it run down the back of my neck. I filled the cup with Tate's lemonade after—it really was the better one.

Preston stood beside me, held out a bottle of vodka. "Tell me when," he said as he poured.

"When," I said, but he kept going. Gave me a knowing grin. Chucked me on the chin like I was a kid who needed a pick-me-up.

I followed his gaze to where Mac and Ruby were walking back up the path, side by side, in silence.

Whitney called out to Preston from the lounge chair, plastic cup held forward. "Me, too, please."

Preston smirked and rolled his eyes. "Think again, little one." And she did, giving him a glowing grin, holding out her cup once more, smiling at his husky laugh as he turned away. A cycle I'd seen before.

Charlotte passed behind me a moment later, squeezing my shoulder. "You okay?" she asked, leaning close—closer than she'd ever been. The way I'd imagine she'd whisper to her daughters, something private and comforting.

As if, finally, I had earned my way back into the fold. The price: shame and public embarrassment, for which I would be welcomed with shoulder pats and chin taps, words of encouragement, the knowledge that I was one of them now.

I nodded, reached a hand for hers, and squeezed back.

Ruby and Mac drifted apart as they passed through the pool gate, neither looking my way. I drank half the cup in several large gulps, then found myself leaning back against the iron bars, Chase beside me.

"Hey," he said slowly, like he was testing me out. "I'm sorry about last night. I went about it the wrong way."

"Did you know about her and Aidan?"

He turned away, staring straight ahead. "God, that was so long ago. I heard rumors, yeah. But I heard rumors about a lot of things."

"Did Mac know, too?" I watched him across the pool, standing off to the side, by himself. I wondered if I'd underestimated him. Whether he knew my weak spots and exploited them.

There was a boys' club here, I could see that now. Even back when Aidan was here, with Javier and Preston and Chase. They'd known he was going to leave before I did. God, even Paul Wellman was probably a part of it. Mac *must've* known. The groups in this neighborhood were not by household unit. They never had been. Those might fracture and strain. But there was a web below that held us together. Held us in place.

Chase's gaze followed mine to the crowd watching the sky with anticipation. "I don't know what Mac knows. Never did. He's not really one for gossip." He took a deep breath. "Listen, Harper, I need to explain, what you heard that night . . ." He cleared his throat. "When I said *Keep it simple,* it was about this stuff. Some of the guys back then wanted to bring up all these rumors we couldn't prove, but they weren't really relevant, other than showing she was a pretty shitty person. But that's all smoke and mirrors and detracts from the simple truth. The solid evidence. And maybe I overstepped because I live here and you all know me, but I thought I was doing the right thing." He turned to face me. "I still think it was the right thing."

I couldn't take a deep breath—coming face-to-face with all the things I hadn't seen. How wrong I had been about so much. "I made a mistake," I said, which was maybe the most honest thing I'd ever said to Chase. And right then I felt like he was the one who could absolve me.

"Harper," he said, "get her the fuck out of here."

I laughed into my drink, draining the rest. "I'm trying," I said. But I feared I had lost the ability to do anything about her. She was here to taunt us, to prove something, to disrupt the foundation of all of our lives. Simpler, even: She was here for revenge. And we all knew it.

When I looked up, Ruby was swaying to the music. She had my blue cup in her hand, had drunk so much she could barely stand upright, her hand wrapped around an iron bar to steady herself.

The first rocket cried through the night, a burst of red flames over the top of the trees, and Preston let out a whoop. Ruby stumbled into the nearest lounge chair, head tilted back, the colors reflecting off her exposed skin.

I looked from her, to Mac, to Javier; Tate, just outside their group, hands resting on her stomach; Charlotte perched on the edge of Whitney's chair, Molly beside them; Tina and her parents around the table, faces tipped up to the fireworks; Margo covering the baby's ears while he began to cry; Paul looking down at his phone, burger in his free hand; Preston with his date in his arms, hands wrapped around the iron bars behind her.

For this brief moment, we could all look away, forget about Ruby Fletcher and all she threatened to uncover here. The bright lights singeing the sky. The explosion vibrating in your chest.

I was betting no one even noticed when I left. With the fireworks show still happening, I grabbed the pool bag and went back home, my brain moving too fast, working through the simplest way to get her out of here. The first step, I knew, was to lock the door behind me.

The second step was to pack up her things, get them out of my house.

THE POUNDING ON THE door began just before midnight. I was upstairs piling the last of Ruby's clothes into that empty suitcase.

Back in my room, I opened my laptop to watch the camera feed, to see which Ruby Fletcher I was dealing with.

But on the frame was Margo Wellman, casting glances behind her as she pounded on the door with the side of her closed fist. I heard her sharp breathing, a single whimper.

"Coming!" I yelled as I raced down the stairs, because she looked afraid, and she was on watch tonight, and I worried Ruby had done something.

As soon as I opened the door, I knew something terrible had happened. I'd seen the expression before. *Chase, turning from the end of the bed, eyes wide with horror, mouth slightly open, choking on his words—*

I placed both hands on her upper arms, her skin clammy and cold. The rough feel of goose bumps or a heat rash covering her shoulders. "What did she do?" I asked, trying to force the words from Margo. Picturing the endless possibilities: the pool water, the lake water, the knife under her bed—

"Ruby's at the pool," Margo said. "She's still there."

I squeezed her shoulders tighter, thinking of everyone who had been down there together. All these people I suddenly cared for.

She sucked in a gasp of air. "She's not breathing, Harper." Hand to her mouth, fingers shaking, while faces scrolled in my mind: Charlotte and her girls, Tate, Tina—

Margo started running toward the pool, and I followed, barefoot, heart pounding.

That moment when Chase lunged toward the bedroom windows, throwing them open, and I caught a glimpse—

The lights at the Seaver brothers' home were on, and a door swung open like they could sense something happening—

Chase's raspy voice that morning as he'd yelled at me, "Call 911. Harper, move!"

The front door of the Wellman house also ajar, the lights off. A baby crying inside, ignored.

Voices yelling from the pool. "Get her on the ground!"

Tina, the first person I saw, in her pajamas under the corner light of the pool. Paul Wellman helping her lower a figure from the lounge chair. The chair I'd last seen Ruby in—

And then I understood. It was Ruby, still at the pool, not breathing. My foot caught on the curb, and my knee hit the grass outside the pool entrance.

The sharp cry of a siren, a flash of red and blue, and Chase's shadow illuminated from up the road, heading our way.

And then time slowing down, my body sluggish, the scene coming in fragments:

The EMTs pushing their way in and Tina stepping back, kicking over my blue insulated cup that Ruby had taken. Tina looking out the pool gates straight at Margo and me, her face set. A single shake of her head.

The street filling up behind me. The sirens and the lights, the gathering crowd. The police arriving in new vehicles, beckoning us back.

And still we watched, standing on our toes, leaning around one another. There was movement on the trail beyond the pool, people sneaking closer for a better look.

Everyone watching her, even now. The commotion she could create, bending the gravity of a room her way. A spectacle, still— living or dead.

FRIDAY, JULY 5

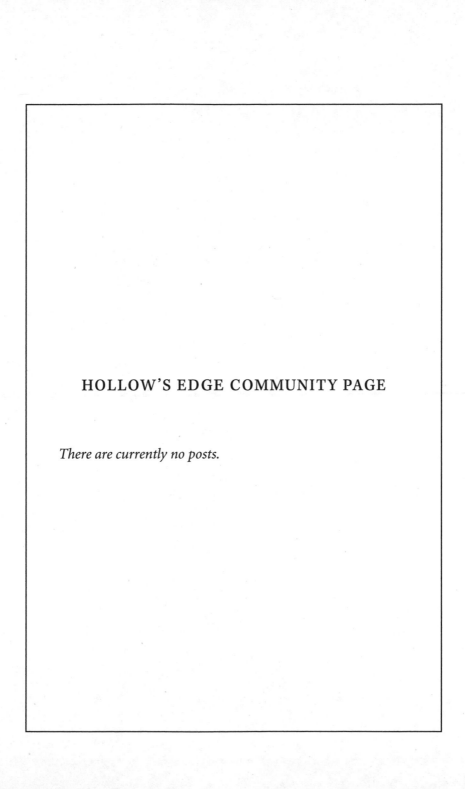

HOLLOW'S EDGE COMMUNITY PAGE

There are currently no posts.

CHAPTER 16

SILENCE.

It stretched up the road and around the corner. No doors opening or closing, or neighbors calling to one another, or voices carrying from backyards or open windows. It moved through with a heavy warning, a physical presence— something worth heeding.

This was the opposite of what had happened after the Truetts, the way we had all called to one another, reached for one another, arms entwining in comfort and relief. The feel of skin on skin, reminding us that we were alive.

The message board back then had been full of notes. All of us checking in: *What happened? Who noticed? Oh my God, is everyone else okay?* The calls, the texts, the community growing even closer in the aftermath, at first.

Now the message board was empty. Not only that, someone had gone through and deleted every previous post.

Even my house was eerily quiet. Nothing but a drip coming from the kitchen, the click of something mechanical in the living room walls. Like time had frozen last night with Ruby's death. Her purple insulated cup that I'd dropped in the sink when I'd first returned, my flip-flops kicked off by the front door, beside the pool bag. I couldn't bear to move anything.

My phone rang from the spot beside me on the couch, Mac's name on the display. "Hey, you okay?" he asked as soon as I picked up.

"Yeah, I mean. I don't know. I think so." My own voice seemed to carry in the silence.

"I wanted to come by last night to check on you, but the police were outside. I didn't want them to see me going to your house after they took all the statements," he said.

"No, that's fine. That's okay." I cleared my throat. "How are you?"

I heard him breathing into the phone. "It's crazy. I can't believe it. Did you see what happened?"

"No, I was back at the house. I'd left early."

"Me, too," he said. "As soon as the fireworks were over. I told the police that. I didn't see anything. Preston and his date barely made it through the fireworks show before leaving, too. Charlotte didn't see anything." A pause. "None of us did."

"You talked to them?" I'd gone straight back home on autopilot after giving my statement. Had walked upstairs and stood in the shower until my skin had begun to prune. Had found myself in her room after, in her bed, staring up.

"For a little bit, outside, yeah. After we gave our statements. Listen," he said, and his voice dropped, his mouth pressed closer to the phone. "No one said anything."

In the silence, I imagined what he was implying: my fight with Ruby; the things we'd said or at least insinuated; the way she'd turned on all of us, fingers pointed and accusations hurled.

"No one is *going* to say anything," he added, like a promise.

I felt a lump in my throat. Felt the memory of Charlotte's hand squeeze my shoulder, Preston chuck me under the chin, Chase lean against the gate beside me. "What happened to her? Did the police say anything?"

"No one knows. Maybe it was the alcohol. She was drinking so much she could barely stand. Tina said she had thrown up. And she was lying on her back . . ." His words trailed off, and I saw her there, head tipped back, the red glow of the fireworks reflecting on her exposed skin—

"And none of us checked," I said.

"Harper," he said, gentle and close, like he was propped up on one elbow beside me in bed. I closed my eyes, thinking how easy it would be to slide back into this. "Don't do this to yourself. You're a really good person, and you did all you could for her."

But I hadn't. I'd needed her gone. Told her she was a terrible fucking person. Wanted her far away and out of my life, never to return.

"What did she say to you down by the lake?" I asked, thinking that whatever she'd confided to him there were the last words she'd ever spoken.

"Nothing really," he said, but I was picturing his arms wrapped around her, the way her body had folded into his. "She was drunk, and sad, and not really making any sense."

"Shit," I said, hearing the catch in my voice.

He sighed. "I'll come by tonight, okay? Help you go through her things? I'll even bring dinner."

The silence was messing with my thoughts—a buzzing in my head I couldn't contain, an emptiness that only seemed to expand. But Ruby's things were already packed up, and I'd ended things with Mac. I didn't want to go back. "I'm doing that now," I said. "But thanks for the offer."

The doorbell rang, jarring me back to the present. "I gotta go," I said before hanging up.

From my spot on the couch, I opened the laptop to see who

was out there. A man I didn't know stood on my porch, looking up at the camera—staring back.

I KNEW THEY'D BE coming.

The police had taken our statements the previous night when we were all out there, in the street. They'd looked at the angle of the houses, the corners of the clubhouse, asking if there was any footage.

But it was Margo who shook her head. Who explained it was a policy not to record at the pool, where we were half-dressed. Who shared that none of the houses on the street had a good angle anyway.

The group of officers from the Lake Hollow Police Department scanned the crowd of us, and we stared back, wide-eyed and silent. Every one of us understanding: She had died in plain sight, with no one noticing, in the one place there were no cameras, with no witnesses.

How very different from what the police had experienced after the Truetts' deaths. Where everyone here was a witness with something to say, something to share, something to prove.

So I was not surprised to see a man on my front step now. This man, so obviously part of the investigation with his gray button-down and black tie, regardless of the soaring temperature and humidity. This was where Ruby had been staying, and I'd told them as much last night.

When I opened the door, I tried to place him from the sea of faces last night. But he seemed out of place, a stranger. Last time, Chase Colby had been part of the investigating team—to put people at ease, we thought. But also, as we learned, to gain access. To share what he learned on the message board, send the detectives our way. To save the recordings we'd posted from our security cameras and forward them to his superiors.

"Ms. Nash?" the man said, rocking back on his heels. "I'm Jay Locke, a special agent with the Bureau of Criminal Investigation. We're with the state police. Can I have a moment of your time?" He looked to be about my father's age, silver hair streaking through the brown, a weathered face, sharp blue eyes.

"Yes, I'm Harper." I opened the door farther, but he lingered on the front porch. His shoes were a shiny black, unmarred, and a dark car with tinted windows was parked behind him at the curb.

He smiled. Then he leaned backward and jabbed a finger at the camera over my door, angled at the porch. "That record whenever there's movement?" he asked.

"No," I said. "It's a webcam. I can sign in to see who's on my porch when someone rings the bell, but not much else."

He nodded, then crossed the threshold, his shoes echoing on the hardwood. "Seems to be the preferred method of security around here. Several of your neighbors said the same about theirs."

I didn't know why he wanted access to my camera or anyone else's. Ruby hadn't left the pool last night. I pictured her again, lowered to the ground by Tina and Paul, and ran my hands over my arms, chasing away the chill.

Agent Locke extended his hand my way in a half-hearted gesture. "I'm sorry," he said. "I should've led with that. I'm really sorry for your loss."

I nodded, unsure what to say. I didn't deserve any condolences, wasn't sure her loss could be mine to grieve. The sharp sting of her death, exacerbated by the guilt that I could have prevented it—and something worse: the muted, whispered relief that she was gone.

"So, Ruby Fletcher was your roommate." He said it as a statement, though it looked like he was waiting for me to answer.

"She was staying with me," I clarified. *Roommate* implied an agreement, not that someone had taken up residence in your house with or without your consent. "Do you know what happened to her?" I asked. Mac had mentioned the alcohol, but I didn't know why an agent from the state police would be in my house, asking about camera footage.

"We're waiting on the autopsy report," he said. "In the meantime, I was hoping you might have some more insight about last night, as her roommate."

"Sorry, I really don't. I wasn't there when . . ." My gaze drifted out the front window, my words trailing off.

"Okay, so let me just make sure I've got it all down right," he said, pulling my attention back. "The guys last night got your statement, I know, but we like to do our own legwork at the BCI. So you left the party pretty early."

I nodded, a beat behind, realizing his statement was really a question and he was waiting for me to fill in the blanks. I heard the echo of Mac's words, promising that no one had said anything about our fight. "Yes, I was tired," I said, trying to appear at ease, standing several feet apart from this stranger in the foyer of my home.

He was watching me closely. "And where was she when you last saw her?"

I flinched. "On that lounge chair. The same chair. During the fireworks, I saw her there."

His gaze also went to the front window, eyes narrowing slightly, lines in his skin radiating outward. "How did you find out something had happened to her?"

"We have a neighborhood watch. Margo Wellman saw her after everyone was gone. Still lying there."

She'd been the one to tell the police last night. Her voice wavering, breath coming too fast, hands shaking. She said she'd seen Ruby lying on the lounge chair on the pool deck as she circled past on her first walk-through. Went to get Paul to tell Ruby to move. Didn't want to approach on her own. It was Paul who said something was wrong with Ruby. Who called 911 and told Margo to get help.

Agent Locke continued. "Yes, I heard about the neighbor on watch. She mentioned running to get someone else for help— Tina Monahan?"

"Yes, Tina is a nurse. Two doors that way." I jutted my thumb to the left.

"Makes sense, then, that Margo would stop here on the way back. With you being Ruby's roommate."

I nodded, not sure what he expected me to contribute. I was one of the first to leave the party—it was the only thing people seemed sure of. Last night, no one could agree who was the last to leave. Everyone took their things when the fireworks ended, then they scattered.

No one noticed Ruby? A question directed at the crowd last night.

A shrug. A glance passing from one to the other. Until Charlotte cleared her throat. *We had been doing our best to ignore that she was there . . .*

Agent Locke walked closer to the window, peering out, though the only thing visible was his car in the road and then the trees in the distance. "Do you know what she was drinking?" he asked.

And there it was, what Mac had been implying. A vast consumption of alcohol. I wondered if our neighborhood would be liable, since she'd died on our shared property. If *I* would be liable, since she was seen as my guest.

"She made sangria for the party," I said. "But I don't know."

Agent Locke let the silence stretch between us until the discomfort became something physical, like the tension between me and Ruby in this house, growing until one of us had to break it.

"There was a lot of press around her release," he said. "We're trying to trace Ruby's path since she'd been out, and since she'd been staying with you, we thought you might be able to help."

But it was clear now how little Ruby had confided in me. "Ask her lawyer," I said. "I think they've been in contact."

"Blair Bowman, right. Thing is, she's had a hard time keeping track of her. Said Ruby hadn't been returning her calls. The last time they spoke was after some news program that she'd been on."

I ran my hand across my neck, felt a wave of heat flush through me. Ruby had lied about needing my car to meet her. Of course she'd lied. Preston had seen my car on campus. And Chase believed she'd been here—that she'd tried to get into his house. What the hell had she been up to?

"Her lawyer didn't even know where she was staying." He stepped farther into the house. "Can I take a look at her things?"

"You can have them," I said. They were already in a suitcase. I'd searched the room myself—there was nothing there.

Agent Locke followed me up the steps, through the loft, to Ruby's room. I gestured to her suitcase on the other side of the room, but I remained at the entrance. The agent went in alone, moving slowly through the room, leaving large shoe prints in the carpet.

Koda leaped from the foot of the bed as the agent bent to look through the luggage. Agent Locke jolted as the cat darted from the room, giving me a wide berth as well.

"Jesus," he said, hand to heart. Then, peering closer, "Is all of this new?"

"Yes," I said. "She showed up without anything."

He sighed, hands on his knees, pushing himself back to standing. He took one last glance around the room. "Looks like she wasn't planning to stay long."

I watched as he stepped to the side, peering into the bathroom. And I held my breath, willing him not to look up. The money, tucked out of sight.

"She didn't tell me what she was planning," I said as he exited her room. And that, at least, was the truth.

Back downstairs, he handed me his card before leaving, in case I thought of anything else. I closed the door behind him and retreated from the window just as he turned around to look back. I watched him from the laptop on my couch as he opened his car door with one long glance in each direction, up and down the street. As if calculating something. And then I watched him sit in his car, unmoving, for five minutes. Then ten. Until I thought my video feed had frozen. I was on my way back to the front window to check when I finally heard the sound of the engine pulling away.

And then I grabbed my keys, locking up behind me. I knew what they were doing from the last time. They were making a time line. Sliding us all into place. They wanted to know what Ruby had been up to since her release, wanted to piece together her movements—and so did I. They must've been wondering—like all of us in the neighborhood of Hollow's Edge—why she'd come here at all. Why she'd come to *me*.

I knew why no one was going to say anything about the fight, and it wasn't just because they were protecting me. It was because of what Ruby had implied with her thinly veiled accusations. *A crime I didn't commit,* she'd said.

It had sounded like a defense at first, like she'd said to the police when they'd come to my door: *Tell them, Harper, tell them I didn't do it—*

I'd thought she had come here for revenge, and maybe that was true. But twisted inside that motive was something else at the heart, fueling it.

She'd come here to prove her innocence.

That's what she was implying as her eyes skated over all of us last night.

She'd come back to prove that someone else was guilty.

CHAPTER 17

RUBY HAD BEEN ON campus. With my car. With my keys.
Chase thought she'd been trying to get inside his house, too, in the days when we thought she'd been gone.

Which meant she was looking for something. And there was one place I could go to start tracing her path.

Campus remained eerily empty, the July Fourth holiday bleeding into the long weekend. At the staff entrance, I passed the security center building, the electric vehicles all lined up in a row, unused. Every lot I passed was empty, the wind whipping up the brittle leaves, scattered across the narrow road.

When I pulled into the lot behind my building, I half expected to see the white car again under the oak tree, but mine was the only car here. Maybe even on the entire campus, judging from the drive in.

Before entering the building, I peered through the glass panel beside the back door, but the motion lights remained off. I paused at the entrance when I stepped inside, taking it all in—trying to see things as Ruby might. This place where she once gave student tours, and joined me for lunch, and asked for advice, and smiled when Aidan stopped by to say hi.

Everything about her, a deception.

The lights flicked on one by one as I moved deeper inside. I moved fast, using my key for my office, imagining Ruby doing the same days earlier. How compliant I must've seemed to her. How easily manipulated. *Ruby in my house; Ruby in my car; Ruby in my place of work—*

Was there any part of my life she hadn't tainted?

Standing in the glass doorway to my private office, I tried to look for signs of her. But everything looked exactly as I thought I'd left it the week before. Only my mug on the blue bookshelf was off-center—HELLO THERE! now barely visible—but that had been my doing, when I'd watered the plant.

My desk was covered with files on prospective students and meeting notes and interdepartment communications. I kept nothing personal or private here. Nothing that would be of interest to Ruby. What would she have been here for if not for me? What did she think she would possibly find here? Evidence that I was not equipped to do my job? Proof that I did not measure up to Brandon Truett?

There was nothing else here except for a plant on the verge of dehydration and a closet full of junk: the detritus left behind from when Brandon Truett worked here. I couldn't think of a reason that would interest her, but I crossed the room, throwing open that closet door for the first time in months.

It was empty.

My breath left me in a quick gust. The closet was completely, totally, empty—except for a faintly stale scent, from disuse and uncirculated air. The file box where I'd stored the remnants from Brandon's desk, the photo of him and Fiona—all gone.

It had been so long since I'd looked in here that I couldn't say for sure. Couldn't tell whether the contents had disappeared sometime in the previous year, with Anna at reception, or the janitor, or someone with an attachment to Brandon Truett—or Ruby.

Absences were harder to find. Negatives harder to prove. To know for sure that it wasn't someone else, over the last year, who had gone through here and cleaned things out. To take the leap that it must've been Ruby.

But she'd definitely been here.

I remembered her expression when I had caught her outside on my way home with Mac—when I told her I'd been to work. The quick frown. The worry. Had she been concerned that I'd noticed what she'd done?

If that was true, then Ruby Fletcher believed there was something worth finding in Brandon's things. More important: She knew that the Truetts' deaths had not been solved with her conviction. Her words at the party were not empty threats. And she believed that, here, she might find some proof.

I pictured her again, the moment she arrived at the party last night—the knowing looks she gave everyone; the way she flaunted her presence; the things she said: that we had somehow conspired against her. That she knew what each of us had done.

It seemed like maybe she had found that proof after all. A note he'd scribbled in a margin, maybe. A photo slipped behind another in the photo frame. Something that had eluded meaning when we were all so focused on Ruby. Something out of my grasp still.

But whatever she'd taken from this closet must exist.

Whatever she'd uncovered must be able to be found.

SHE'D HIDDEN THINGS, YES, distrusting all of us who had wronged her. But there were only so many places she could keep things close by.

All of them in Hollow's Edge.

There were barely any signs of life outside by the time I returned home. No one running, or watering the grass, or talking out front. The pool was abandoned, with a black and red sign out front that I couldn't read but which must've declared the premises closed. I wondered if there were guidelines in the bylaws for this.

As I passed Charlotte's house, her front door opened. Chase slipped out, jogging down the steps, then paused on the sidewalk as he noticed me pulling into my driveway.

My mind was already three steps ahead, thinking through where Ruby might've left a box of Brandon's things that I hadn't yet uncovered—the bathroom cabinet, under my old tarp in the garage—so it took me a moment to realize Chase was waiting for me, standing in the Truett yard.

"What's going on?" I called, meeting him halfway, the overgrown grass itching my ankles.

"I tried your house a few minutes ago. Just missed you," he said, like we were friends. How death could alter everything, swing you from enemies to allies or the other way around. "Has someone from the BCI been by to talk to you?"

I was still trying to figure out how Agent Locke fit in. But Mac had implied we were together in this. All of us on the same side.

"Yes," I said.

Chase nodded. "The local PD won't be allowed to handle it. Not with the lawsuit pending."

"Handle what?" I asked.

He glanced to the Truett house, the dark, empty windows, narrowing his eyes. "They suspect foul play," he said, leaning closer.

I blinked twice, trying to process. Foul play, such a generic euphemism. Downplaying the truth: *They suspect someone hurt Ruby. They suspect someone killed her.*

"Did they say how?" I asked, and I could hear the waver in my own voice. I pictured Ruby on the lounge chair, how she'd looked the night before, under the corner light. No blood. No signs of a struggle.

"This isn't official," he said with another glance to the Truett house. "Just friends on the job. Small town, you know?" I nodded, urging him on. "They suspect she was poisoned."

I stepped back, hand to my mouth, something churning in my stomach. Could taste the vodka from yesterday, the acid rising, the scent of chlorine in the back of my throat.

"Shit," Chase mumbled, stepping closer even as I backed away. "Look, it's not official, right? Just something I heard. I wasn't sure if I should say anything, but I didn't want anyone to be caught off guard by it if they hear from somewhere else."

I shook my head. "No, right, thank you for telling me." I stepped back again, itching to be inside, behind the closed door, all the dangers held at bay.

He rocked back on his heels, hands in his pockets. "What did he ask you?"

"What?" I asked. "Who?"

"The guy from the BCI."

"Nothing," I said. Then I shook my head. "Just where I last saw her. How I found out. He wanted to see her things, but there was nothing there." I swallowed. "He asked if my video feed records."

Chase's gaze went to the front of my door, where the camera was positioned.

"I told him no." Another step back, so I could get away from Chase and this conversation. "He asked what she was drinking. I told him she made sangria." I sucked in a gulp of air, heard myself wheezing. "I thought it was because she drank too much. I thought she had died because none of us had checked on her . . ."

"Hey," he said, one hand at my shoulder, the closest I had ever been to Chase Colby. His breath, up close, smelled of mint and cigarettes. "There's nothing to be afraid of. But you should know that's what they're looking for. You don't have to talk to them, Harper. Remember that."

I blinked slowly, waited for him to remove his hand, back away. Wondering if he thought I had something to hide.

"Let's keep this between us," he said, but he gestured up and down the street. And I realized he'd been going door-to-door, telling each of us. Warning us.

I was shaken as I walked up the front steps. Couldn't steady my hand to unlock the front door until I'd leaned my forehead against the wood, taken deep breaths, counted to ten.

Inside, my plan had been to search the hidden corners of my house—see what she might've found in my office. But I only got as far as the kitchen.

I saw her purple insulated mug in the sink. The purple cup I had found abandoned on the concrete. That I'd rinsed out and drunk from when I'd been unable to find my own.

I pictured that moment last night when Tina had backed away from Ruby's body on the pool deck, kicking over the blue cup by her side.

The one that had belonged to me.

I couldn't breathe. I opened the fridge, pulling out anything Ruby had drunk from, anything she'd eaten, imagining all the places death could be hiding—all the ways she could've been poisoned. Desperately tossing any open containers. The wine, the orange juice, the open containers of fruit.

There was a second batch of sangria, and I poured that out, too—splashes of red staining the sink, chunks of fruit clogging the drain.

I washed everything down, let the faucet continue to run, scooping up handfuls of water and gulping them down to purge it all. But I couldn't shake it—a grit I could feel on my teeth; a taste I imagined on the back of my tongue.

I CHECKED THE GARAGE, every closet, each bathroom cabinet. Under the kitchen sink, the upper shelves in the laundry room, the small attic accessible through the pull-down steps over the loft.

But there was nothing hidden away. Nothing but dust and old paint cans and things I'd had no use for in all the years I'd lived here. I was starting to doubt myself, thinking that maybe that box in my office had been missing for months; that it hadn't been Ruby at all.

I was still searching the house, hoping some new alcove would reveal itself to me, when my doorbell rang, jarring me.

I peered out the front window, saw Mac standing on my porch with Chinese takeout in a white plastic bag and a haunted expression. He had a hat on, though it was dusk, and the dark circles under his eyes looked even more pronounced—like he hadn't slept, either.

I opened the door, and he sheepishly held up the bag of food. "I know you said you had already gone through her things, but I figured dinner couldn't hurt." He let himself in as I stepped to the side.

"Thank you. I don't think I can eat, though," I said.

"Then at least you'll be all set with leftovers," he said, giving me half a smile. He made himself at home in my kitchen, pulling the containers from the bag, taking two plates down from the cabinets. I was captivated by the way he kept moving, like the way we'd continued to celebrate at the party, everyone trying to push through to normalcy by persistence alone.

"She was poisoned," I said, in case he hadn't heard.

He paused, standing over my counter, spoon deep in the sweet-and-sour chicken. "They don't know for sure," he said. "They don't know what happened."

I felt nauseated, staring at the food. At him. "Chase said—"

He dropped the spoon, turned to face me. "Chase isn't even part of the investigation. Alcohol is a type of poisoning, right?"

"He said foul play," I whispered.

Mac took off his hat, ran a hand through his light brown hair. "Hey, I'm here, and Chase is going to take over for Tina on watch tonight. We're all safe, Harper."

But I didn't know how he thought that was true. All these deaths that had happened on our street. Maybe it was the degree of removal in them—as though there was nothing to fear if it wasn't where we could see it. As though that didn't make it something scarier at heart—that we couldn't see it coming; couldn't see where the danger might be hiding.

The poison; the carbon monoxide. As if someone preferred to kill without having to look at the victim while doing it. A level of deniability. Something that required the hand of fate, absolving you of guilt.

A car turned on; a death that could occur only if you kept on sleeping. Poison left for someone else; but it required the other person to consume it.

He stepped closer, hands on my shoulders, but I shook him off. "It's all horrible, but I'm not sure what else we can do right now other than eat dinner, go to sleep, face tomorrow."

We brought our plates to the kitchen table and ate in silence. Or rather, I watched him eat, and I moved the food around my plate. Nothing but the sound of utensils scratching against the dinnerware and the ticking of the mantel clock echoing through the room.

"Thanks for dinner," I said, standing from the table and clearing our plates.

"Do you want me to stay?" he asked, slowly rising from his chair. "I don't mean . . . I mean, I could just, stay. You look like you haven't slept."

"You don't look so hot yourself," I said, feigning levity. "Thanks, but I think I'm about to crash."

Because all I wanted was to be left alone. Alone with my fears. Alone to work it through. To trace each thread through the night of the party, as if something new would suddenly emerge.

Because as he was eating, I'd felt myself fracturing. My thoughts had disconnected from the present, circling back to the events of the last few days.

I saw Ruby again, holding her purple mug in the air—*The gang's all here!*

I couldn't stop my mind from taking the alternate path. Step by step, from the day Ruby had returned to the day she had died. *On the lounge chair, being lowered to the ground, my blue cup rolling across the concrete—*

Foul play.

Poison.

Working it through, day by day, to its inevitable end.

To the sudden fear that maybe this ending wasn't meant for her but for me.

SATURDAY, JULY 6

HOLLOW'S EDGE COMMUNITY PAGE

Subject: Meeting today

Posted: 8:02 a.m.

Charlotte Brock: For anyone who was at the party. Noon, at the Seavers'. Tell any neighbors not on the board. I'll be deleting this ASAP.

Preston Seaver: BYOB, friends

Tate Cora: Seriously, what the fuck is wrong with you?

Preston Seaver: Sorry, I deflect with humor

Charlotte Brock: Humor implies something is funny.

Javier Cora: I mean, I thought it was a little funny . . .

CHAPTER 18

NOTHING WAS ANY CLEARER by the morning. Whether I was safe; whether I was in danger.

Alone, in the middle of my kitchen, with the chill of the tile floor under my feet, the emptiness, the quiet—I felt the need to call someone. To tell someone else what was happening here and what I was afraid of. So someone would come looking for me should I disappear. So it wouldn't take a barking dog for people to realize that something was wrong.

My friends from work would be home from their trip by now, unpacking their luggage. But what could I say? *Ruby came back while you were gone, and now she's dead, and I'm afraid.* They'd missed too much, were too connected to Brandon. And my position at work made that type of confessional friendship no longer possible.

My dad had always been the person I went to for advice—I'd stayed primarily with him after my parents separated—but we'd distanced since Aidan. I couldn't stand that he was right. That he'd seen the worst in Aidan, and it had played out exactly as he'd predicted. When I called him after Ruby's arrest, I could feel his words, so close to the phone: *Jesus Christ, Harper, you've got to stop taking in people like this. You've got to cut out this affinity for people who walk all over you. And look now. Look who you were living with. I could've gotten a call from some stranger telling me my daughter is* dead—

He'd choked on his words, half anger, half fear, and I saw myself as my brother then. Understood that my father could never handle this sort of role, could not accept a future of uncertainty. He spoke like there were pieces of me that existed outside my own control. Forces at work that were always looking for a weakness. He seemed to feel that the world endangered you just by your existing within it, and it would look for your faults to exploit.

And I hadn't even told my mom about Ruby's arrest in the first place. Wasn't sure how much she knew, either from my father or from Kellen. I'd always worried she had too much on her plate with Kellen, and I'd never wanted to add to it.

I laughed to myself, close to delirium, thinking how the most unreliable person I knew was suddenly the only person I could trust.

Maybe this was why I'd told him about Ruby and the trial the first time, at Christmas. Maybe it wasn't the eggnog or the lack of sleep but this need for someone else to know—just like now. Maybe I'd needed someone else to tell me I had done the right thing. But instead, all I'd gotten was a questioning look, a questioning statement: *Shouldn't you be sure?* Something that had kept me from confiding in anyone else.

I held the phone with two hands as it rang. My stomach dropped as the call went to voicemail. I was about to leave a message when my phone chimed with an incoming text. Thinking it was my brother—*Why are you calling me so damn early, Harp??*—I hung up.

But it was from Charlotte: *Just making sure you saw the note on the boards about the meeting.*

How different things were now from last weekend. When I had been kept out of the loop, not part of their meetings.

I'll be there, I responded, dropping my shoulders back, starting the coffee.

I SPENT THE FIRST half of the day doing a deep clean, as if I could purge everything that had happened over the last week. Everything felt unsafe and stagnant, and this scent kept lingering as I cleaned—like wood and drywall. Like the bones of the house.

Just before noon, I saw Tina Monahan through the front window, arms crossed, head down as she strode quickly past my house, as if moving through a rainstorm.

I threw open the front door. "Hey," I called after her. "Wait up."

She flinched, then put her hand on her chest as she turned my way. A flush rose to her cheeks, in sharp contrast to the ashen tone of the rest of her face. "I didn't see you there," she said. "Sorry."

"You heading to the meeting?" I asked, jogging to catch up with her.

She nodded too fast, still flustered. "Sorry, everything's just . . ." She moved her hands around, searching for words.

"Yeah, me, too," I said.

Up close, her eyes were bloodshot and hollowed, her short hair was pulled back in a tight ponytail, her bangs clung to her forehead from the humidity. When she frowned, I could see the shadow of her father in her.

"I haven't had to do that before," she explained with a shudder. "Guess I should count myself lucky that I made it this far without . . ."

I placed a hand on her shoulder briefly, remembering the nightmares I had after we found the Truetts. The image I couldn't shake of them in their bed, faces turned toward each other. The unearthly stillness that looked neither peaceful nor real. I wondered what image would haunt Tina.

"Your parents okay?" I asked, walking side by side with her toward the Seaver brothers' place on the corner.

She took a slow breath in, then let it out. "As okay as any of us, I guess. My mom wants us to move. Like that's an option right now. She's demanding an alarm system, at the very least." She paused and squeezed her eyes shut at the base of the Seavers' front porch steps. "I can't believe this is happening again."

The front door opened above us, and Charlotte appeared in the entrance, like she was the hostess. "Tina, Harper. Good, come on in."

I wondered if she had an attendance list. She was the only one of the three of us who didn't look like she'd been through hell since the last time we saw one another.

When I stepped inside, a small group was already gathered in the family room, hovering between the sofas and the television, like some awkward middle school party. Chase sat on the arm of the sofa, glancing periodically out the side window like he feared someone might be watching.

Mac waved me over from the kitchen, where he was opening a beer. For however much he was trying to channel calm and controlled, his hand was shaking as he twisted off the cap.

"Sleep okay?" he asked.

"No. You?"

He tipped his head in camaraderie, then raised the bottle of beer to his mouth.

Tate and Javier Cora arrived next—all of us always prompt to Charlotte's meetings, lest we be judged accordingly. I wasn't sure what we were doing here. People whispered. Cleared throats. Avoided direct eye contact.

"Was this Charlotte's idea?" I whispered to Mac.

"No," he said.

Just then, Margo came through the door, drawing attention.

Nicholas was on her hip, complaining—something between a whimper and a wail—and she had a diaper bag slung over her other shoulder. "Sorry I'm late," she said to Charlotte, her neck turning a blotchy red.

"Where's Paul?" Charlotte asked, peering out the front door before pushing it shut.

"He's busy! Can't always drop his life at a moment's notice for you, Charlotte." Margo's voice carried through the quiet of the house, and we all watched as her free hand went to her hair, then to the baby.

Even Charlotte seemed caught off guard by Margo's reaction. Charlotte must've touched a nerve because Margo suddenly appeared on the verge of tears. "I don't know," Margo said. "He's just . . . stressed. And apparently, I'm part of that stress, expecting too much, so I'm just trying not to ask *too much* of him right now, to hold everything together, but—"

"Okay, come inside, come on," Charlotte said, ushering her further into the house, lowering her voice accordingly. She took the baby from Margo, parked him on her hip. "Go on to the bathroom," she said, gesturing to the powder room at the base of the stairs. *Pull yourself together,* the implied message.

There was no room for us to fall apart now.

Charlotte pulled out her phone with her free hand, a move she must've made before. "Come get Margo's baby, please," she said. After a beat, she rolled her eyes, hardened her voice. "No, you are not being paid, for the love of *God,* Whitney." She hung up and sighed, smiled tightly when she saw me looking. "Two teenagers will be the death of me, I swear." Then she froze, her shoulders stiffening. "Sorry. That wasn't funny."

Charlotte watched through the blinds of the front window until Whitney hopped up the steps. Charlotte met her at the front door, passing Nicholas into Whitney's outstretched arms just as Margo returned from the bathroom.

"Oh," Margo said, hands held awkwardly in front of her, like she was reaching for something.

Charlotte pushed the front door shut, put a hand on Margo's shoulder. "No worries. Come. Relax. You can pick him up after at my place. The girls will keep an eye on him."

Margo's gaze trailed after Whitney through the dining room window, but she nodded, following Charlotte into the Seavers' living room.

There were two brown leather sofas with matching ottomans, all angled toward the large-screen television over the fireplace. The layout of their house was almost identical to mine, except in mirror image, and they'd closed in the upstairs loft, turning it into a third bedroom, which they used as a shared office.

Mac had saved me a spot beside him on the couch. Tate and Javier were on the sofa beside ours, Tate looking slightly more nauseated than normal. Tina squeezed in beside Tate, and Tate winced as she shifted to make room.

"When are you due again?" Tina asked, like we were here for a friendly catch-up.

"Three more months," Tate answered.

Charlotte seemed to be waiting for something. "Is this everyone who was at the party?" she finally asked, eyes skimming over all of us.

We looked at one another, each performing a silent tally.

"Not Pete," Javier said. "Or the Wilsons." Those must've been the people who'd left as soon as Ruby arrived.

"I meant the people who were there . . . during the fireworks," Charlotte amended.

"Preston's not back yet," Mac said.

"Well," Charlotte said. "You can fill him in later. Go ahead, Chase."

Tina's parents weren't here, either, but no one mentioned that, not even Tina.

Chase stepped to the front of the living room, and Charlotte took his place, perching on the armrest. Apparently, Chase had worked his way back into our good graces, too. How we needed him. How we welcomed him.

"Some of you may have noticed the agents from the state police," he said.

At that moment, the front door opened, and Preston walked in, then stopped abruptly in his tracks at the sight of us.

"Where've you been?" Mac called.

"With Madalyn. Sorry I'm late." The second statement was directed Charlotte's way.

Chase gestured for Preston to join us in his own living room. "As I was saying, there are agents from the state police who've been going door-to-door, asking questions. Preston, what's going on with Madalyn?"

"Well, she's totally freaked. I told her to go home for a little while. There's nothing for her to say anyway. She didn't see anything."

"She's a student?" Tate asked, cutting her eyes at him.

His jaw tensed. "Grad student. But yeah, she's going back home to Ohio for a little while, I think."

"She okay with it?" Chase asked. I couldn't keep up with the conversation. I felt like I had just walked in instead of the other way around.

Preston nodded, then addressed the rest of us. "Madalyn wasn't feeling well, so we left early," he said, and it took me a minute to understand what he was saying. That she didn't see anything. That none of us did. That she wouldn't discuss any fight with the police or the things Ruby had said—the way she had turned on us all.

Chase nodded. *Keep it simple.* Keep it contained. For once, I was on the inside.

"The agent came to our house yesterday," Tate piped in. "We didn't answer the door."

Tina nodded in agreement. "My mom answered the door, so we had to talk to him. Just gave him the general rundown." She flicked her hand like we'd all been through it. Knew what she had seen, what she had said.

Margo raised her hand and started speaking. "I'm sorry, is no one going to mention the *foul-play* suspicion? We were all there. We were all witnesses."

"What are we supposed to say?" Mac responded. "I sure didn't notice anything."

"Well, it looks pretty fucking suspicious that we were all there, and no one saw a damn thing," Tate said. Her eyes flicked from person to person, challenging us.

This was how it began. When we started to winnow down the group, deciding whom it would be. Whose image would first raise suspicion when it appeared on one of our security cameras. Whom we were willing to feed to the masses. Did they even see what they were doing?

"Listen," Mac said, the first time I'd heard him take control of anything, "it was a public event. It's not like we live in some gated community. We've all noticed things happening on watch."

"Javier, you said you heard people down at the lake on your shift, right?" Margo asked.

Javier nodded. "There were definitely people out during my shift at night. And Tate heard something the night you were on watch, too, Harper. Right, Tate?"

"Yep," Tate said. "At like two-forty-five, a loud noise somewhere out front. I'm getting to the point where I can't sleep, anyway."

Was this how it really was? Were these truly the people I lived beside? I could feel it, this idea gaining momentum, that the danger was *out there* and not in this very room. Just like Ruby had claimed in her own denial. *Someone else was out there. Someone else did it.* It didn't have to be one of us. We didn't have to look at one another and wonder.

"We were ignoring her, mostly," Charlotte said, and everyone nodded, though that wasn't true. Maybe we'd tried to, but we hadn't ignored her—we couldn't, when she'd turned so clearly on all of us.

But there was something so alluring to it, a momentum I couldn't stop. Something I wanted to be part of. An idea we could develop together, a puzzle we could solve, each of us with our own small piece. An image we could bring to light only collectively. Something that seemed suddenly possible.

Because we were friends and colleagues. Had known each other for years. Mowed each other's yards when we were injured; thrown baby showers and graduation parties; pulled in the garbage cans when people were working late. We knew each other—we knew more about each other than any of us cared to admit.

"There were footprints at the pool," I said, "the night I was on watch." The gate swinging open. Footprints disappearing at the black pavement. "And a car driving off behind our homes." I thought about that white car again—the one at the office. Who might've had cause to go there. "What about Brandon's brother?" I was grasping, but it was another possibility. Someone who might've been keeping an eye on Ruby. Who might've been angry about her release.

Tate nodded. Finally, I was on the inside as we cast our suspicions outward.

"Listen," Javier said, "I say we make a pact. No one tells them anything. No rumors or gossip. You know how it goes, right? We were all together. We can all vouch for each other. Let's not complicate things."

And I now understood what Chase had meant when he said

not to dilute the evidence with rumors we couldn't prove. The answers were simple. There was no great conspiracy. The simplest answers were most often the right ones.

Everyone seemed to be in agreement as I looked around the room. Even though the simplest answer, we all knew, was that someone here had done it.

Maybe it was because we each understood. There was a collective motive, and the focus could turn to any one of us. We had each testified. We were each afraid. We were protecting each other as much as ourselves.

We were just ignoring her, going on with our lives. We don't know what happened. We didn't see.

We were all good people here.

MARGO WAS THE FIRST to leave, heading for Charlotte's to pick up Nicholas. I had started paying attention to things like this—who was leaving and who was staying. The order in which we arrived and left.

Several others stuck around to talk to Chase one-on-one. The bathroom by the stairs was occupied, but there were two upstairs, and I headed that way so I could catch Chase after, ask if he'd heard anything more from his friends—whether they were sure it was poison. Whether I had cause to be afraid.

Mac had the master bedroom with its own bathroom, the mirror image of my own. But when I went to let myself in his room, the door was locked. I guessed he had done this knowing there would potentially be a large meeting downstairs. But I found it odd.

The door to their converted office was ajar, connecting to Preston's room through the Jack-and-Jill bathroom. I peered inside the office space, but his bathroom door was closed on the other side.

It felt like an invasion to use his private bathroom. Especially since we weren't particularly friendly.

I heard the front door close and was about to return downstairs when a balled-up piece of paper caught my eye. It lay beside a metal trash can under the long table used as a shared desk. As if the paper had just missed.

But it was what I could see through the page that caught my eye. The bold black print. Something so familiar about it. I dropped to my hands and knees under the desk and gently unfurled the sheet of paper, flattening it against the beige carpet.

My hands began to shake as the three words stared back at me, a quick chill in the silence: I SEE YOU.

The same format as the warning I'd received with the photos tucked inside. As if other versions had been printed out here and decided against.

I balled it back up, dropped it in the trash can, stumbled down the staircase. I didn't know if anyone saw me barreling through the front door. If any of the cameras caught me stumbling toward home. My flip-flops catching on a sidewalk square before I regained my footing.

I had to slow my breath, slow my heart rate. Get inside my house and regroup.

But my stomach churned over the thought of Mac. Of Mac, who had been in my house, whom I had let inside my life—

I threw open the front door, barely enough time to notice the square of paper wedged into the door. It flopped to the floor, the photo facedown.

Not again. Not this. I was still thinking of Mac, but I had just been with him the entire time.

Preston, though. Coming into the meeting late. Preston, who had ample time to leave this here.

Not Mac, then. But his brother.

The sheet of paper with that same bold print I'd seen beside the garbage can: HELLO THERE! Friendly and ominous at the same time. Like the mug behind my desk at work.

I picked up the photo, feeling nauseated. My hands shook. It was so clear. The trees and the lake and the dog-bone key chain. The Nike swoosh on the side of the sneaker, the ponytail, the face caught in profile. Looking to the side to make sure there was no one watching.

That first message: YOU MADE A MISTAKE.

The second: WE KNOW.

They were right, of course. I had made a mistake.

Anyone who saw this picture would know.

Anyone could see it was me.

CHAPTER 19

THEY WEREN'T MINE.

That was the defense I had worked through, sitting in my backyard patio, key ring in hand. What I'd tell the police. What I'd tell the neighbors.

They weren't *mine.*

But they'd been in my house, and my fingerprints were all over them, and this wasn't just the Truett key. Oh, no. If only it had been, maybe I would've called someone, turned them in.

But this was something more, and I heard the echo of Chase's advice, his low words through the fence: *Keep it simple.*

Get them out of the house.

Away from you.

Now.

I'D FOUND THEM THREE months ago, in the spring, planting flowers in the mulch bed of my patio. Spade in the soil, digging beneath the mulch into the cool earth.

My shovel struck something hard six inches down—something I thought at first was an accumulation of small stones. But I reached my gloved hand into the soil, and my fingers hooked into a ring. A glint of metal in the sun as I pulled it out.

A large ring of keys, deliberately hidden in the corner of the garden.

That dog-bone key chain was the first thing I recognized, attached to a larger ring by a small loop. But the large ring was full of keys. Each labeled with a small black letter written in Sharpie.

I pieced through them one by one, wiping the dirt and grit from the surface of each key to reveal what was written below.

The *T,* the *B,* the *S,* the *C* . . . I was halfway through the key ring before the realization settled in: that these were the keys to other houses on the street. The *T* for Truett; the *B* for Brock; the *S* for Seaver; the *C* for Cora. On and on they went.

I didn't know what this meant. Why Ruby had all of these keys. I assumed she'd hidden them during the investigation after denying she'd had the Truett key. Asking me to back her up, to tell the police: *I don't have their key anymore.*

A bold-faced lie, while she buried the truth.

Not only did she have the Truetts' key, she also had the keys of nearly everyone on the street. And they probably had no idea.

I could only imagine that this was an accumulation of keys she had amassed over the years, living here. From all her time walking dogs, or bringing in mail, or house-sitting. The keys that were left for her under doormats, or spares that were temporarily lent her way. Either she hadn't returned the keys, or she'd copied them. My guess: copied them. So that no one knew she had them anymore.

But these were also more keys than I thought she'd had access to. There were plenty of people who had never trusted Ruby, wouldn't have left her in possession of a key. But we were all connected here. Access to one house could grant her access to another—a neighbor's spare key, for emergency, labeled and hung on a key hook on the wall or in a kitchen drawer.

Years ago, Tate and I had swapped keys in case one of us was ever locked out. Though our friendship had cooled, we'd never asked for them back. Such an admission would be too direct. Too confrontational. And so Tate and Javier Cora's key was still buried at the back of the top drawer of the entryway table, should they ever need it.

Ruby had plenty of chances to find it, copy it, use it. From the look of it, she had gotten us all. Every one. And now this set of keys was in my hand.

I'd debated what to do with the ring of keys that day, sitting on the brick patio, as the late afternoon turned to evening. And then I thought of the lake, of fingerprints disappearing—a hand of fate that might or might not drag them to the surface someday in the future, freeing me of any role or suspicion.

So I'd headed that way in the dark, passing the closed front doors, the glow of porch lights. The jangle of keys in my pocket was too jarring in the quiet night. I'd clenched them tightly in my palm, cut down the path in the woods by the pool, heading toward the water. Believing I was alone.

But someone had seen me. Someone had stood at the back corner of the concrete pool deck, watched as I ran by—and caught me.

NOW I KNELT ON the cold wooden floor of the front foyer, this photo in hand, with all the things I knew it could imply—all the ways it could be twisted against me. Wondering why someone was taunting me with this and what they were planning to do with it now.

Though Preston and Mac shared that upstairs office space, Mac had been with me at the meeting. He'd already been there when I arrived. It was Preston who came in late. Who had time to leave this threat in my door.

Preston had been so quick to turn on Ruby after the Truetts were found dead. And when Ruby was gone, his distrust seemed to transfer to me, by rule of proximity alone.

Preston, who had been at my place of work, watching me. Preston, who had a master set of keys at work. Who had printed other warnings in his office, the I SEE YOU crumpled under his desk. Preston, who lived three doors down, who had walked straight through my front door when I'd been out on watch.

I'd thought these warnings had been to try to push me to get Ruby to leave. A threat that, if I did not, this could be revealed—to others, to Ruby herself.

But Ruby was gone now, and this newest picture had still arrived. And I no longer knew whom I could trust.

I didn't know whether Mac was a part of this somehow. I didn't know how much the brothers shared with each other, whether family mattered above all else. I felt entirely afraid and alone.

I was remembering the way Mac came over at the start of summer break, beer in hand, crooked smile on his face—the coincidence of his timing. Whether the rumors of Ruby's case had brought him to my front door once more. And if so, what he was truly after.

I called my brother again, sitting on the cold floor of the foyer, the photo in my hand.

This time he answered on the first ring. "Harper? Is it Dad?"

"Sorry, no, everyone's okay," I said.

"Oh," he said. "Good." He paused for a beat. "It's just, you've called twice on a Saturday. I have a missed call from you from earlier." Our calls were infrequent, our relationship existing primarily on holidays and via parent updates.

"What kind of person would you say I am?" I asked abruptly. I was staring at a photo of evidence I'd hidden. Had listened as Ruby called me an opportunist, unable to be happy as myself.

"Are you drunk?" he asked as answer.

"No. Just if you had to describe me to a friend. Like *My sister is . . .*"

"The good one," he said without pause.

"Ha," I said.

I heard his sigh through the phone. "I guess I would say: *I wish I knew her better growing up, but I fucked up our family pretty good. I would say: She gave me more chances than I deserved, and she's a better person than me.*"

I'd forgotten this about my brother: that he was direct and honest, always trying to atone for himself but unable to stop the cycle. I was wrong—nothing existed in him that reminded me of the true Ruby.

In the silence that followed, he said, "Is everything okay? You're not having some sort of breakdown, are you?"

"Well," I said, thinking of how to even begin. How to present this without inviting judgment. And then I stopped worrying. It was my brother, and I'd seen him at his worst, and maybe it was only fair that he saw me at mine. "The verdict in my neighbors' murder was thrown out."

"Oh, shit," he said.

"Ruby came back here. To my *house.* It was a mess, and she's dead." Silence on the other end. "The police think she was poisoned."

More silence.

"Hello?" I asked.

"Are you in trouble?" he asked, quick and low.

"No." A pause. "I don't think so. I don't know. Kellen, my God, it's all horrible." A horrific mess, with three people dead and an investigation just beginning.

"You should come visit me."

I laughed. "I don't need Mom breathing down my neck right now, too."

"No, I've got a new place. God, it's been a while, Harp." Our last real conversation was the one on New Year's Eve, I thought now. Over seven months with neither of us reaching out. "I'm in Philadelphia," he said. "Well, close to Philadelphia."

"What?" That was six hours away.

"Long story. But I have a job here, and other than dealing with Mom's constant calls, it's a pretty quiet time." *Quiet times* was the term Mom used for his good times. As if *quiet* were a positive thing and not an immense blanket of deception covering what was potentially brewing below.

But I was stuck on his prior statement. "You moved to a new city, you're only six hours away, and you didn't tell me?"

"I don't want to impose."

"You wouldn't be," I said.

"You weren't always thrilled to see me when I came to visit Dad . . ."

Because my dad expected too much of Kellen, was never able to let the past go. He'd bring it up somehow—on day two or day three—and I'd have to watch my brother harden, never able to exist in the present. "Not because of you," I said.

"Well," he said, "I also don't have a car right now, either."

I laughed then, remembering how his excuses always existed in layers. But knowing I could reach him in a day's drive if needed. "I'll call you later," I said. "It's good to hear your voice. Just don't tell Mom and Dad, okay?"

He laughed then, too. "Harper, it is my absolute pleasure to begin repaying that debt to you."

And then I pushed myself off the floor with that photo in hand. I wondered what Ruby felt the first day when she was home, reaching her hand deep into the soil—coming up empty.

The first day Ruby was back, even before she'd gone to the kayak for the money, she'd gone into the backyard in the middle of the night and reached her hand down into the dirt, looking for this.

I was seeing her more clearly now: She wanted access to all of us here—our secrets, our lives.

When I'd found the keys this spring, Ruby had already been gone for so long. She had been convicted.

Back then I'd wondered what she had been doing with those keys. Whether she used them to piece through our lives, stirring up gossip with a throwaway line—if our discomfort had been all for her entertainment.

Chase told me the guys had wanted to bring up the rumors they knew but couldn't prove during the investigation. And now I was thinking again about the way Aidan had left, so fast, desperate to escape something.

Chase was right: She had always been dangerous, just not in the way I had assumed.

I remembered Preston telling the police that Ruby had once been inside, broken dishes, while Mac and she were fighting. And Fiona looking in her wallet, confused. How everyone was quick to throw suspicion on Ruby after her arrest, in a myriad of ways. The access she had, not just to our things but to our secrets.

They sleep in separate rooms, you know, she had said about the Truetts. And none of us asked how she knew. None of us doubted the veracity of her claim, either.

Because we all believed that Ruby knew things. We just didn't always know how.

IF PRESTON TOOK MY photo as I ran down to the lake, I wondered if he knew what I'd done with the keys. If he'd seen me after, as I stood at the edge of the lake, surrounded by the noises of the night, moonlight glinting off the metal.

If he'd seen that I had not tossed them into the water at all, afraid of the sudden openness, the currents, the cameras that might place me down here. The way beer cans washed up the morning after kids had tossed them from their boats at the mouth of the inlet.

How I'd gone deeper into the woods instead, letting the darkness protect me, the noises insulate me. Farther around the inlet, where I believed that no one could see or hear me. To the boundary of our woods, with the sign on the tree warning us: PRIVATE PROP-ERTY.

The roots of that tree were thick and exposed from the soil, and I'd used my bare hands to dig out a spot at the base of the gnarled trunk. Then I'd wiped the keys carefully of any prints before depositing them in the earth, and pushed the dirt back over the top, dispersing the leaves and the twigs.

Ruby had buried them, and so had I. But out in the woods, they couldn't be traced back to me.

And then I'd kept going, to the other side of the inlet. Through the trees, with the dense underbrush, to the plot of land cleared but never built upon. A dusty circle of dirt with the remnants of an old campfire in the center, though all that remained was ash in a pit.

The dirt access road dipped and curved, marred by large rocks and mangled roots, and my footing was unsure in the dark. But in that dark, from the distance, I could see the lights from our neighborhood through the trees. I cut through the woods, hands in front of me, until I emerged across the street from the house on the corner where Tina Monahan and her parents lived.

I returned home from the other end of our street, feeling lighter, like I had rid my life of the last of Ruby Fletcher.

But in that moment, for the first time, I could see how she did it: The keys, to the Truett house, to the lake. The woods, to the clearing, to the access road, following the lights home. Sneaking around back to hide what she had done.

In that moment, a year after her arrest, months after her conviction, I finally believed she had done it.

I HAD NO IDEA if the keys remained, especially if Preston had seen me down there. And now I feared that someone might've had access to our homes all along—finding that key ring for themselves.

I had to wait for dusk, though we still had a neighborhood watch going. It was supposed to be Charlotte's turn tonight.

It was easy enough to wait for her on my webcam. To watch as she passed my house on her way back home.

Thirty minutes later, I went out, locking the door behind me.

I did not try to remain hidden; that never worked out for us here. I strode right in front of the homes, right past the cameras— *just taking a walk,* like Ruby once claimed.

At the Seaver brothers' home, I saw flashes of the television screen through the blinds. I turned at the path across from Margo and Paul Wellman's house, remembering the camera that had caught Ruby running. I walked slowly down the dirt path, careful not to make much noise. But I turned my face to the pool as I passed by, imagining someone standing there once before, watching me. Now the pool appeared vacant.

To my left, the noise in the underbrush, down at the water's edge, grew louder. A cacophony of insects and animals that drowned out my footsteps. Trying to keep myself hidden, I used the light from my phone only once to judge the way.

I had just reached that sign, my fingers brushing over the warped metal edges, the nail protruding from the trunk, reminding us to keep away, when I heard footsteps echoing over the plywood on the path in the distance.

I ducked down, stared back, and saw the outline of long hair and long legs in fragmented glimpses through the trees. I thought it was either Whitney or Molly, and I remained perfectly still, hoping she hadn't seen me—and wouldn't ask what I was doing down here, in the woods, in the dark.

She moved closer, her steps resounding on the plywood, not trying to remain hidden at all. She seemed to stare directly at me. "Whitney," she said. "Whitney!" A little louder this time. She took out her phone and used the flashlight to illuminate the area to my right, down by the water.

I held my breath, and she took another step—off the plywood path, into the rougher terrain. This was Charlotte, then, thinking her daughter was out here in the woods.

A sharp peal of laughter echoed off the water—high-pitched and fast—before being smothered by the other noises. The crickets and frogs, a low buzzing that seemed too loud for an insect.

"Shit," Charlotte mumbled. I could see her clearly now, illuminated by the screen of her phone. She held the phone to her ear, but no one must've picked up on the other end. "I see you out there," she said before hanging up.

She stood there, hands on hips, staring into the darkness over the water, before turning back for home.

My eyes had adjusted to the dark, and I could see the shadow of a boat out there in the moonlight. Whitney and her friends, then. What Javier must've heard, his night on watch. If only Charlotte would've told him as much—that it was probably Whitney out there—we wouldn't have thought it was someone keeping an eye on Ruby.

The pool gate at midnight, footsteps trailing away, the car driving off: They could all be traced to a group of teenagers, bored in the summer.

There was truly no one else to blame out here. There was only us.

I was tracing my hands over the roots of the tree, making my way to the base of the trunk, when I heard someone cough. Closer than the kids on the lake.

I stood slowly, staring out at the water, looking for movement. Another one of their friends, maybe, planning to meet them out there.

At the other side of the inlet, I thought I saw the shape of a man. But I couldn't be sure. He did not call out to them, but the shadow moved slowly and deliberately, as if trying to remain undetected.

None of us was alone out here.

So much for this quiet little neighborhood. All of us were alive, at night, in the dark. All the things we needed to keep hidden during the day, set loose at night, when we revealed ourselves.

From the distance, I couldn't tell if the person at the edge of the lake had seen me, too. If they were turned my way even now. A prickle on the back of my neck, and I ducked down quickly, with the sudden feeling that he was looking straight at me, too.

I held my breath and scratched my nails at the surface, tearing away chunks of compacted dirt. Then I reached my hand down into the cooler earth, deeper, deeper, panicked that I was wrong, that I'd forgotten, that time or animals or someone else had been here first. That rainwater had washed it away. But my index finger brushed something cold and curved.

I hooked my fingers into the ring and pulled.

SUNDAY, JULY 7

HOLLOW'S EDGE COMMUNITY PAGE

Subject: Did you all see this?

Posted: 12:30 a.m.

Margo Wellman: Just saw this article—THIRD SUSPICIOUS DEATH IN LAKE HOLLOW NEIGHBOR-HOOD. Anyone else seriously considering moving right now?

Javier Cora: What do you think this does for property values? Asking for a friend.

Charlotte Brock: This is in really poor taste. Go to sleep.

CHAPTER 20

I T WAS ONE A.M. and the key ring lay before me on the kitchen table, drying on a heap of paper towels, after I'd run them under the sink—mud and sludge and dirt sliding down the drain. I went through the labels more carefully this time, making a list of each key:

> *T—Truett (Tina?)*
> *B—Brock*
> *S—Seaver*
> *M—Monahan (Margo? Mac?)*
> *C—Cora? Chase Colby?*

I was betting on the letter being the initial of the last name; it seemed to be a pattern that fit with each name, though there were some with more than one possibility. And there was one easy way to check—as long as the bank hadn't changed the locks after taking ownership of the house next door.

There was no way I was going to be caught out front, trespassing at the Truett house. Not with the cameras and people walking by, the neighbors not sleeping, watching out their windows

247

instead. Not when the police were questioning us and what we were each doing. Charlotte might still be on watch, and I'd already evaded her once.

I knew the Truett fence had somehow become unlocked; I'd seen it swinging ajar my night on watch. As if someone else had been in there.

Maybe someone was able to jimmy it with a golf club from above.

I left through my back patio, but in the dark, I collided with the white Adirondack chair on the way to the gate, forgetting that Ruby had moved it from the other side of the yard. I cursed to myself, hoped Tate and Javier hadn't heard me—or the wood scraping against the brick patio—then hoped they didn't hear my own gate creaking open in the stillness. Tate had said noises woke her the last several nights, that pregnancy was starting to affect her ability to sleep.

I latched the gate carefully behind me, then peered once into the trees before sliding along the edge of the fence to the back gate of the Truetts' house.

Their gate was easy to unlatch from the outside, without the lock engaged. But the squeal of the hinges through the night made me cringe. I left it ajar, so as not to create any more noise than necessary. Charlotte's house was just on the other side, and her master bedroom was downstairs, near the back.

Key ring in hand, I walked up their patio steps. I slid the *T* key into the lock, but it was unnecessary. I could tell before even attempting to turn the key. The handle moved freely, and the dead-bolt lock had sharp gouges around the edges. So did the wooden strip where the door met the frame.

I twisted the key back and forth, just to check, but it wasn't working. Either it wasn't the key for this house, or the bank had indeed changed the locks.

But someone had been inside here. From the look of the dead-bolt and surrounding wood, someone had forced their way in.

I ran my finger along the deep grooves, the wood splintered in sections. Wondering who had been in here. If they'd tried to force their way into my place, too.

I'd noticed the unlatched gate here a few nights ago. My own gate had also come unlatched, swaying loose in the wind, though I was always careful to keep it locked. It seemed likely that both had been opened by the same person. Like someone was spying on each place. Or like someone was moving back and forth between our patios.

Ruby had gone out back the first night she was here—I'd heard that creak of the back door. And the next morning, she'd been sitting in the Adirondack chair, her feet up on the wooden ottoman, while Tate and Javier were arguing next door.

She'd moved the chair, I thought, for the single square of sunlight on the patio. But maybe she'd moved it sometime in the night. The base of the chair was solid wood, and the arms were sturdy, and it was now positioned just beside the Truett fence.

Maybe, after looking for the keys and finding them missing, she'd decided to find a way in by any means necessary.

I shook the fence between our properties to check for stability. It didn't budge. These fences were meant to withstand storms and wind and wear and accidents, connecting from yard to yard, reinforcing the strength.

I felt a chill running down the length of my arms, up my back. Like she was here with me now. Of course it was her. It was always her.

I could picture her clearly, her determination: Unlocking my back gate, to be able to return after. Dragging the chair to the other side of my patio, perching on the base, climbing on the armrest, slinging a leg over the sturdy flat-top posts of the fence, falling to the bricks on the other side, where I now stood.

The marks around the deadbolt—my knife in her hand to wedge her way inside.

Ruby had been here, I was sure. Ruby had gotten inside.

I walked up the brick steps again, twisting the handle, following her trail. Desperate to know what she had found, what she had discovered.

The door pushed open on the first try.

Inside, I was hit by a wave of thick humidity and uncirculated air. I flipped the switch on the wall, but nothing happened. The electricity had long since been cut. And with that, the air-conditioning and any hope of circulating air. I breathed shallowly into my sleeve, like I'd done that day when we'd found them.

Shadows emerged from the darkness as my eyes slowly adjusted. Random pieces of furniture that had been left behind after Brandon's brother had either sold or donated what he could—a hard-backed chair against the wall, a coffee table in the middle of the room, a stool at the kitchen counter—creating the skeleton of a house.

Even breathing into my arm, there was something off about the smell. Everything in this house reeked of wrong.

I used the light on my phone to guide the way, looking for any signs of an intruder here. But the silence and the stillness had their own presence.

I passed the kitchen window that I'd once thrown open in a panic. I kept the light pointed down so no one would see me in here.

Next, the garage door, where Chase had yelled for me to hit the automated opener—the responding mechanical hum painfully slow in the chaos—while Charlotte had run for the living room windows, throwing open the back door, too.

I followed the hallway, swooping my light up to the ceiling, to that small, discolored circle where the carbon monoxide detector had once been. The stairs to the right, where I'd followed Chase.

I'd found him at the foot of their bed. I'd never forget the look on his face. Sometimes I couldn't look at Chase without picturing them, too. I couldn't imagine why anyone would want to break in here now. Especially Ruby.

At the end of the hall, the scent suddenly changed. It became something beachy, more fragrant. A scent to mask another smell. The closer I moved to the front of the house, the more the scent grew.

The Truetts had converted the formal dining room at the front of the house into Fiona's office, with French doors. One of those doors was ajar, and the source of the smell revealed itself: a blue candle in the middle of the wood floor, currently extinguished but burned all the way down to the melted wax. The label declared it *Ocean Breeze*.

I approached it slowly, this single sign of life in an otherwise barren house. The office was empty except for a stand-alone desk shoved against the far wall, and I didn't want to use my flashlight in here—too visible, with the uncovered windows, from the front sidewalk.

I almost didn't see it in the shadows: the heap of fabric in the back corner under the desk, stuffed against the wall.

Keeping my light off, I got down on my knees, inching closer, hand extended toward the fabric. A rustle of material, the shape of something rolled up—

A sleeping bag that had been tucked into the corner space.

Like someone was squatting in here. I'd heard of this problem in other abandoned places, people breaking in and taking up residence. But not here. Not in this neighborhood. Not with everyone so close to others who would notice people coming and going, who would hear something in the night.

I slid the sleeping bag my way, and a small black notebook dislodged from where it had been balanced within. I took the notebook and backed out of the room to where I could use my flashlight without fear of being seen.

A pencil marked a page in the middle like a bookmark. Opening to the marked spot, I recognized the handwriting immediately. Knew for certain who had broken in and who had been staying here.

This belonged to Ruby.

At the top of the page was a date. The day before the party. The day before she died: July 3. Her notes seemed to be written in a complex system I couldn't quite work out. Letters and arrows, dates and times.

I flipped to the front page to see if I could make sense of it. In faint print, she'd written a series of numbers on the inside cover: 62819

6-28-19.

The date of her release.

I turned the page, and a square of folded paper slipped out.

I unfolded it to reveal an old computer printout. Like something from our message board.

But it wasn't recent. I recognized it from long ago. This was a screenshot of our message board from the early days of the investigation:

HOLLOW'S EDGE COMMUNITY PAGE

Subject: CHECK YOUR CAMERAS

Posted: 4:48 p.m.

Chase Colby: You all saw the video from the Seavers—looks like Ruby, but it's not a clear shot with her hood pulled up. What we need is footage between midnight and 2 a.m. We need to track Ruby, and it has to be airtight. Check your

doorbell cameras, any security footage, anything that picks up noise . . . let me know what
you've got.

Margo Wellman: What if we find something else?

Chase Colby: Don't.

Javier Cora: Lol

Preston Seaver: He's just being honest. There can't be anything else. A lawyer will take that and try
to cast doubt, twist the story around so
that it's someone else instead. Anyone who
might've stepped outside. Suddenly you're
the other suspect. Just saying.

Chase Colby: He's not wrong.

Tina Monahan: It's obviously her.

Charlotte Brock: Delete this.

This exchange had barely appeared on the message board before
Chase went back and deleted it. But it was enough. And Ruby had it.

The post that had kicked everything off. The focus on her time
line that ultimately led to her conviction, yes. But also her release.
The screenshot that found its way to the lawyer months after the
trial, that started the internal investigation into the police. That got
her conviction overturned.

Ruby had a copy of it, and as with a list of suspects, she was
watching them all.

The paper shook in my hand as I scanned through the names.
My neighbors, people who once were my friends. It had seemed
so innocent then: an idea slowly gaining momentum—evidence
conforming toward its support.

I had thought everyone had good intentions. But maybe I was
wrong.

The people of Hollow's Edge, subconsciously conspiring against her, to end her. To put her in her place. To show: *Here—look what we can do.* That we, as a collective group, were powerful. And once we began, it was a steamroller gaining momentum, and there was no stopping it.

She had come out of prison on a mission. Had lied and broken into this house; followed us, watched us. Taunted us with what she knew.

This neighborhood may have become something different in the time since she'd been gone, but oh, so had she.

I wasn't sure if she would've done this before or whether prison had changed her. Or if everything that had happened before had changed her view of the justice system. What was the point of playing by the rules if you were the only one? If the system had failed you?

Not that I was ever sure Ruby had played by the rules. She'd had these keys, after all.

But two weeks ago, I wouldn't have been here. I wouldn't have dug up the keys and let myself into this home that did not belong to me.

Turned out, we were all so close to criminal. All you needed was a good enough motive.

I TOOK THE JOURNAL with me. Had no intention of staying in this house any longer than necessary. Wasn't sure how Ruby had managed—in the oppressive heat, with the stifling scent—knowing all that had happened here. I couldn't lock the back door, since the key didn't work, but I retraced my steps, out the patio gate, back through my own, and then sat on the edge of my couch, trying to make sense of Ruby's notes.

CHAPTER 21

BY NOON, I HADN'T slept, but I believed that I had worked out Ruby's system; that I knew what she was doing in that house at night, curled up in a sleeping bag in the front room.

Ruby was watching us. Tracking each of us.

She'd been in that house even when I thought she was gone.

From her journal, it was obvious she'd been here all along, watching us.

Under the heading for each day was a list of initials, and arrows, and times, kept in columns. I realized she was keeping track of who was passing in front of the window and in which direction. She watched us during the day, and she watched us at night.

I wasn't sure when she slept, other than the few times I'd seen her in the upstairs bedroom of my house.

I could find myself, even, on these pages. *HN,* passing the front window of the Truett house, going to the right—when I was heading to the pool or to Charlotte's. A chill ran through me as I realized I'd seen Ruby there once. That the chill at the back of my neck had always been her: a flash of movement in the front window as I passed. The feeling that someone was watching me.

She noticed Mac coming and going, too. *MS to the left*—to see me. A wave of nausea rolled through me, even though she was gone. Of course she'd known. She must've known about Mac almost from the start.

In the evenings, she marked the movements of the people on watch: Mac and Javier and me, passing by, on each shift.

All these mundane movements—she'd been keeping track of them all.

Beginning June 29, she knew there was nothing quiet about this neighborhood. She knew she'd caused a stir with her return and that people would show themselves, reveal themselves. Believing we'd be afraid.

And we *were*.

Not of the physical things she was capable of but something more—something she might know. The year before, we had been a steamroller gaining momentum, but that momentum had shifted direction. She had endured, she had returned, and she knew what we had done.

This time, she had the power, and we were afraid.

I WASN'T SURE WHAT she'd done with my car in the days when I'd thought she was gone. Why she wanted to take it from me. Whether she wanted to trap me here.

Or maybe she just wanted time when people weren't looking for her, looking at her—to watch, one-sided, without the fear of being watched.

We didn't need cameras in Hollow's Edge. We only needed to open our eyes.

The notebook captured page after page of this activity. As if Ruby had lost herself in these details, circling deeper, so sure that some pattern, some truth, would emerge from the page.

But the part that struck me as odd was the way she'd been keeping track of Margo. The *MW* at night, always followed with a question mark, like she couldn't be sure what Margo was doing. Like there was something that struck her as odd. Something worth noting.

We knew Margo wasn't sleeping much. The baby kept her up, she'd told us as much. And she and Paul were obviously having issues. Maybe she took the baby for a walk when he woke in the night, to lull him back to sleep. Maybe she went out by herself, for the freedom, whenever she could.

But Ruby marked her name often, and only late at night. With an arrow pointing left.

Always heading toward me, toward Tate and Javier Cora, toward Tina Monahan—to the left.

FROM THE MESSAGE BOARD, I could see that Margo was up late last night. But so were others: Javier, Charlotte. Me. None of us seemed to be sleeping much.

Ruby had kept that post, using those names to guide her way. She'd had keys to most of their homes. Must've known that our neighbors were hiding things.

Now those keys were in my possession. There was a certain power to the feel of the ring in my pocket as I walked out back again. To imagine Ruby doing this as well—listening in.

The secrets we told inside our high back patio gates, as if that protected you. The arguments that carried through open windows or poorly insulated glass. The churning air-conditioning units outside that acted like a white-noise machine before abruptly cutting off, exposing you.

The things people revealed when they were afraid.

I passed Tate and Javier Cora's yard—silent, empty—but

heard Tina Monahan's parents on their back patio, arguing about lunch. About whether to wait for Tina, to see what she brought back from the store. Tina was gone. No one would be inside her house right now. My muscles twitched with nervous energy, but I had to know.

It was curiosity, mostly. I had no intention of going inside. Just wanted to see whether the *M* was for Monahan or Margo. Both their names had been on the message board post that Ruby had kept.

And her repeated note—*MW?*—kept haunting me. The way she was tracking Margo made me nervous. Like I was missing something.

I wanted to know whose privacy Ruby had invaded. Who might've had something to hide back then—and something still worth keeping hidden.

At the corner, I circled back to the front of the street, turning up the path to Tina's house. Not worried about being seen at the Monahan house—*What would I need a security camera for, Officer?*—as I walked up their front steps, hand on the keys in my pocket.

I planned to check quickly. Slip the key into the lock and turn, before heading away. Pretend I was just knocking, and no one had answered, with Tina at the store and her parents out back.

I gripped the ring of keys in my hand, sliding the one marked *M* into the lock—

The front door swung open with force, dislodging the key, still tight in my grasp. Mrs. Monahan stood in the entrance, wide-eyed and friendly. "I thought I saw you heading up the steps, dear," she said. "It's been so long since we talked!"

My hand dropped quickly to my side as I attempted to hide the entire ring of keys in my closed fist. "It has," I said, pasting a friendly smile onto my face. I could hear my own heartbeat echoing in my skull. Feel it pounding against my ribs. The fear. The rush. The thrill of coming so close—

"Is Tina home?" I asked, dropping the keys back in my pocket.

"No, she's picking up food. But we could use your help if you have a minute. Come," she said, not waiting for my response.

I found myself following her deeper into the house, passing the kitchen, through the living room, to the back door, left ajar.

"George is stuck," she said, peering over her shoulder as she opened the back door to the patio.

"I'm not stuck," he said from the edge of the wooden patio ramp. He frowned when he saw me, like he'd been expecting someone else. It was the same look he'd given me when I ran into him and Tina during my watch shift. The only thing he'd asked me then was if Ruby was back.

"He is so stuck," Mrs. Monahan whispered.

Mr. Monahan's wheelchair was wedged at the base of the wooden ramp. The bottom lip of the ramp looked like it had broken or chipped, and it seemed neither could maneuver the front wheels up the incline.

"Chase said he was going to help us fix the ramp this weekend, but I think he got distracted. Understandably. But it's gotten worse, and I can't quite manage it on my own," Mrs. Monahan said.

"No problem," I said, heading down to the base of the patio. I leveraged the seat back and then forward, easing it over the start of the wooden ramp.

"There we go," Mrs. Monahan said, following us inside.

"Chase was going to come?" I asked.

"Oh, yes, he helps out a lot. Whenever Tina isn't around. He's a good man, that one."

I wasn't sure she'd agree if she knew everything that had happened during the trial. If she understood that he was under internal investigation, that his hand in the case had tainted everything.

"Do you want something to drink while you wait, dear?" she asked as Mr. Monahan moved farther down the hall, toward the dining room at the front of the house.

"No, thank you, I'm sure I'll catch up to her later—"

"That girl is back," Mr. Monahan said, eyes narrowed at the dining room windows, facing the front yard.

A shudder rolled through me. The same thing he'd said when I was out on watch that night, when he was with Tina, asking if *that girl* was back home.

"What?" I said. I turned, expecting to see the ghost of Ruby. If anyone could return, fake her own death, convince us she was gone when she was really still here, it would be her. I caught a streak of dark hair—a blur at the edge of the window—and then it was gone.

He grunted. "She thinks she's so clever. Hugs the front porches so the cameras don't catch her, so no one will see her. But we do. We see her." He moved closer to the window, and I stepped beside him, peering out.

"George, don't make trouble," Mrs. Monahan called. He waved off his wife, though she couldn't see him.

"Who was that?" I asked.

He shrugged. "One of Charlotte's girls. She figured the trick," he said, eyes narrowed as he kept watching. "Stay close enough, and the motion lights don't catch you, the cameras look right past you." He shook his head. *That girl back?* he'd asked just after one of Charlotte's daughters had been dropped off at home—not asking about Ruby at all.

"Where is she going?" I asked.

"Down to the lake. Cuts through the trees. There." His finger jabbed at the windowpane, and my gaze followed. The trees across the way. The other side of the inlet, with the dirt access road, the abandoned campfire.

"Ha," Mrs. Monahan called from the kitchen. "Like you would know. What, you following her now?"

"No, but people talk around me like I'm not here. Like if I'm not on your eye level, I can't tell what you're saying. I can hear *just fine,*" he called back, raising his voice. "She and that young man were making plans at the pool party, standing right over me. Before . . ." His words trailed off. Before the fireworks. Before Ruby was found dead. Before she was poisoned.

Before someone poisoned her.

But I was stuck on his earlier comment. "What young man?" I asked.

"You know," he said, waving his arm, seeming to search for something. Mrs. Monahan entered the dining room and gave me a knowing look. Like his mind wasn't all that it should be anymore. Like I should take whatever he said with a hefty dose of salt. "She told him there was a party out there. That they were meeting at the pit the next night. Asked if he'd be showing up this time."

The pit. That must've been what they called it—the small clearing on the other side of the inlet. Where Javier thought the kids were launching a boat. Where I'd seen the shadowed figure watching the kids on the lake last night.

"They're just kids, George," Mrs. Monahan said. "You weren't even sure which girl it was." She turned to me. "They look so similar, don't they? For a long time, George called them both Whitney."

"No," he said with a grin. "I called them both Molly."

I saw Ruby's journal again. The initials she put in the page at night with a question mark.

Not Margo Wellman.

She couldn't be sure whether it was Molly or Whitney. Ruby had seen one of them sneaking by in the evenings—and so did Mr. Monahan.

"Anyway," he continued, "it's the older one. The one we had the graduation party for. She's the one who was making plans to meet up at night. She's the one who sneaks out there."

"Whitney," I answered.

"You sure you don't want something?" Mrs. Monahan asked, a polite way of telling me it was time to go.

"No, thank you," I said. I opened the front door, and Mrs. Monahan retreated to the kitchen.

"I told Charlotte," Mr. Monahan said in the entrance, one hand on the door. He lowered his voice. "I wouldn't want my daughter out there with everything going on. Scary enough she was out there that night."

I blinked twice, trying to process. "What night?"

"The night the Truetts . . ." He trailed off, hand to his hair again, as if trying to keep track of something.

"You saw Whitney out that night?" I asked, keeping my voice low in response. Ruby had claimed she heard someone else out there, and maybe this was it. Maybe she had been telling the truth about that all along.

"Yeah, I told Chase that. Saw one of Charlotte's daughters heading down there earlier in the evening." He shook his head again. "I saw her and Ruby both. But we don't have cameras, and apparently, an eighty-five-year-old in a wheelchair is not the most reliable witness in the middle of the night. Like I said, I'm not *blind*. I could've helped. But I guess they didn't need it."

"Wait," I said, eyes closed. I knew it by heart: the path she had taken that night. The direction she'd gone. The direction she'd returned. The tight time line of it all. "You saw Ruby?"

She'd gone down to the lake to the right, past the Brocks, the Seavers, the Wellmans. She'd come back home from the other direction, behind our homes. Sneaking in the back gate.

"Yeah," Mr. Monahan said. "Clear as day. She tripped the

motion light in our driveway. Guess she didn't know the trick. Shielded her eyes at the house and scowled." His eyes widened. "You know how she could scowl." He seemed so sure, but he must've had it wrong.

"You saw Ruby heading that way, down to the lake?" I pointed to the left, toward the trees across the street, in the direction he'd just seen Whitney going.

"No," he said. "No. Heading home." Thumb jutting to the right.

I started walking down the porch steps as he closed the door behind me. Trying to make sense of it, I stood in their yard, staring down the street. Past Tate and Javier Cora's house. Straight to mine.

No wonder Chase didn't believe him, didn't trust him.

If Ruby had been heading home, she would've been on Tate and Javier's camera. She would've been on their feed. But neither one of the Coras had seen or heard anything that night. They'd come in late, there was nothing on their camera.

Behind me, a car engine rattled as Tina pulled into the drive. *Shit.* I was stuck in the yard, working through an excuse—*Just checking in on everyone*—when Tina spilled out of the driver's seat, already speaking.

"Did you tell them?" she asked, and I shook my head because I had no idea what she was talking about.

"My God, it's so horrible," she said. She glanced to the front porch, then back at me. "Chase called me. I'm not sure how I'll tell them." She looked even more haunted than the last time I'd seen her. "Antifreeze," she whispered, shaking her head, her eyes drifting shut.

I felt the blood draining from my face, pooling in the pit of my stomach. The word buzzing in my head. "Are they sure?" I asked, pretending I was in on the information, that yes, of course, I'd come here to make sure she had heard, too.

"They found evidence of it in her system," she said. "It's in the autopsy report."

And Chase had called her. I hadn't heard any texts coming through, any calls. And I started to fear that they understood—that I would be the main suspect—and had started to distance themselves accordingly.

"Wouldn't she have felt sick?" I asked, feeling on the verge of illness myself.

Tina must have been feeling the same, because her hand was on her stomach, and her face seemed pale, her skin dehydrated. "More likely, she would've seemed drunk at first," Tina said. "And she *was* drinking." She crossed her arms, rubbing her hands over the exposed skin of her forearms, as if chasing away a chill. "It might've tasted sweet, we learned about that in school . . . it's a common cause of accidental poisoning because of that." Her eyes closed, but I could see them moving behind the lids. "She had thrown up when I found her—"

But this—this was not accidental. This was at a pool, at a party, after a fight—when we were all afraid. Antifreeze could be in any of our garages, with the sudden winter freeze and the cars left out in the cold.

Something anyone could've done.

The police, I knew, would be coming back. Would be looking closely. Going through our lives, searching for our motives, shaking out our secrets.

The Coras' front door swung open, and Tate came out, hurrying our way. "Did you hear?" she asked, arms crossed over her abdomen. Her face was pinched and her eyes were bloodshot, and I could tell from her expression that she'd been crying.

"My God, it could've happened to any of us," she said. "We were all there. We were all drinking . . ."

The pitchers of lemonade, the sangria—we had all been

drinking from the same sources. Our cups left out. The communal ice in the chest below that we scooped into our glasses.

Tate looked to each of us, wide-eyed, so unlike how she usually seemed, focused and determined. She seemed suddenly vulnerable and exposed. This realization that we didn't know where the danger was—that we hadn't been able to see it coming. Had stood nearby while it worked its way in silence, slowly killing her.

"Someone at the pool," Tina said in a whisper, and I saw Tate's throat move. The lines we'd stuck to at the meeting, the things we wanted to believe, were no longer possible.

There was no escaping the truth now.

It had to be one of us.

"How can there be two people willing to kill . . ." Tate said, hand to the base of her throat. Like she couldn't believe it. The darkness at the heart of us here, with our view of the water and our lazy summer days. Our barbecues and friendships and parties. Such a close familiarity. Such a quiet place.

I caught Tina's eye, and I knew she was thinking the same thing. There were not two killers here. There never had been. There was always just the one.

I TRIED TO STAY up that night. Watching out my bedroom window, like Ruby must've done. But the sleepless nights caught up with me, the fear like a spike of adrenaline, rapidly subsiding. I saw Preston Seaver walk past around ten, taking his turn on watch. But now I wasn't sure what he was watching for.

I checked the locks. Pulled the curtains. Dreaded what I might find waiting for me in the morning. But I was drifting, and there would be nothing I could do to stop it.

All I could do was lock all the doors and windows, keep my phone close, sleep with a paring knife under the mattress, and wait.

MONDAY, JULY 8

HOLLOW'S EDGE COMMUNITY PAGE

Subject: They're back

Posted: 9:06 a.m.

Tina Monahan: Going door-to-door for follow-up statements. Just a heads-up.

/ɪ\   /ɪ\   /ɪ\   /ɪ\   /ɪ\
\ɪ/   \ɪ/   \ɪ/   \ɪ/   \ɪ/

Subject: STOP

Posted: 9:23 a.m.

Preston Seaver: Whoever is leaving these baseless, threatening notes, knock it the fuck off.
Margo Wellman: Seconded.

CHAPTER 22

I WASN'T THE ONLY ONE who got messages.

Someone had been leaving messages for others, making us all on edge. For Margo Wellman. For *Preston Seaver*? Judging by his post, I'd been completely wrong. Maybe that note I'd found on the floor of their office—I SEE YOU—hadn't been meant for me but had been left for Mac or Preston. Something one of them had found and balled up in a rage.

The line between culprit and victim kept shifting.

How much had I misinterpreted because I'd held my secrets close? We all had.

Ruby was right about that—how none of us ever talked face-to-face. How we talked around one another, about one another, aired our grievances in thinly veiled comments on the message board. One-upping each other in passive aggression.

How long had others been receiving the notes? How many more of us were there? All of us frantically keeping them a secret. Fearful and ashamed of what they might expose—until Preston, of all people, had the guts to mention them.

I WANTED TO TALK to them. But Preston seemed to hold me at arm's length. And I didn't have Margo's cell. All this time living on the same street, and we communicated by message board or when our paths crossed.

It was Monday morning, and Margo would probably be home. I could catch her before I left for work if I hurried.

Before I could talk myself out of it, I threw open the door—then jolted backward from the figure standing on my front porch.

Agent Locke stood there, blue eyes sharp, mouth a tight line. He was dressed the same as the last time I saw him, in the uniform button-down and black tie, but there was a graying stubble along his jawline today, which made him seem older, more solemn. "Am I interrupting you, Ms. Nash?" he asked.

"I was heading out . . ." I trailed off. "I have work." I didn't see his dark car, but it must've been parked around here somewhere. Like Tina had warned, he must've been going door-to-door.

"I just wanted to share some updates with each of you," he continued as I stepped out on the porch, pulling the door shut behind me. "But it seems like most people are out this morning," he added, with a glance toward Tate and Javier's house. Javier's truck was no longer in the driveway.

I didn't reply, didn't feel the need to explain why my neighbors may or may not be home on a Monday morning. The pause stretched awkwardly until he said, "The medical examiner is calling Ruby's death a homicide."

I swallowed nothing, could feel a cold sweat breaking out. "Oh," I said, the panic rising, even though I'd known this call was coming.

He raised his eyebrows, motioned to my front door. "Are you sure you don't want to take this inside?" He looked up and down the quiet street as if I should fear what he was about to share. As if I should fear being seen with him. Maybe he understood this place better than the rest of us did.

I shook my head and gestured for him to continue.

He sighed, shifting on his feet. "There was an insulated cup found beside her," he said. "Since it seems everyone got their drinks from the same pitchers and appeared just fine, we have to wonder if the cup itself was the source."

I nodded, even as my eyes drifted shut. Just as I had imagined. My blue cup with the poison inside.

"There are a lot of fingerprints on that cup besides hers," he said, and my eyes shot back open. "Seems like it was handled by a bunch of people."

"The cup is mine," I said, trying to get ahead of it. Because of course my prints would be among them. "Everything she used was mine. Everything in this house was handled by me."

I kept it to myself that the blue cup had been the one I was using that night, because it didn't seem like the truth would set me free. It seemed like it could trap me, corner me: *Someone who had access to that cup. Who had it in her possession. Who had motive and opportunity.*

"Of course," he said, nodding slowly. "That's the impression I've been getting."

I didn't know whom he'd been talking to, or what they'd been saying, but I worried how easy it was for them to tilt the investigation my way. How much sense it would make—to the police, to the neighbors. *They were fighting; that was Harper's cup; she had plenty of time to poison the drink.*

"Did you notice anyone else handling it?" he asked.

I shook my head. "People put their cups down on tables. You know what it's like at a party. People move cups around. Serve drinks to each other. We all do it."

Anyway, if you were going to poison someone, my guess was you'd be careful not to leave your prints on the cup, but I kept that thought to myself. It was probably a good thing that people weren't answering their doors this morning.

"We'd really like you to come down to the station and give an official statement. Clear up any discrepancies."

Discrepancies. I didn't know to what he was referring, and it seemed he wanted me to ask. But he was forgetting—we'd been through this before. We'd seen it happen to Ruby. We knew the steps and understood how truth was determined by the evidence presented, and even then, it was subject to the way it was framed.

I had no idea what he was looking for. Whether these threatening notes, and all they implied, had found their way to the state police, too. I needed to know what was happening here before I spoke to him further. Before I gave any statement binding me. I had to be sure.

"This is all so horrible," I said, the catch in my voice authentic. "But I have work. There's so much to catch up on after the holiday week. And . . . my mind has been scattered, with everything."

"Tomorrow, maybe?" he asked, and when I didn't agree, he added, "I'll give you a call, Harper."

"Thanks for letting me know," I said.

After a beat, he finally took a step down the porch. "Well," he said, "I'll let you get on your way."

I remained on my porch as he walked down my front path, and I watched as he strode past the Truett house, heading for Charlotte Brock's house next.

I needed to wait until he was gone before trying to catch Margo. It was too late to ask about those pictures before he rang her doorbell. And I'd just told him I needed to be at work.

I wondered how many of us here were checking in our garages, under our kitchen sinks, over the laundry room cabinets, to see whether we had antifreeze in our homes.

How many of us would look at the people we lived with and wonder.

I HAD JUST COME back out with my purse, heading for my car, as Javier's truck pulled up at the curb behind me. Tate stepped down from the passenger seat before he took off again. She hitched her bag onto her shoulder, keeping her eyes down.

"Hey," I called.

Tate froze on their front path, gaze flicking my way. "Hey," she said back.

"That guy from the state has been going around. He just tried your house."

She nodded, continuing up the path.

"Everything okay?" I asked, gesturing at the spot where Javier's truck had just been.

She eyed me suspiciously. "I had a doctor's appointment," she said, hand to her stomach again. "All good, except for the endless sugar craving. Javi's getting donuts."

I walked closer, halfway across her yard, and felt like I was encroaching on her life. "Tate," I said, lowering my voice. "Have you been getting notes, too?"

She crossed her arms, gaze sharp, with none of the vulnerability I'd witnessed yesterday. "Have *you*?" she countered.

"Yes." I peered over my shoulder again but couldn't see Agent Locke anywhere. "It's a homicide, Tate," I said, his words echoing back, the fluttery panic in my stomach. "It's official."

She looked at her front porch, at the camera pointed in our direction. Her throat moved. "Do you want to come in?" she asked.

Inside, Tate and Javier's house had started to transform. They'd repainted the walls a warm gray, added a low table to the open area of the kitchen. A pale green glider with matching ottoman was positioned in the corner of the living room, where there had once been a bar cart. Everything seemed softer inside, as if they were rooting out any potential sharp edge.

We were standing in front of the kitchen window while Tate leaned gently against the counter, shifting from foot to foot. From here, I could see directly into my living room: the arm of the couch, a corner of the television screen.

I'd heard their fight, carrying from this very window, last week:

Maybe you should just calm the fuck down for once.

Maybe you should get the fuck out of here.

"I saw the comments on the message board this morning," she said. "But I haven't gotten any notes."

And here, I'd thought she was preparing to make a confession about notes left for her or Javier. "Oh," I said, disappointed. "I had thought maybe it was all of us." I shook my head. "I thought it was Preston at first who was leaving them for me. I found a paper at his house that looked like the one left for me, but going by his post this morning, I think he or Mac must have received it." Though Preston seemed to be the one who had found it, I wasn't sure which of them it was meant for.

"God, it sounds like something Ruby would've done," she said, pushing off the counter.

"Well, it's obviously not Ruby anymore," I said, staring out the window, straight through to my house. And yet the notes had accomplished what Ruby would've wanted—turning us against one another, suspicion mounting. Keeping us on edge. "Why us?" I asked. They were left for me and Margo and one of the Seavers, at least. "Why go after the group of us?"

"Well, what did it say?" she asked. Her head was tilted gently to the side, like she was genuinely curious. Curious to know whether I'd answer. Whether any of us trusted one another with our secrets here.

"I found the key," I said, forcing the words out as Tate's eyes

grew large. I put my hand up, palm out, a proclamation of innocence. "I didn't find it back then, during the investigation. I found
it this spring when I was digging in my garden. But it wasn't just
the Truett key." I lowered my voice as if someone were listening,
just below the window frame, hidden out of sight. "She had more
keys than just that one. She had a lot, Tate. Keys to most of the
houses on this street. She must've hidden them during the investigation."

I wasn't sure if Ruby had hidden them because of the Truett
key or whether she understood what they would imply: She was
not an innocent person. She might not have been a murderer, but
not everything she did was legal, either. The police could probably
arrest her on one thing while working to build a case on the other.

"You didn't tell the police?" Tate asked.

"What was the point?" I said. "She was already in jail. Convicted.
I was afraid the keys would be used against me somehow. I didn't
know what to do, so I went down to the lake to get rid of them,
and someone saw me. Someone took my picture." I let out a slow
breath. "That's what I keep receiving. That picture of me with the
keys." And the implied threat within.

"Was my key one of them?" Tate asked.

"I think so," I said. Ruby had probably copied the one I'd had
from long ago, when we were friends.

I saw a quick flash of anger cross her face before it subsided.

"So that's me. I have no idea about the rest of them, though.
What they're so scared of . . ."

Tate drummed her fingers faintly on the counter beside her.
"Margo's even jumpier than usual. I thought it was just Ruby being
back, but who knows."

"She used to be much more mellow," I said.

"She also used to sleep," Tate said with a grimace. Her eyes
darted to the side, and her hand went to her stomach, and I could

see, for the first time, fear. Fear, maybe not just of this but of what was to come.

"Paul seems like he's shit at helping, to be fair," I said, because I worried Tate was seeing her own future, the person she might become against her will. And Javier was nothing like Paul.

"There's that," she agreed. She bit the side of her thumbnail, eyes narrowed at the window. "This isn't about Margo, but." She cleared her throat. "There were some rumors . . . from the girls on the team I was coaching in the spring."

"About who?" I asked, my spine straightening.

She ran her fingers along the base of her collarbone, like she was too hot. "Preston." She put her hands out in defense, like she'd already said too much. "They didn't exactly say it, but I sort of put it together. I heard some of the girls talking about one of the guys in security, the guy who uses the weight room." She lowered her voice. "How he takes pictures in there sometimes." She cringed even as she said it. "I don't know for sure if it's him, but I reported it. So someone at least keeps an eye out."

"Do you think it's him?" I asked.

She raised one shoulder in a half-hearted shrug. "I've heard things before. Little things. How he breaks up parties and drives some of the students home. It's the way they talk about it, you know? Just sounds a little too friendly." She shifted her jaw, and I remembered his date at the July Fourth party—Tate had asked him if she was a student, then given him a cutting look.

"You think someone else who works at the college knows? That they're leaving him notes about it?" I asked.

"Honestly, I don't have a clue. I'm just telling you what I know."

"I sometimes got the feeling Preston was taking pictures at the pool," I said. "I thought I was paranoid."

I heard Ruby's words echoing back: *Something about those Seaver boys, huh?* And this unspooling suspicion that she knew something. If only I had pressed her on it. But I hadn't asked, because I'd wanted to avoid the conversation, wanted to veer away from any reference to Mac.

Tate scrunched up her mouth, shook her head. "I feel so bad for that girlfriend of his. She has no idea."

I blinked twice, feeling the hot pulse of shame roaring to the surface again. All the things Tate must've known and chosen to keep hidden.

"Did you know about Aidan? That he was going to leave?" I asked. The past suddenly right beside us. "You didn't seem surprised."

She looked off to the side and shook her head, her high ponytail swishing back and forth. "No, not me. Javi told me right before you showed up. He said Aidan finally decided to leave, to leave *you,* and then the doorbell rang. I didn't know how long he'd known, but I swear I had just found out. Just a few minutes before you told me, that's all."

"I thought you knew about Aidan all along. I was mortified that you knew and hadn't said anything."

"You acted so standoffish after," she said. "I thought you needed time. But then it seemed like maybe you only wanted to be friends as a pair. That I wasn't worth it on my own."

"That's not what I thought," I said. "You totally ignored me after."

She whipped her head in my direction. "I did not ignore you. I was giving you time. I sent you flowers."

"What?" And then, as it slowly dawned on me, "Did you send the lilies?"

Her eyes widened in a gesture I used to know so well, like *Of course I sent the lilies.* "Yeah, I left them on the porch. I wrote you a letter. I signed my name to it, Harper. It really wasn't a mystery."

But I was shaking my head, wanting to go back in time, to see the simple truth when it counted. "I never got it," I said. "Ruby told me they were from her."

Tate's expression turned sharp, her jaw tensed, and I knew that if Ruby were alive, Tate would've made her pay. It was Ruby who had caused that divide between us. Who'd pushed that narrative. Telling me that my friendship with Tate was unhealthy. Letting me believe that she was the one who cared. The only one.

I wanted to ask Tate what the letter had said. What she'd wanted to tell me. I wanted to reach out to her, go back, make different decisions that would land me in a different place. But it felt impossible, too large a gap to bridge—how one small move led to another, until you were too far down a path to undo it all. Wondering how to even begin.

"Well," she said. *Well.* Here we were, all the same.

We fell to silence—the hum of the refrigerator, the click of the air-conditioning unit turning on, white noise circulating, keeping our secrets.

"Tate, can I ask you something?" I said, voice low.

"Shoot," she said in her straightforward way.

"Mr. Monahan said he saw Ruby that night," I began, easing my way to the question.

"What night?" she said, turning away fast, her ponytail whipping behind her, like she'd just forgotten something. Like she knew what I was going to ask.

"The night the Truetts were killed," I said.

"Okay," she said, opening the fridge, taking out the lemonade, pulling two cups from the cabinet. "Do you want some?"

"No, thanks," I said as she poured, one hand at the base of the pitcher to hold it steady. "He said Ruby was walking up the front of our street on her way home. But then she would've been on your camera, too. Right?"

She eased the pitcher down, sipped from her drink, then tipped the cup back further, gulping it down. "God, this doesn't really do the trick anymore." She laughed to herself, then stopped.

"Tate," I said. Remembering what Ruby's lawyer had said on the news program, that there was evidence that had been destroyed. And Chase telling them to *keep it simple*. The fight I'd heard between Tate and Javier, their voices carrying out the kitchen window. The tension brewing behind these walls. "Did you see her that night?"

She dropped the cup on the counter too hard, so the liquid splashed out over the rim. "She's dead. It doesn't really matter anymore."

"It does, it matters," I said. Because someone had killed her, and I had invited myself into the house of the people who might've destroyed evidence, and Javier would be coming back soon.

"No, I promise you. It doesn't."

"Was there someone else on your security camera? One of Charlotte's daughters?"

Her expression jolted in surprise. "Charlotte's daughters? No, why would you say that? It was her, it was only ever Ruby."

The truth, then. Mr. Monahan was right. And Ruby had been on Tate and Javier's camera.

"Then why did you hide it?"

"Because!" She threw her hands in the air. "Because there's no way to just turn in a thirty-second clip of Ruby walking by. Because I'd have to turn over the entire evening. From midnight to two, that's what the police wanted, right?"

I nodded, not understanding.

"I am a teacher," she said. "A middle school teacher. We both are, me and Javier. You can't have *anything*"—her voice broke, nearly a whisper now—"anything on your record. Nothing."

"Tate, I'm not following you here."

She finished the lemonade, then twisted the cup back and

forth on the counter, looked me dead in the eye as if deciding on something. "We got back after midnight," she said.

I nodded, encouraging her. I'd heard this much, after all. "You were at a friend's party."

"We were. And we drank too much."

So they'd been caught on camera, stumbling in the front door, a little drunk? I hardly thought the police would care. I hardly thought they'd be able to charge the Coras with anything and make it stick.

"We hit a deer." As soon as she said it, her eyes wide, the rest of the words started spilling out, like she'd been holding it back for too long. "It was bad, Harper. The car was a mess. Like we needed a new bumper. Like we're lucky we got home in one piece." She squeezed her eyes shut. "We're lucky we got home at all. It was a horrible, horrible idea. But we kept driving after, figuring we just needed to get home, and that's what you'd see on that camera out there." She pointed to the front door. "Us, practically falling out of the car, barely able to stand. We moved the other car out of the garage to hide the damaged one inside. Because we couldn't bring it to get fixed until we were sober. Because we had to pretend we'd hit a deer another time. We decided we'd say it happened the next day. And then we'd go into the shop and get the car fixed."

Her hand went to her mouth, her fingers trembling. "It was supposed to be simple," she continued. "But then the police arrived early in the morning, and at first I thought it was about us. I'd had nightmares that night—that we'd hit something other than a deer. How close we had come . . . to ruining our lives."

A shudder ran through her, transferring straight to me. All the little things we hid to protect ourselves. All the small mistakes that could lead to the incrimination and ruin of someone else.

"Javier had to get a rental from the dealer, and the neighbors wanted to know why, of course, because they didn't know why

there was a vehicle they didn't recognize lingering on the street.
Scared Charlotte's girls, even. We were all so scared back then, remember? So we said we bought it. Traded the old one in. Kept this
one instead. So yes, it was reckless and stupid, but it was unrelated,
I promise. It wouldn't have exonerated her. All it would've done
was ruin our lives."

"It did matter," I said. Ruby's time line was the *only* thing that
mattered. And they had to make it stick. "No one knew she had
been out front. It didn't add up in the time line."

"That was your fault," she said, turning on me—a new place
to shift the blame.

"What?"

"Your insistence that she'd come in at two in the morning.
Maybe you heard wrong—the front door, the back door, you were
upstairs, right? But the timing was off, from what you were saying.
We were going to tell the police we saw her, just not say it was
on the video. We were going to *tell,* because we thought it was
the right thing to do. But Chase said it was best to keep it simple.
It wouldn't change anything. And cameras counted more than a
witness."

"Chase said that?" He had lied. When he'd told Javier to keep
it simple, he was, indeed, trying to close up her time line. Trying
to make it stick.

"What time?" I asked.

She looked to the clock over the oven, then back to me.
"Four a.m."

"You're sure," I said. "You're sure it was her. That she was
coming back home at four a.m."

She shrugged. "That's what we saw."

It didn't make any sense. It was possible Ruby could've left
again, come back. But she would've stayed hidden. It was incon-
sistent, and Ruby was nothing if not consistent—in the way she

tainted my friendship with Tate, in the way she sowed discord; she thought she was better than all of us here. She would not have made that mistake.

There was only one answer, and it nauseated me. Made me take a step back even as Tate called after me. "I have to go," I said.

"This is why we didn't say anything," she said. "It only complicates a simple case."

But she was wrong. The explanation was alarmingly simple. Horrifyingly clear.

Ruby had come home at four in the morning, not two.

Someone else had been out there, just like she said.

And whoever was out there had been the one to sneak in the back door of my house that night.

Whoever I'd heard—it was not Ruby.

CHAPTER 23

EVERY TIME THAT BACK door creaked open in my memory,
I shuddered.

It was someone else. Someone else in this house. Someone else who had access. Who found a way in.

There was no way I was heading into work anymore. I quickly called Anna at reception, so they wouldn't be expecting me. "I'm so sorry, I'm not feeling well—" I began.

But she was already talking. "Oh my God, everyone's been talking about . . . what happened . . ." I couldn't tell whether it was a statement or a question.

"It's horrible," I said, because all I could do was stick to the truth. "Anna, is there a car in the lot? A white one?" That car had been in the lot twice, and I thought it might be a reporter, following Ruby's case. They'd be coming back for sure now.

"No," she said. I could hear her straining for a better look. "No, it's just us. Is it the media? Should we lock the door?"

Last time we had to, before they walked right in—for a statement, for a photo. Ruby's death would be splashed across the news, circulating through the community, if not further.

I peered out my front window, on the lookout for Agent Locke passing by again. "Yes," I said. "Lock the door."

I NEEDED TO KNOW what had really happened that night the Truetts were killed.

Ruby might've been desperate to prove her innocence, but now so was I. Those were my fingerprints on that mug. That was my image on the photo left in my house. There were too many pieces that could be twisted against me, should someone want to do it.

It was possible that whatever Margo had received could provide answers. All these secrets we kept from one another—Tate, and me, and others.

I watched as Javier returned home, and then as the state agent drove off in his dark car. He'd probably noticed my car still here, just one more piece that could be used to craft a story.

No one appeared to be home at Charlotte Brock's house, or at Mac and Preston Seaver's. All of the cars that were usually parked out front were gone. Maybe everyone had gone back to work, in a show of normalcy and routine, except for me.

I couldn't tell if anyone was home at Margo and Paul Wellman's house—there were no cars in the driveway—but I rang the bell, hoping I didn't wake up a sleeping baby. No one answered. I had just started walking down the front steps when I heard laughter coming from the direction of the pool.

Crossing the street, I could see the bright yellow of Nicholas's pool float standing out among the greens and browns of the trees.

There was no longer a sign posted at the pool gate, keeping us out. Apparently, the scene of Ruby's death had been released back to regular use.

Margo was the only person inside, standing in a growing puddle of water on the pool deck and wrapping Nicholas in a towel. She was standing maybe six feet from where Ruby had been found.

"Margo?" I called.

She straightened slowly, pulling up the front scoop of her bathing suit. "Hey," she said. But she didn't come closer.

"I don't have my key. Can you let me in?"

She looked from me to the baby, then placed him in his stroller. "Just a minute," she said, taking her time buckling him in place, adjusting the shade, pouring Cheerios into the front snack tray. I had started to think she'd forgotten about me until she finally headed my way, though she kept peering back at Nicholas as she walked. She took a step backward at the click of the gate, already turning for the stroller, cinching the towel around her waist.

"I just went by your place," I began, following her inside.

"Oh?" she said, busying herself with packing up the rest of their gear.

I scanned the pool deck, a chill running through me; I was aware of where I was standing. Where all of us last stood. "I didn't know the pool was open again."

She nodded quickly, her hair starting to come loose from the bun on top of her head. "We have to get out," she said. "I have to keep him busy and stick to routine, and then he'll take a good afternoon nap. But otherwise?" She shook her head.

"Margo, I've been getting letters, too," I said, and Margo finally stopped moving.

"I shouldn't have said anything," she said quietly, still looking down at her pool gear.

"I'm glad you did. I thought it was just me." But she didn't respond. "Margo." I put my hand on her shoulder. "Margo," I repeated, stepping even closer.

"Is it horrible?" she asked, peering up at me, her blue eyes wide and glassy. "The picture? Is it something that could really hurt you?"

I nodded slowly. "It's pretty bad." I closed my eyes, saw the image again. "I hid something after the trial," I said. I understood now—I had to give information to get it in return. And I had nothing left to lose. "It looks really bad."

She stared at Nicholas again, then leaned closer, the words spilling out. "A few months ago, I needed a break, and I left the baby with Paul. He must've gone to run some errands. Two birds, very Paul." She took a deep breath in. "I was sleeping when he came back, but I heard him. And I didn't hear the baby." She took a step closer to the stroller. "Nicholas was in the car, Harper. Paul *forgot* about him." Her hand fluttered to her mouth, like she couldn't believe it. "He was fine. He *is* fine. It was just a few minutes. We had a huge fight, and he thinks I don't trust him with the baby anymore, and maybe that's true—"

I could see her hands were trembling, and I grabbed one to still it. "It's okay, Margo. You're right, he's fine. Nothing happened."

"No, but someone must've . . ." She trailed off, eyes on the empty road behind me. "Someone must've seen him there. Someone took a *picture,* Harper. A picture of my baby in a car. You know how hot it's been this year." A noise escaped her throat. "Do you know what happens to people like that? They have charges brought against them, in the best case. In the worst?"

"Oh, God, Margo, I'm sorry." Her recent behavior was understandable—a reaction to that fear. Always with the baby, never wanting him out of her sight. The fear, and stress, of knowing someone had witnessed it. That one of us had seen. "We would all vouch for you, you know. You're a great mom. And you can't tell from a photo whether it was a minute, or five, or ten. It wouldn't prove anything."

A visible shudder rolled through her. "You know what gets me the most?" she asked. "Whoever it was, they didn't try to help. They didn't knock on our door to tell us. They just took a picture, Harper. What kind of person does that?"

I felt a chill in the air, even in the heat. A cold sweat breaking out, because I wasn't sure what kind of person would do that, either. "Maybe they would've come back," I offered. "You said you noticed quickly."

"I don't know," she said. "I don't know about anyone here anymore."

She cleared her throat, took a quick step away from me. I followed her line of sight, out the pool gate. Chase Colby was walking down the sidewalk and changed direction to cross the street when he saw us.

"Don't say anything," she said, damp hand on my forearm. "Please."

"I won't," I said, walking beside her as she pushed the stroller out the pool gate.

Chase stopped on the cement square beside us, where grass was starting to push through the gaps. His sunglasses were on, and I couldn't read his expression. "I was just coming to check on you guys. Make sure everything went okay with the state police."

I stared at him, no longer sure what side he was on. What side he was ever on. He knew what Mr. Monahan had seen that night. He knew Tate and Javier had seen Ruby, too.

"Everything's fine, Chase. I've got to get Nicholas settled," Margo said, weaving the stroller in the other direction.

I felt Chase's gaze on me, even behind the glasses, like he was waiting on me to fill him in. "You shouldn't be involved," I said as soon as Margo was out of earshot. "You're not supposed to be. This is all because of you, you know." I waved my arm in front of me, trying to take in the entire neighborhood—the past and the present, all of it, because of his involvement. I had a place to focus my anger. My fear.

But his face barely changed, his voice steady and measured. "Oh, no, Harper, don't you dare. I only went with the information you provided me."

"You pushed us to it," I said, remembering the message board post that I'd found in Ruby's things.

"No one needed any pushing. You were all too willing."

I stepped closer, lowered my voice. "I know what Mr. Monahan saw. What Tate and Javier saw. And you buried it."

His face went slack. "Two people who think maybe they saw someone in the dark? Eyewitnesses don't hold up the same as hard evidence, especially in the dead of night. We had the evidence. The rest was just noise. I've done nothing but give you all full transparency. Every one of you. If I made any mistake, it was that."

"It wasn't for you to decide."

"You're right," he said, his words coming faster, with more bite. "It was *their* decision not to say something in the end. You want to blame someone? Look in the mirror, every one of you. I only tried to keep this place safe. I only tried to keep you *all* safe. You were my friends. My community. I knew you all. I knew you wouldn't do it. Tell me, was I wrong?"

"You must've been wrong about someone, Chase."

He breathed in sharply through his nose. "Okay, Harper, go ahead. Who do you think it would be if it wasn't Ruby?" He raised his sunglasses like he expected me to understand. And I did, even as I was fighting it. The same truth that we all understood: If it wasn't her, it must've been one of us. And none of us wanted to believe it.

"I don't know," I said.

"Really, now?" He leaned closer, just slightly, so I had to tip my head up to look at him. "I know what Ruby said to Mac down by the lake."

I flinched, and I could see in his face that he knew he'd made a mistake. Mac had told me that Ruby didn't say much, that she was drunk and not making any sense. Mac had lied. "What?" I asked.

Chase waved a hand between us, took a step back.

"What did she say, Chase. You said transparency, so prove it."

He nodded once, as if conceding the point. "Apparently, she said, *Harper, of all people, can you believe it?*" And then he smiled. "What do you think she meant by that?"

I shook my head. She meant because I'd been seeing Mac. She had to. Or maybe because I'd taken the keys she'd hidden. Or because I'd yelled at her just then, at the party. She couldn't mean what Chase was implying. But the others here could make it seem that way.

Mac had known and said nothing. But he'd told Chase. The boys' club, making sure to keep one another safe.

"You're all just protecting yourself," I said, taking a step back. And Chase was no different. Trying to clear his name. So he could convince himself everything he'd done was worth it. I took another step back, and he stood there, watching.

"I told you from the start to be careful, Harper. I *told* you she was dangerous."

And I remembered that we were in the one place with no cameras. That someone had poisoned her, standing feet away from where we stood. That someone had seen Margo's baby in the car and left him there, too.

That we were all dangerous people here.

EVERYTHING WAS SPINNING OUTSIDE my control again. I could feel it, circling around me. Circling *toward* me.

I needed to know who had been inside my house the night the Truetts died. And how they'd gotten in.

My patio gate might've been left open—we didn't lock it often back then, believing in our perceived safety—but the back door to the house should've been locked. Especially since Ruby appeared to leave from the front.

I stepped down onto the patio. Ruby had always had a key, of course. But I was starting to wonder if she'd left a spare out here. She'd already hidden the large key ring out here. But I couldn't imagine she'd bury a spare.

There were only so many places it could be. There were no potted plants or doormats to conceal a key. I ran my fingers along the top of the doorframe but came away with only dirt and grime, damp moss clinging to my fingers. I tried lifting the bricks at the edge of the patio to see if anything was wedged underneath, but they were adhered firmly to the base.

The only furniture out here was an Adirondack chair and matching wooden footstool, the perfect spot for reading. I ran my hands under the armrests, checking the spaces between the slats. I came away with nothing but the debris left behind from weather and time.

Last, I flipped the wooden stool over, and my stomach dropped. A silver piece of duct tape ran across the bottom slat, the corners of the tape grimy and pulled away from the wood from repeated use.

Peeling back the tape, I felt like I was following a ghost across time.

Flecks of paint dislodged as I pulled, and there, adhered to the sticky side of the silver tape, was a single spare key.

I shivered, imagining how secure I'd felt behind my locked doors and my latched windows. How utterly unsafe I had been all along. There had always been a way in.

Ruby knew better than to trust such a thing as a lock or a door. Had slept with a knife under her bed to be sure.

That horrific night last spring, someone else knew this key was here. Someone who'd been told they were always welcome here.

Someone who'd let themselves in the night the Truetts were killed. Someone who'd crept up the steps and used the shower to rid themselves of any evidence.

To wash away everything she had done.

/ı\ /ı\ /ı\ /ı\ /ı\
\ı/ \ı/ \ı/ \ı/ \ı/

I HAD TO TALK to Charlotte. But how did one say to your neighbor: Is your daughter leaving me threatening messages? Is your daughter a criminal? Do you know where she was on the night Brandon and Fiona Truett were killed?

I didn't understand what had happened that night. Why anyone would want the Truetts dead.

Ruby must've suspected something—must've uncovered something as she'd watched us. Something that had ultimately gotten her killed. And now I was following in her footsteps.

I didn't know whom to trust. Not Chase, who had lied, pushed the facts onto Ruby, kept the investigation focused there. Not the police, who were the subject of an internal investigation relating to Ruby. Not this state agent, whom I barely knew. Because, just as my brother had warned, you had to be sure. Before a system churned you up.

Even innocent, you wouldn't emerge the same. *He* didn't. The past always following him, refusing to let him go.

The system wasn't infallible. It was made of people and the rules we had established with moves we deemed fair—or not.

Once it turned on you, it was hard to find your way out of it. It followed you, became part of you, just as you became a part of it.

I COULDN'T TELL IF Charlotte was home. I'd been waiting all afternoon for some sign of life from her house. I'd texted her, even, something innocuous—*Can we chat?*—but there had been no response.

While I waited, I kept going through Ruby's journal pages, her notes of Whitney passing by the house each night. I was assuming it had been her. Then and now.

Someone who had been told that they could always come to Ruby should they need her.

Someone who knew where the cameras were and how to avoid them.

A girl who had been to my workplace in the spring for a college interview—that mug staring back at her from across the room: HELLO THERE! Something she'd used to taunt me with instead.

But the timing of the notes—I couldn't figure out what had set them off. The first one—YOU MADE A MISTAKE—had arrived the evening when we'd been at the clubhouse meeting, all of us signing up for the neighborhood watch. The second—WE KNOW—had arrived the night I'd been on watch myself, boldly placed inside my house.

As the day was drifting to evening with no response, I grabbed that photo and stalked two doors down to Charlotte's house.

The Brocks' security camera was pointed at the walkway over the sidewalk. I strode up that way so they would see me coming. I rang the bell and saw a flicker of movement behind the window. Someone looking out. But no one came to the door.

I pounded on the door with the side of my fist until it abruptly flew open, Molly's long hair swaying into view. "What?" she said, somehow managing to walk the line between whispering and yelling. The same expression she'd given me last week when I'd come looking for her mother before the clubhouse meeting. Full of suspicion and fear.

"Where's your mom?" I asked. The house behind her was still, the lights dimmed. Like she had been pretending not to be home.

"Not here," she said, face stoic, starting to close the door once more.

"Wait," I said, placing my foot in the gap between us, propping the door open. Because I thought I finally understood what had kicked off the arrival of those messages.

It was me.

Me, standing in this doorway, telling Molly that Ruby had not been proven guilty.

And Molly insisting that she was.

I saw her expression again—the distrust and uncertainty. Not of Ruby, so close to her house. But of me knowing something. Of me marching up her porch that day, looking to talk to Charlotte. Me implying that Ruby might've been innocent.

And Ruby couldn't be innocent. If she was, it meant that someone else was guilty.

HELLO THERE! the last message had declared. From someone who had been inside my office. Preston, I'd thought at first. As a member of campus security, he'd have access to the buildings and to my office.

When I marched over here, I was thinking of Whitney. Whitney, who had applied for admission and would've had the opportunity to see into my office. Who might've noticed that mug with the bold text.

But Whitney had been interviewed by someone down the hall. It was Charlotte and Molly who'd sat with me, waiting.

"I'm actually here to talk to you, Molly." I took the photo from my back pocket, held it out to her, watched her eyes widen, her throat move. "I'm happy to have this conversation right here, if you'd like." I stepped back to the edge of the porch, where I knew the camera feed would pick up our conversation.

Molly let the door swing open, stepping back into her house.

Their house appeared perfect inside, like always. The counters cleaned, dishes put away. But I was starting to see the cracks in the facade. The things that had gotten away from them. The door of the cabinet under the sink, off its top hinge. The family photos that hung from the walls, that hadn't been changed—Bob standing beside Charlotte, the girls barely up to their shoulders. As if they still existed like this. As if Charlotte never wanted to acknowledge the truth.

I slapped the photo down on the island between us. "Hello there," I said. "Want to tell me why you keep leaving this for me?"

Molly swallowed, hand to the base of her neck. "Looks to me like you're doing something illegal," she said, but her voice was soft, and she looked behind her, like she was afraid. I could tell I'd surprised her, caught her off guard. That she had never expected someone here to be so direct.

"Oh, but I'm not," I said. "And Margo . . . What are you doing, Molly? Why are you threatening us? What do you think they'll say when they find out it's you?"

"You all act like such good people," she said, crossing her arms. "But I see you all. I see what you do."

"This is blackmail," I said, even though she didn't say what she wanted in return.

"It's just what I see," she said with a shrug. She gave me a sly grin. "Did you know Mr. Wellman once left their baby in the car?"

The room hollowed out; a pit formed at the base of my stomach. "Yes, Molly. I did. And I know you did nothing to help."

She frowned. "He's not a good parent. He got distracted by a phone call when he pulled into the driveway, left that kid in the car when he went inside. But Mrs. Wellman, she had a fit. An absolute *fit*." She shook her head. "It's not safe to do things like that."

Like Tate said, such a small thing could ruin your life.

But Molly wasn't some innocent bystander. "And you just left him there. You didn't think to knock on the door? To tell them?"

She blinked rapidly, as if it hadn't occurred to her. "He was *fine*," she said. "I would have. *Obviously*."

But I could tell I had rattled her. "I think you don't understand the things you see," I said.

She narrowed her eyes. "I understood just fine. I see more than all of you. I mean, Preston lives *next door,* and he flirts with my sister, who is *eighteen.* And no one says anything. You know he brought her home once? Last year?"

I shook my head. "I didn't know that." But I had learned to stay quiet, that the best defense was a strong offense, and that's exactly what Molly was doing. She was revealing it all—what everyone fought to keep hidden—to justify her actions.

"She went to some party at the college, and I guess he broke it up, found her there. Brought her back home."

"That sounds like the responsible thing to do," I said.

"Does it?" she asked, making a face. "Rumor at school is that there's a guy in security who will come to the party to break it up. But sometimes he doesn't. He just acts like he will."

I SEE YOU.

That note I'd found in the Seavers' upstairs office had definitely been left for Preston. Me, Margo . . . and Preston. That was the common thread. We had each testified in Ruby's trial.

The threat was implied: *Say it was Ruby. Stick to your statements. It had to be Ruby.*

There was so much here that we wanted to keep secret, and she was reminding us of the one fact we'd always been sure of: Any one of us could turn into a suspect. If it wasn't Ruby, it might've been one of us.

"None of you are paying attention," Molly continued. "Watch him. Ruby was."

"Ruby was watching him?"

"She knew. She asked me about it once—I had her for class, you know. She asked me, and she asked Whitney, if there was anything we wanted to tell her. Promised us that she was someone we could tell, and she'd make sure no one found out it had come from us." She rolled her eyes. "But knowing Ruby, I'm sure she just wanted to screw him over."

Preston knew she'd been watching him, and he didn't trust her. Maybe he thought I knew as well. Maybe Ruby had told Mac about it when he went to visit her. And he'd come to me after, to see what I knew.

Maybe I was being paranoid. Seeing danger everywhere, in everyone. Doubting every motivation, every interaction. As if the foundation of this entire neighborhood had been built on half-truths and white lies.

"You took his picture?" I asked.

"He shouldn't be talking to my sister. Should he even be allowed to live here?" She put her hands on her hips, channeling power. "You think people will be mad at *me* when they find out?"

"Yes," I said. Because it wasn't just Preston. "I think people are going to be very angry."

Molly handed the photo back to me like a reminder: It was time to go, and I needed to remember who had the power here. But I wasn't done.

"Ruby told you both she was someone you could always turn to," I said. "I remember that."

"Yeah, well, good thing I never did."

"She left a spare key out back," I continued, "told you where you could find it."

Molly swallowed, saying nothing.

"I know Whitney was out that night," I said. And Molly must've known, too. Charlotte knew. They all knew. Casting suspicion outward to protect someone else.

There was a duffel bag packed up to get her daughters out of here after Ruby's return. To keep them away. Just like they'd been sent to their father's after the Truetts' deaths. Not just because of the dangers Charlotte feared for her daughters. Because of what she feared they might have done.

Molly lifted one shoulder in an exaggerated shrug. "She goes out, meets friends from the other side of the lake. So what?" But her eyes cast to the side.

"Molly . . . what did you do?"

"Me? Nothing." She crossed her arms over her chest. "Oh, don't act like Ruby was so innocent. Don't you dare. She was an ex-con." I heard an echo of her mother then. "She had you all fooled. But you know what she's been doing? Messing with you all."

No, I thought, *she's been watching you.* Trying to work out what happened. Coming to terms with the truth. And now she was dead.

"Ruby lies about everything," Molly continued. "My mom told us that. And she's still doing it. You know she's got a car, right?"

"What?" A chill ran through the room, and Molly smiled. Like she knew she finally had me. I had forgotten what seventeen was like. So close to adulthood, you could taste it—the freedom of it, the power.

"She's got a white car, parked off the road, down by the pit. Whitney saw it there. Ruby could come and go whenever she wanted, but I heard she took your car anyway. She was messing with you," Molly said. "Because she could."

I closed my eyes, shook my head. Of course it had been Ruby. Of course. "I didn't say she was a good person," I said. "But that doesn't make her a killer."

Her face turned hard. "My mom said they're going to retry the case. It *has* to be Ruby." Her voice cracked midsentence.

I felt for her then. Even after everything. The things you would do to protect your sibling. The ways you weren't sure whether you were helping or hurting, but you tried anyway because doing nothing seemed worse.

The little lies we told our parents—*No, he wasn't out*—that became like second nature. The way I'd lie awake at night, listening for the sound of him returning home.

A fear that fueled the bigger lies, deep at the heart of a family.

I left her there, in her empty house, all alone. Knowing, one day, she'd have to come face-to-face with who she was—and what she had done.

CHAPTER 24

A WHITE CAR.

According to Molly, there was a white car, off the road, down by the pit.

But it was dark, and the investigators from the state had been going door-to-door, and the arc of a flashlight swept across the sidewalk in the distance, coming closer. It passed Tate and Javier Cora's house, then paused briefly in front of my own.

I remained perfectly still—a shadow in the dark, looking out. Feeling like Ruby must've felt, watching as each person walked by the Truett house, unaware that someone was inside, seeing everything.

His face turned briefly toward the front porch light—Preston—before continuing on, moving slowly down the sidewalk. Maybe he was patrolling again tonight. Maybe he was watching for something. Some threat that he knew was out there but couldn't find.

I SEE YOU.

Did any of us ever see each other here for what we truly were?

AS SOON AS HE was out of sight, I left through my back gate, carefully locking up behind me. I kept to the fence line, hearing the nighttime routines of each house I passed, the homes winding down to silence, the drone of the air-conditioning units churning in the night.

When I rounded the corner, the sounds of the outside gained force, the cacophony of the lake growing louder as I darted across the street. The crickets, the call of the frogs—beckoning me closer, into the trees, thick with the promise of something.

Inside the tree line, I was fully disoriented at first. There was no clear path here, just trees and branches and things moving through the underbrush. It was easier on the way back, when you could see the lights from the neighborhood guiding your path.

I closed my eyes, listening to the sounds to orient myself. The water lapped at the shore in front of me, so I headed left, deeper into the trees. It was impossible to get lost—the woods were not that deep here. Eventually, I'd hit either a road or the water. I could feel the breeze coming in off the lake, from my right.

Every few steps, I turned on the light from my phone to guide the way, but I didn't want to draw any attention to myself, in case other people were out here. Slowly, my eyes adjusted to the woods. The moonlight was crisp and clear, and the shadows became more distinct—the shape of trees, of branches, of dense underbrush scratching at my legs.

And then, abruptly, I was out. The trees gave way to nothing. To openness.

I shone my light around the space: a flattened circle of dirt, the ash pit in the center. Little signs that others might've been here in the past: cigarette butts where the flame had once been; a bottle of beer at the border of the clearing; drag marks across the dirt, like someone had pulled a boat through the woods.

There was no car that I could see. From where I stood, to the right, was the water—where the kids must've been launching their boat. I headed to the left, where the clearing gave way to the dirt access road. The path was narrow and rocky, dipping and swerving with the terrain, not the place for any vehicles. You'd easily lose a tire or worse.

But at the bend of the next corner, I saw it: A flash of metal in the moonlight. Bright white, tucked off the side of the dirt road.

I moved faster until I was almost upon it. Until I knew it was the car I'd seen before. Tinted windows and mud-streaked tires. No plates.

There was no way to know whether this was Ruby's car, though. To know why Whitney or Molly had assumed it was hers. Or whether Molly was just spinning another story, trying to keep Ruby at the center.

I circled it carefully, as Preston had done when it was parked in the lot at my office. Between the dark and the tinted windows, I couldn't see inside. I shone my flashlight into the window but could make out only darker shadows.

I braced myself as I tried the handle, ready for a siren that blared through the night, but the passenger door was locked, and no alarm sounded. I tried the other handles, but every door was locked. There was a keypad under the handle of the driver's door.

Keys couldn't keep you safe—

I searched on my phone for the make and model of the car, to see if there was a way to reset it. All I discovered, per the car manufacturer, was that a five-digit code would grant me access, but it would also lock me out for good after three attempts, requiring a call to the dealer afterward.

I almost left. I had no proof this car was hers, and no way to get in. But I had three attempts, and I decided to take them.

The first code I tried was Ruby's birthday. I knew the date by heart, subtracted backward to calculate her birth year, and hoped the locks clicked open.

They didn't.

What other codes could there be? Knowing Ruby, she'd think she was being clever, subverting all expectations. Not even bothering to try to outwit someone.

I punched in 1-2-3-4-5, because what other options did I have? Nothing happened.

I was down to the last attempt, but I could think of no other date. Pacing back and forth, I tried to remember her dad's birthday or anything significant that had happened in her life—and then I froze.

The date she'd written inside the front cover of that journal. 6-28-19.

The date she'd been released from prison. Something meaningful. Not just arbitrarily dating her book but writing down her code.

I held my breath as I tried it now: 62819.

The locks clicked open, cutting through the silence. And I knew, without a doubt, that this car had belonged to her.

She'd parked it at my workplace, knowing we were all on vacation. Moved it after discovering I'd been there and must've seen her car.

Molly was right. Ruby had taken my car and gone absolutely nowhere. Taken it for my set of keys. Because she could. Acting like she hadn't driven in over a year. Acting, always acting.

Like she'd been planning this for so long. Something stirring inside her for fourteen months. Not arriving in her car but by cab. Acting like she needed help, needed me.

She wasn't back only for that cash or the set of keys she'd left behind. She was planning to dig to the bottom of things by watching us all. To get her revenge.

God, how she must have hated us. Fourteen months for that hatred to take root deep in her heart and grow.

I opened the driver's door now, and the overhead light turned on, exposing me.

Ruby, the liar. Ruby, the criminal. Ruby, the victim.

I wanted to know which one I was dealing with. Which one was the true Ruby.

There was nothing but a bill of sale in the glove compartment. Candy wrappers and a soda can littered the cupholder, as if a child had been hiding out in here. I moved to the backseat, where a blanket lay over the space between the seat and the floor—like she might've slept here or been planning on it.

Or maybe she was just preparing. Always ready to leave. In case the district attorney decided they were ready to retry her. She couldn't trust that the system would work in her favor, ever again.

I moved the blanket and found what she'd been hiding: a file box, lid on.

The box from my office of Brandon Truett's personal effects.

I opened the box and saw all the things I'd stored away: the photo of him and Fiona smiling up at me, on top of a stack of magazines routed to the wrong address. A Visa gift card, removed from the birthday card, wedged into the corner of the frame now.

Tipped on its side was the small box that had been delivered to the office after his death. I turned it over, but Ruby had already torn it open. The edges were mangled, the sides compressed, but the top was folded back on itself.

I pried the cardboard sides apart, looking at what lay within, as a wave of sickness washed over me, heat rising, goose bumps running down my neck.

It was a white box labeled in simple print: *carbon monoxide detector.*

The picture below the label showed the make and model that had been inside his house. The same model in all our homes.

As if Brandon Truett had placed this order and accidentally

clicked his business address for the delivery. As if he'd used the gift card we'd given him, sitting at the desk where he worked, to place this order.

And by the time it arrived, he was dead.

I closed my eyes, trying to take a deep breath, as I finally understood what Ruby had uncovered.

No one had taken the carbon monoxide detector from their house. No one had hidden it or thrown it in the lake after planning their dark and heartless deaths.

More likely, the Truetts had removed it—an incessant beeping that wouldn't stop, a broken model that needed to be replaced— and the new one had not arrived in time to stop it.

Who had known it was missing? Did that person take advantage of the situation, planning how to kill them, silently, at night, without needing to dispose of the carbon monoxide detector?

Or—

Or . . .

Had Ruby believed something else.

I heard a noise in the woods, and my head jerked to the side, my heart thundering.

A raccoon scurried across the dirt road in front of the car, disappearing into the brush on the other side.

Was it possible?

I had to see. Had to walk it through to believe, as I knew Ruby must have, that simple, horrible truth: that no one had killed them at all.

I STARTED RUNNING, THE box with the carbon monoxide detector tucked under my arm—the only thing that mattered anymore. Proof. Proof, if I could make sense of it.

Proof, but I had to see it. I had to be sure.

I raced through the woods, the twigs scratching at my bare legs, my breath catching. Seeing the flicker of lights through the trees in the distance—Hollow's Edge, leading me back.

What had we done? *What had we done?*

Had we covered up a tragic accident? Blamed it on Ruby?

Because negatives were harder to prove. Absences, harder to find.

I burst out into the road, not worried about being seen anymore. Not even looking for Preston, or the investigators from the state, or the neighbors who might be watching out their front windows, who might hear my frantic breathing on the other side of the back patios.

There was only one thing that mattered anymore.

That house. What had happened in that house.

I didn't stop at my backyard, continuing on to the Truetts' house instead. Opening their back gate, sprinting across their patio, where the dog had been left. *Where he might've been left all night—*

Pushing open the back door and stepping into the living room, where I was hit by a wave of humidity again. Walking to the center of the hallway, looking up. At the discolored circle left behind. *Not removed by the killer, but by the Truetts, days earlier: an incessant beeping that wouldn't stop, a malfunction that needed to be replaced—*

Stopping at the garage door at the base of the stairs that had been left ajar. Fiona's car keys in the ignition, which had been hanging beside the garage door.

Fiona leaving in the car, Brandon trying to get her to stop, closing the garage door—

A fight. The bang of her car door, picked up on the Brocks' footage, as she followed him back inside, just for a second—

Please, just let's talk about this . . .

An argument that had trailed into the kitchen, up the stairs, not realizing what they had forgotten.

I followed them now—the ghosts of them—up the steps to the front master bedroom. Over the garage.

Imagining them succumbing to exhaustion, emotionally spent, not thinking. Or succumbing to something else. A slow but heavy fatigue setting in.

I stared into the empty room from the same spot I'd stood long ago, where they were both found—not in separate rooms, as Ruby had promised us—but together.

I took a slow, wavering breath in, my throat hitching from the memory—and heard it.

A creak at the base of the stairs, shattering the stillness.

My shoulders tensed, everything on high alert.

Another step, and then I was sure: I was not alone.

TUESDAY, JULY 9

HOLLOW'S EDGE COMMUNITY PAGE

Subject: Did anyone else hear that??

Posted: 12:13 a.m.

Margo Wellman: Was that a fucking GUNSHOT?!?

CHAPTER 25

I HAD THE BOX WITH the carbon monoxide detector tucked under one arm, and I fumbled for the phone in my back pocket.

"Hello?" a woman's voice called from the bottom of the stairs. "Is someone in here?"

"Charlotte?" I called back, heading for the stairs.

She was all in shadow, standing on the second step from the bottom. "Oh my God," she said, stepping back, laughing slightly to herself. "You scared me to death. What are you doing in here, Harper?"

I descended the steps, though she still had a grip on the railing, like she needed it to orient herself in the dark.

"I found something," I said, arm tight around the box. Proof. Proof that Ruby was innocent.

"In here?" she asked. "Did you break in here? I heard something, and the back door . . ."

I looked down the hall, where the back door was fully ajar. "No," I said. "Ruby did."

Charlotte scoffed. "Of course she did." Even in the dark, I could see her hair moving over her shoulders as she shook her head. "And what's that, Harper?" She pointed to the box under my arm. But there were things I had to explain to her first. Things I had to know.

"Can we just . . . can we get out of here? Go back to my place?" It was so hot, and I couldn't breathe inside this house, and I couldn't read the expression on her face.

I reached around her, to unlock the front door, to get *out*— but her hand circled my wrist, stopping me. There was barely any force behind it, but the intent was clear.

"You're trespassing, Harper," she said in that calm, unwavering voice. "Tell me now what it is you found."

Even in the heat, I felt entirely cold. This was my neighbor, and I'd known her forever. Had been in her house, taken her advice, accepted her help—

But right now she was a stranger to me.

"I found Ruby's car," I said. Something true, something innocuous, that would get us both out of this house. I wished for the cameras out front. For the perception of safety, the threat of being watched. "I can show you."

But Charlotte didn't move, and she didn't release her grip on my wrist. Her fingers felt cold against my skin in the oppressive heat of this house.

"She had a car?" she said. "God, she really had us all fooled. She really was a terrible person, Harper." Just like I'd said to her at the party. Charlotte's grip loosened, and I pulled my arm back. But she still stood between me and the front door and made no indication to leave.

"She didn't do it," I said, taking a step back. There was another door, another way out—

"She did. And she's dead now. It's time for us all to move on, to heal."

My neighbor who was the voice of reason, who was in complete control, calm and efficient, who said, *I think it's best to ignore Ruby.*

314

"Harper, stop," she said. Only then did I notice I'd been backing slowly down the hall and that she'd been matching me, stride for stride.

"Listen," I said, hand held up to keep her back, though I didn't know what I feared her doing to me. We were the same size. We were not violent people here. We ignored confrontations, performed them in thinly veiled comments instead. "I know Whitney was out there the night the Truetts died. She was in my house that night, too. I thought it was Ruby, but it wasn't. Whitney was in my house."

I heard only her sharp intake of breath in the silence. "Do you have any proof?" she asked. But I was chilled, wondering why she wanted to know. What she was after. The threat of proof could keep me safe. Safe, until she found it for herself.

"You knew," I said. "You thought it was Whitney, too." Mr. Monahan had told her she was out that night—

Charlotte stepped closer, lowered her voice like there were people listening even now. "You would do the same," she said. "One day, when you have children of your own, you'll understand."

"Did you ask her, Charlotte?" I said, my voice rising with the horror of it. "Did you even ask her?"

"Sometime, when they're teenagers, you lose them," she said, like she was back in her typical role, giving advice. "They go quiet, and you just have to pay attention, have to anticipate their needs."

My God, everyone here, not talking to each other. Not asking each other directly. And look what we had become. Look what we had created.

"Whitney didn't do anything," I said. "She was out at a party on the lake. Ruby heard them down there." *Someone else was out there,* she'd promised, to anyone who would hear. "Whitney came to our house after because Ruby told her she would always be welcome there. But Ruby wasn't there." That tight time line we'd traced of Ruby's path. Like she'd gone down there only to dispose of evidence before heading right back.

I wasn't sure whether Whitney needed help that night; whether she wanted to talk to someone; whether she just wanted to wash away the evidence of a night out before returning home. It was all forgotten the next morning when we discovered what had happened.

We hid everything else we had done that night.

"I promise, Charlotte," I said, speaking more forcefully. "Whitney didn't hurt the Truetts."

Charlotte froze only for a beat before nodding once. "Then I did the right thing. Ruby was guilty." Creating in herself, once more, a righteous person. Someone justified in her actions.

I shivered. Who was this person I'd lived beside for so many years? "Did the right *thing*? You *poisoned* her! Were you going to say anything when I picked up that mug?" Realizing, with horror, that the antifreeze had been in Ruby's mug all along. That Ruby must've put it down, forgotten where it was, and taken mine after. But she'd already consumed it earlier at the party—had appeared drunk, increasingly unsteady on her feet. And we had watched her slowly succumb to it, unaware.

"I saw you rinse it out, Harper. Don't be so dramatic."

"Don't be so . . ." I closed my eyes, the rage within me growing. "No one did it, Charlotte!" I was yelling now. "No one killed the Truetts! It was an accident. A terrible fucking accident. A tragedy. But no one did it." I showed her the box under my arm.

"What is that?" she asked, because it was so dark inside, and nothing could be clear in here. Not what we had done or what we were doing. Everything felt buried under a haze of heat and disorientation.

"Come on," I said, walking toward the back door, and she didn't object.

But she wrapped her hand around my upper arm as we descended the back steps. To an outsider, it might look like she was helping me.

"Stop," she said as we stood in the center of the patio. I took a deep breath of air, turned the box to face her. The print was visible in the moonlight. The words on the label clear to see.

"A carbon monoxide detector," I said. "Brandon had ordered this before his death. Their old one failed. No one took it and hid it anywhere. It was just a terrible accident. It was no one's fault."

Her gaze met mine, and the whites of her eyes reflected my own horror in the moonlight. "You don't know that," she said. "The police would've found that. Or seen it on his credit card."

"He ordered it with a gift card," I said. "It came to the school, and I never opened it. Ruby found it, though."

Ruby had fourteen months to run through the series of events, unspooling every one of them, knowing that she wasn't to blame. And if she wasn't, then who was?

The suspicion fueling her search. The sickening truth that she'd uncovered. A defense so difficult to prove—there wasn't somewhere else to cast the blame. There wasn't someone else to reveal.

There was no one.

"Let me see," Charlotte said, wresting it from me. But I had a tight grip on it and pulled it farther from her reach.

"Don't you see what you've done?" I asked, expecting her to give something—some show of remorse or regret. To show something real. But she couldn't do that. She was too far gone, too committed to the path. There was no way back and no way out.

I saw her then, saw everything she had done to get to this point, and what she must've been willing to do to maintain it. The righteous cause: to protect her family. Built on presumptions and lies.

She stared at me, and I saw her gaze roam around the patio, the open doorway to the house—and I knew she couldn't stop now.

I raced out the back patio, the gate creaking sharply, the wood hitting the fence on the other side. I had to get home, lock the door, call someone—

"Stop it!" she called, and I felt her arm wrenching mine back, just outside my fence line.

"What are you doing?" The voice came from beside us. We turned to face it together.

Tate stood before us with a gun in her hand, haphazardly pointed toward the ground.

"Why do you have a gun, Tate?" I asked. Her hair was in a bun, and she was wearing a matching pajama set, and she looked so young—so disconnected from the gun in her hand.

"Why do you think?" she asked, gesturing with it. "For protection. For our protection. Why were you in the Truett house?" Her arm swung wildly in the direction of the open gate behind us, and I cringed as the gun arced my way.

"Tate," Charlotte said, "my God, put down the gun. We're just talking things through—"

"I heard you," she said as her back gate creaked behind her, swaying in the wind. "I heard yelling."

"Everything's *fine*," Charlotte said. "Tate, go back to bed. Put the gun away, and—"

"Charlotte killed Ruby," I said. I blurted it fast. So someone else would know. So that the proof—the truth—could not disappear. Could not be buried by someone casting the suspicion elsewhere first. *Get help, call the police, do something.*

But Tate only stood there, gun at her side, looking between the two of us.

"Harper, stop," Charlotte said through clenched teeth. "We're all on the same side here. It's over, it's done. She's gone."

318

"Because you *killed* her," I repeated.

"Stop saying that. I kept us safe. She was dangerous. Tate, you know that. You know the things she did. She was so dangerous."

She was dangerous, but not in the way they meant.

"She didn't kill the Truetts," I said.

"That's not possible, Harper," Tate said. "I told you, there was no one else on the camera—"

"*No one* killed them, Tate," I said.

"What?" she asked, her voice impossibly small.

"It was an accident. A horrible accident, but no one did it. And I think I can prove it."

"Tate," Charlotte said, making a calming motion with her hands. "Everyone played a part. We're all liable here." She gestured to the box tucked under my arm. "Take that, please."

Tate looked between the two of us slowly, as if debating. Deciding. Working through each path to see which would work out the best in her favor.

Ruby was right, we had all done it. Had conspired against her even if we didn't mean to. Individually, we couldn't have done it. But together, we were powerful. We could set laws, enforce rules, make someone feel welcomed or ostracized.

All these things we knew about one another; all these things we had on one another. Everyone so afraid to speak up, to disturb that balance and give ourselves away.

"Tate," I said as she took a step closer. "Please. You don't understand. Ruby found this. Ruby *knew*—"

"Stop talking," Tate said, the gun rising in my direction. "Both of you. Just. Stop."

We both raised our arms on instinct.

I had no idea who I was dealing with anymore.

Everyone taking pictures of each other, recording each

other, and so we had to exist on two levels. The one where we knew we were being watched, and the one where we believed we weren't.

A secret, simmering existence behind the facades.

"Tate, you understand," Charlotte said, her voice no longer calm but pleading. "The things you would do for your children. The things you would do to protect them."

"I do," Tate said, widening her stance.

I'd thought she wanted safety. I'd thought the gun was for her protection. But there were different types of safety. Different things we wanted to protect.

I didn't know any of them at the heart. I didn't know what any of us were capable of doing.

Tate flicked a latch on the side of the gun: I could hear it from where I stood; could hear my heart racing, too.

"Wait, wait, wait," I begged.

But her arm kept lifting until it was pointed directly over her head. She squeezed her eyes shut and shot the gun into the air, the noise deafening.

I crouched on impulse, dropped the box, covered my ears, until the ringing subsided. When I opened my eyes, Tate's eyes were wide open, staring at the gun. She had taken several steps back, been unprepared for the recoil—like she'd had no idea what would happen when she pulled the trigger.

Only that people would come.

The sound of steps approaching, the back gate screeching open, and Javier spilling out into the night in his boxers. "Tate?" he called, skidding to a halt.

"Javier," she said, waving the gun in our direction as she spoke. "Pick up that box."

He did as he was told, eyes barely skimming over me as he bent down in front of me, taking the box from where it had fallen. He looked at it carefully, eyebrows furrowing, then back at his wife, like he'd never seen her before.

Chase arrived next, sprinting from the other direction, in tune to the sound of a weapon firing. "Whoa," he said. "Everyone calm down." He looked behind him for anyone else. "Shit."

Charlotte's gate creaked open slowly, and I saw eyes peering out from the darkness. "Mom?" Whitney stepped out in an over-size T-shirt, messy hair, rubbing at her eyes. She looked so far from adulthood right then, with no understanding of all the steps that had led to this moment. No idea the role she herself had played.

Molly emerged behind her, eyes wide, meeting mine—as if she understood. Someone else who quietly watched.

All of us stood there, in the trees behind the fence line, with no cameras and no other witnesses.

"What the hell is going on?" Preston asked, standing beside Chase as if they were the people in authority here and not the three of us—with the knowledge and with the gun.

"Call the police," I said. I begged it, really. The fear of inaction, the danger of it.

"Harper, stop," Charlotte said. "Listen, we're all a family here. Every family has secrets. Things we need to keep together. A bond that makes you stronger."

Another back gate opened, and everyone turned to look.

"Girls," Charlotte said, taking control, hands still raised, afraid to make any sudden move. "Go back inside. Don't say a word."

But they both remained, staring at the scene unfolding before them.

Preston looked to Mac, slow to arrive, slow to react. Chase looked between all of us, trying to unravel it all.

"Harper says that no one killed the Truetts," Tate said. And they looked to each other, considered each other, eyes wide, voices silent.

"Ruby was innocent," I said. "The Truetts' death was an accident, and Charlotte doesn't want anyone to know."

Molly whipped her head from her mother to her sister.

"She poisoned Ruby," I said, though I had no proof. Just the conversation inside the house that no one else had heard.

We weren't a family.

Us, with our taste for true crime and gossip. With our view into each other's homes, our voyeuristic desire to be part of something bigger than ourselves.

Yes, we were as powerful as we had imagined, in our search for the danger, our yearning to lock it up. We had deluded ourselves. Turning ourselves into liars and worse. Buying in to our brand of reality. Because we had to believe it—accept that there was a killer, one who must've lived so close, *right here*.

It could just as easily be one of us. It could just as easily be you. Every one of us, inching one step closer.

It had to be someone else.

We'd conjured monsters from nothing. Manifested fear.

Truth by mob; death by fiction.

"Is no one going to call the police?" I yelled, my voice wavering. "Seriously?"

And Tate, with the gun, arms wide, gesturing to all of us like a threat. "You heard her. Call the fucking police!"

Javier made a show of patting at the sides of his boxers, then turned for the house. Preston had his phone out in his hand now.

But I was suddenly afraid. Of what they would say. Of whom they would protect.

Of what they envisioned as safety.

I slid my phone out from my back pocket, fingers shaking. Everyone watching as I pressed the buttons. No one stopping me as I held it to my ear. As I told them where to come. "This is Harper Nash. There's a situation in Hollow's Edge."

Everyone kept watching, the tension growing. This realization that we were all complicit. That we'd made mistakes or told tiny lies—little things that added up. That ended with the conviction of an innocent person.

That we'd all had a hand in the events that led to her death.

"My neighbor killed Ruby Fletcher," I said, so it was clear, so it was on tape somewhere.

A pause.

"Charlotte Brock."

We stood there waiting, the call of a siren coming closer.

All of us staring at one another, trying to unravel the steps that had gotten us here. To Tate, with a gun. And Charlotte, with her hands up, begging us not to call the police. And me, with the proof.

To three of us dead, and the rest of us standing out back in the middle of the night like we were seeing each other for the first time.

We had searched so hard for the evil lurking under the perfect veneer, the thing we were so sure existed. Like we had conjured it here.

We were good people with bad intentions. Or bad people with good intentions.

We imagined ourselves judge and jury, protectors of our community.

Turned ourselves into monsters, to murderers.

We became the very thing we feared.

THURSDAY, AUGUST 1

HOLLOW'S EDGE COMMUNITY PAGE

The page you are looking for does not exist

CHAPTER 26

I WAS STAKING THE FOR-SALE sign in the front yard when the car pulled up behind me.

I heard the window lowering, the questions beginning: "Harper Nash? Can I get a moment of your time?"

"No comment," I said with barely a glance over my shoulder. The reporters were becoming less frequent, but a few persevered.

"You sure about that?"

The sound of her voice registered first, and I stood slowly, wiping my hands on the sides of my shorts.

Blair Bowman smiled tightly from behind the wheel of a black SUV as she turned off the engine.

I looked quickly up and down the street as she approached, sleek dark hair tucked behind her ears but dressed casually in jeans and a T-shirt, like she was just out for a drive.

"Let's take this inside," I said.

Her smile grew. "I thought you might reconsider."

INSIDE, BLAIR BOWMAN PEERED around the house carefully, like she was imagining Ruby here.

But the house had changed since I'd prepared it to put on the market. The downstairs smelled of fresh paint and polished floors. I'd already removed half of my things to make the space look bigger. Upstairs, Ruby's old room had been converted back into an office. There were no personal touches anywhere—a blank slate for other people to imagine their life, their future.

Some days, if I was lucky, I wouldn't see her ghost.

"So, you're moving. Where are you going?" she asked.

"I'm not sure yet," I said. But I felt the pull of some trajectory, away from all of this. From Ruby, and Lake Hollow, and the life I'd built here. The possibilities that existed elsewhere. "My brother lives close," I said. "I'm going to visit him for a while."

She nodded. "That's probably a good idea right now. Though I guess you'll be back eventually, if there's a trial."

There wasn't much yet to prove it was Charlotte—just the things she'd said that night: to me, to Tate, to the neighbors who were listening. Just the antifreeze in her garage (in so many people's garages). It was still so early in the process. Too early to know what she would do, what others would do. Whether she'd take a deal. Whether there would be enough to convict.

Blair walked deeper inside, down the hall, toward the kitchen. "I suppose you know why I want to talk to you," she said, turning around.

Because Ruby was staying here. Because I was the one to call the police that night to tell them Charlotte was guilty. To share what Ruby had uncovered.

I said nothing, though. Waiting for what she would reveal.

She smirked. "It's not that difficult to trace an email, Harper."

I flinched, though I supposed I'd suspected it—the reason she had shown up at my door. I thought I'd been so careful.

"An anonymous email, sent from the college campus, with a post from that message board . . . It was a short list, Harper."

I crossed my arms. "There are plenty of us who work at the college and live in this neighborhood," I said. It didn't have to be me.

She shook her head, hands up, conceding the point. "If it came down to it, it wouldn't be difficult to prove. Do you have any idea of the information stored in digital images?" She closed her eyes briefly. "Look, I'm not here to give you a hard time. But there's so much interest in this case—in Ruby's release, in her death—that someone else is bound to come looking."

And yet she was the only one here.

"I don't know what you want me to say," I said.

"I guess I'm just here to satisfy my own curiosity," she said. "Closure, you could call it." She shifted on her feet, looking at me closely. "Did you always know she was innocent, Harper?"

"No," I said. The truth. "I just wasn't sure she was guilty."

I'd sent the email to the lawyer in January. After Christmas with my brother, when I'd told him about the trial and my part in Ruby's conviction.

He'd asked if I knew she was guilty, and I couldn't answer. That look in his eyes—that question—it stuck with me.

It must've stuck with him, too, for him to call me about it again on New Year's Eve. His apology, though, had not absolved me.

Was I *sure*?

Were we ever?

I believed back then that the system would shake it all out— but that was naive. We *were* the system. Decided what went in and what stayed out.

And so, spending the end of winter break alone in this empty house, I'd revisited everything, trying to convince myself.

I'd saved every post from that message board—so sure, like we all were, that the truth would emerge between the lines. I'd prove it to myself. So I knew we had done the right thing, the good thing.

331

When I saw that post, I'd barely remembered it. But I started to imagine the motives behind the comments. The meaning within the questions. Margo asking, *What if we find something else?* And Chase telling her: *Don't.* Javier, Tina, Charlotte, and Chase, each of them doubling down on Ruby. And I wasn't sure why.

"I thought it would get the case looked at again. Get her an appeal, if there was something to it," I said. "So we could all be sure. I didn't know it would take everything back to square one. I didn't know it would get her *out.*"

There were times when I held tight to her innocence. There were times later, like after I'd found the keys buried in my yard, when I believed she was guilty.

And now Blair Bowman was in my house, talking about closure, like that was possible. I was responsible for Ruby's release—not sure, at the time, if she was innocent or guilty. I'd felt responsible for her: for what she did and what was done to her.

"Do you think it was worth it?" I asked Blair now. Ruby had been set free, but she was killed because of it. If it was justice we were after, I didn't think we had achieved it.

Blair didn't answer, looking around the house again. "I told her not to come back here," she said. Like she was trying to excuse herself, too, for all that had come after. Like she felt some of that same guilt. "I told her not to see you. She promised me she wouldn't."

I stared back at her as the realization hit me. "She knew it was me?"

"Of course. She saw that email and she knew right away."

Goose bumps rose on the back of my neck as I remembered those last words—the ones she'd allegedly spoken to Mac at the edge of the lake. *Can you believe it? Harper, of all people.*

"She never said anything," I said. How many things would be

332

different if she had said it? If she had asked? If we had talked about all the steps that had gotten us to where we were?

"I guess she wasn't sure of your motivations."

I looked to the clock. I had to finish packing, had to hit the road soon, if I wanted to make it before dark. "I've got to get moving," I told her, leading her back to the front door.

"Some advice, Harper?" she said as she stepped outside.

"Shoot."

"If you don't want someone else to dig it up, delete the account. Make sure nothing's on your computer. Pretend it never existed. If someone else comes by? Pretend you're not home."

And then she started walking away, down the steps, back to her car.

"Don't worry," I called after her. "I know how to stay quiet."

She gave me a quick, uncertain look over her shoulder as she opened her car door.

Like she had forgotten, already, what great pretenders we all were here.

The things we had feared—and the things we had become.

ACKNOWLEDGMENTS

THANK YOU TO EVERYONE who helped guide this book from the spark of an idea to the finished product.

My agent, Sarah Davies, whose wisdom and guidance I have relied on at every stage of the process, for each and every book. Thank you for believing in these stories.

My brilliant editor, Marysue Rucci, for the sharp insight, feedback, and support, from initial idea to the very last draft. And to the entire dream team at Simon & Schuster, including Richard Rhorer, Hana Park, Elizabeth Breeden, Maggie Southard Gladstone, Kassandra Rhoads, Jackie Seow, Marie Florio, Laura Wise, and so many others who have had a hand in bringing this book into the world. I'm very grateful to you all!

Thank you to Elle Cosimano, Ashley Elston, Megan Shepherd, Beth Revis, and Carrie Ryan for the brainstorming sessions, the early reads, the encouragement along the way, and the friendship.

As always, thank you to my family for everything.

And lastly, to all the readers. Thank you.

ABOUT THE AUTHOR

MEGAN MIRANDA IS THE *New York Times* bestselling author of *All the Missing Girls*; *The Perfect Stranger*; *The Last House Guest*, a Reese Witherspoon Book Club pick; and *The Girl from Widow Hills*. She has also written several books for young adults, including *Come Find Me, Fragments of the Lost,* and *The Safest Lies*. She grew up in New Jersey, graduated from MIT, and lives in North Carolina with her husband and two children. Follow @MeganLMiranda on Twitter and Instagram, @AuthorMeganMiranda on Facebook, or visit MeganMiranda.com.